Death by Design

Death by Design

Marjorie McCown

CREATIVE ARTS BOOK COMPANY
Berkeley • California 2000

Death by Design is published by Donald S. Ellis
and distributed by Creative Arts Book Company

For Information contact:
Creative Arts Book Company
833 Bancroft Way
Berkeley, California 94710
(800) 848-7789

ISBN 0-88739-244-x
Library of Congress Catalog Number 98-83079

Printed in the United States of America

For my extraordinary mother,
Helen E. McCown

Death by Design

One

Now that the dust has settled, I have to ask myself why I didn't catch even a whiff of the storm brewing just on my horizon. No prescient prickle up the back of my neck, no warning inner voice. My instincts are usually better than that. When I can't sleep at night, and these days that's more often than not, I keep going over it all in my head, haunted by what I didn't see in time. By what I might have been able to prevent. Although, in truth, the real damage had been done years ago. But it will be clearer if I start at the beginning, or at least at the point when I joined this particular band of very unmerry players.

And that would be on an unseasonably warm and humid afternoon in early March, the day I met Sara Landesmann. She arrived, punctual to the minute, scrupulously polite. I could see she'd been crying. And she seemed to be having some trouble organizing her thoughts as she sat across from me nervously twisting her hands on the secondhand loveseat in my small and rather dusty office. "Office" is actually a bit of a euphemism. I rent a room that adjoins my friend Joyce's store, Auntie Em's, on Hyperion Avenue in the Silverlake district of Los Angeles. Sara was a friend of Joyce's. Well, more accurately, she was a customer, but for Joyce it's the same thing. She has a seemingly limitless capacity for love and compassion. I, on the other hand, tend to be on the "guarded and suspicious" end of the scale. But this girl got to me. There was a sweetness and a sadness about her that made me want to protect her. I was already too late, but I didn't know that at the time.

"I almost hit someone on the way over." The words came out in a soft rush of breath. "I shouldn't be driving — I can't concentrate at all. This whole thing has been such a nightmare. And then with all the Oscar craziness on top of that . . . "

She broke off and looked up at the ceiling, blinking hard against the threat of tears, then struggled on in a choked voice: "I haven't been able to sleep. I lie awake just listening for the phone to ring. It's like waiting for a time bomb to go off."

I reached over and filled a coffee cup with water from the Sparkletts cooler, then got up and went around the desk to hand it to her. She took a little sip. I leaned back against the desk and gave her a moment. Though I guessed her to be in her mid-twenties, she seemed childlike, fragile and graceful — a deer of a girl with wide hazel eyes and a pale complexion, her light brown hair caught back in a ponytail.

"Sara," I said gently, "let's back up for a minute. You said you had a problem you needed to talk about, but you wouldn't say what it was over the phone."

"Oh, I'm sorry!" she chirped automatically, and I somehow got the feeling she said that a lot. "It's my mother," she said anxiously. "I'm worried for my mother. She's been getting strange phone calls, mostly late at night. Someone breathing heavily. Almost a mechanical sound. They never say anything. Just that awful breathing. Then they hang up." She swallowed painfully, her voice catching. "And notes. Ugly. Threatening. And then this morning —" Her face suddenly crumpled, tears leaking unchecked from the corners of her eyes.

I handed her a tissue.

"I'm sorry," she whispered.

"It's okay. Take a drink of water."

She did as she was told like an obedient child.

"Now tell me what happened this morning."

She drew a deep, ragged breath. "I found Snow, our cat, when I went out to get the paper. Someone had slit his belly open from neck to tail and left him to bleed to death on the doorstep." One trembling hand came up to shield her eyes as if the ruined body still lay at her feet. "With another note."

I recoiled from the image she conjured with a shudder. "What did it say, exactly? Have you brought any of the notes with you?"

She nodded and opened a large beige canvas shoulder attache bag. She took out a manila envelope and handed it to me. "It's in there."

I opened the envelope and slid the note, creased and smudged with dirt, onto the desktop. Composed with letters cut from periodicals and glued onto cheap white notebook paper, what the message lacked in style and originality was balanced by its clarity: FAYE YOU'RE NEXT.

"This is the note that came this morning?"

"Yes."

"With the body of the cat?"

"Yes." Her hands fluttered like anxious birds.

"I assume Faye is your mother."

"Yes. Faye Symington."

"And who is Oscar?"

She gave me a blank look.

"You said something about 'the Oscar craziness.' Could he be the one behind the threats?"

"Oh," she gave a sigh of comprehension. "I'm sorry. I wasn't being clear."

Well, yeah, no shit, I thought, keeping a carefully neutral expression pasted on my face.

"Mother is a famous film designer," Sara explained, though it was obvious this was information she felt I should already have. "Costumes. She's nominated for an Oscar this year. An Academy Award," she added, just in case I hadn't heard of them either.

"How nice," I observed inanely. Her name meant nothing to me, but I've never been an avid film-goer, nor do I pay much attention to the movie business — quite a feat in a company town like L.A.

"But that kind of attention can bring trouble with it. Have you shown this to the police?" I indicated the note with a nod.

She ducked her head and gnawed on a cuticle. Her nails were bitten to ragged nubs that left her fingertips raw and bald. It hurt just to look at them. "We reported the first two. They tested them for fingerprints, but . . ." She trailed off.

"Nothing?"

She shook her head. "They said there wasn't anything more they could do for us until —" She hesitated. "Until something else happens. They suggested private security. A bodyguard." Her eyes sought mine apprehensively and I found myself wishing I could think of something more encouraging to offer.

"That's not a bad suggestion," I said carefully. "But it's not my area of expertise."

"Mother will never agree to it. She says she refuses to become a prisoner of her own celebrity."

I let that pass without comment.

"How many notes have there been, including this one?"

"Three."

"What did the first two say?"

"They were in the same vein," she began, but then tears rushed up in her eyes. She pressed the heels of her palms against the flow and shook her head. "I'm sorry. I guess I've just blocked them out of my mind. We left them with the police. If it's important, maybe we could get them back."

And maybe hell would freeze over next Thursday.

"Did they have the same format as this one — the cut-and-paste letters?"

"Yes, exactly the same."

"How were the first two delivered and when did they arrive?"

"In the mail." She frowned in concentration. "The first one came a couple of weeks ago, just after we got word about the nomination."

"The Oscar nomination."

She nodded.

"And when did the phone calls start?"

"Just this past week."

"Have you reported them to the police and Pacific Bell?"

"No." She colored slightly and looked down, worrying a button on the sweater she wore despite heat that had forced me into short sleeves. "I didn't think it would do any good unless we were prepared to change our number or go unlisted. Mother would have a fit if people didn't know how to reach her with the Awards only three weeks away."

I passed on that for the moment, too, and studied the note in front of me. The workmanship was meticulous — the letters were evenly spaced and precisely lined up, all the edges neatly trimmed. Whoever did this had taken some pains with it. Then they'd hacked up a cat as a companion piece.

"Do you have any idea who might be doing these things?"

"No." A vehement shake of the head. "No idea."

"Anyone with a grudge against your mother? Has she been involved in any sort of dispute recently — legal action, any very acrimonious professional disagreement, domestic trouble of any nature?"

A wistful look came over Sara's face, and something else in her eyes that was there for only an instant. "My mother is a widow. My husband and I live with her. And my sister's staying with us right now, too," she added as an afterthought. "No. There's nothing I can think of along the lines you describe. I'm sorry." Apology as reflex — I've noticed you never find guys doing that. Whenever it manifests, it's a distinctly feminine trait.

"And what is Faye's reaction to all this?"

"She's upset by it, I know." She paused a moment, considering. "But she's not really worried. More annoyed. She thinks it's someone jealous of her success trying to spoil the highlight moment of her career." The last phrase sounded as if it were flanked by quotation marks, parroting her mother's words.

"Does she know you're consulting a private detective?"

Sara nodded shortly, avoiding my eyes. "She just said I shouldn't bother her with the details," she murmured. "And she told me to be discreet."

I was beginning to get the picture. "Un-hunh. Well, for starters, you need to report the third note and what happened to your cat to the police. There needs to be an official record of the incident to help make a case against this creep once he's caught. And I've gotta be honest — I really don't think there's much I can do for you with this."

She clutched at me in panic. "The police won't pay any attention until something even more terrible happens! Please! Joyce said you could help!" She burst into tears, covering her face with her hands.

"Hey, now, settle down." I patted her shoulder, gabbling nonsense like that until she seemed calmer. "We need to be cool and logical about this," I said firmly. "If you give in to hysteria, you give him all the power. First, you have to report the calls. The phone company has services that might be helpful. Do you have Caller ID?"

She shook her head meekly.

"That should go on right away. And with police authorization, Pacific Bell can put Caller Trace on your line. You'll need to keep a log of the harassing calls. By checking that against their records, the phone company can pinpoint the offending number and report it directly to the police."

The waterworks had stopped, but Sara was looking glassy-eyed, and I wondered if any of these pearls of advice were sinking in. "Make up flyers to distribute in your neighborhood telling what happened to Snow. Offer a reward for any information leading to the arrest of whoever killed him. And talk to your neighbors. See if someone noticed any strangers or unusual activity around your house last night or this morning."

Sara stirred and looked up at me hopefully. "Would you be willing to help us implement those suggestions?" she asked in a small voice.

"I'm not unwilling, but I don't think it's anything that requires the services of a private investigator. It's mostly common sense. If you're going to do any hiring, consider a bodyguard. Or buy a big, mean dog. Whoever this sick piece of work is, he's probably too cowardly to try anything bolder than brutalizing small animals, but it's never wise to assume."

"No. I'm afraid that's out of the question," Sara said adamantly. "Mother would have a stroke." She looked at me beseechingly. "Please, I feel completely overwhelmed. I need help — I need someone to help me now. Say you'll at least try. Money's not a problem," she added hastily. "Not even a consideration when it comes to my mother."

I confess my ears pricked up at that — I'm only human. And I didn't have much else working at the moment, so chasing clients out the door wasn't fiscally sound behavior. But I had serious doubts about being able to produce any helpful results. The work would be difficult enough without the additional obstacle of a balky client. Faye, Ms. Prisoner of Her Own Celebrity, sounded like she might be a handful. And yet the young woman in front of me looked so lost. I have in the past been too intimately acquainted with despair to turn from it lightly when I encounter it in another.

"If I do work on this, I'll need your mother's full cooperation, or there'll be no chance of making any progress."

Sara gave a little gasp. "Oh! Thank you!"

I held up a cautionary hand. "I haven't done anything yet. And I'm telling you candidly that if we don't get a lead through the phone records, we may never find out who's doing this unless the notes start coming with an autograph." I shrugged. "But if you're that determined, we'll give it a shot and see what we come up with. My fee is fifty-five dollars an hour plus mileage, and I'll want an advance to get started. I keep a log of how my time is spent, and you'll get a full accounting of that as well as a hard-copy summary of whatever information I turn up. For now, I'll keep you posted verbally. We'll sign a letter of agreement detailing the terms, and either one of us can terminate the arrangement at any time without notice. Is that acceptable to you?"

"Completely."

"Then shall we start tomorrow morning? I'll meet you at your home at, say, eight-thirty?"

She gave me an address on Nichols Canyon Road in the Hollywood Hills, and we wrapped up our business. I typed the appropriate information into the blanks on one of my form-letter agreements, and Sara wrote me a lovely advance check for $1,000. As she got up to leave, she grasped my right hand in both of hers. "Thank you again. I feel like you've thrown me a life line."

We made some goodbye noises at each other, and she was almost out the door when a thought suddenly seemed to occur to her. "You should come to the exhibit tonight!"

"Exhibit?"

"At FIDM!"

"FIDM?" She'd lost me.

"The Fashion Institute of Design and Merchandising. It's downtown. There's a show of costumes and sketches from movies that have been released within the past year, especially featuring the Oscar-nominated designs. The opening is tonight, so Mother will be there since she's one of the star designers. You can meet her this evening!"

"I don't know," I began doubtfully, thinking a more private venue would be better for our first meeting. On the other hand, it was an ideal opportunity to meet a cross section of the Hollywood fashion crowd. I could start to get the lay of the land.

"That sounds interesting," I about-faced. "What time does it start?"

"It goes from six to nine. They'll serve wine and snacks, and people generally dress up a bit, but it's by no means formal. I don't have an extra invitation with me, but I'll leave your name on a list at the door, so you'll have no trouble getting in," she beamed.

She was radiant — so completely transformed from the tearful waif who'd walked into my office just thirty minutes earlier that I gave myself a little pat on the back for doing my bit that day to make the world a better place for at least one of my fellow creatures.

I should have quit while I was ahead.

Two

After she'd gone, I poked my head in next door at Auntie Em's, where Joyce and her clerk/bookkeeper/tarot card reader and best friend, Gail, were setting up a new display of aromatherapy products. Joyce is an aging hippie, well-traveled with eclectic tastes, and her store is the retail personification of its owner. A catalogue of its wares would include a countless selection of incense, soaps, bubble baths, massage oils, scented candles, and all manner of candle holders, cards, wind-up toys, carved wooden boxes, painted masks, artifacts from Asia, Africa, Mexico, and South America, funky clothing fashioned from antique silk kimonos, handmade pillows, rattan slippers, rubber ducks, wall-hangings — well, you get the idea. Although my office adjoins the shop, I also have a separate entrance on the street. It's not exactly the setting one might expect for a private investigator, but hey, this is L.A. And Joyce and I have known each other for years, since we both lived in Manhattan, when I was a cop and she ran a vintage clothing business. We met when I went to investigate a burglary at her warehouse. Been friends ever since. Joyce owns the building, so my rent is nominal. Sometimes when my work is lean or Joyce needs another pair of hands, I man the sales counter to pick up extra cash. Walking through our common door is always like stepping through a time machine. The Strawberry Alarm Clock was playing "Incense and Peppermints" over the speaker system. The air in the shop was heavy and sweet.

"Hey, Grils," (our friendspeak mangling of "girls") I saluted.

"Hey, Maggie." (That's my given name, by the way.)

"Joyce, I just met with Sara Landesmann," I said, picking up a bar of soap embedded with foliage and sniffing. I grimaced and quickly set it down. "Thanks for sending her over."

"Oh, the poor little thing," Joyce clucked, her bright brown eyes soft and sympathetic. "She seemed so upset."

I'm always fascinated by Joyce's wardrobe. She has a distinctive style that pays no heed to current fashion and eludes any consistent definition. That day she wore gauzy Indian-print pajama trousers, a brocade vest, and a long, flowing robe of cranberry-colored silk. Silver necklaces, amulets, and charms hung in metallic profusion around her neck, and wide silver bangles decorated her wrists. Her dark hair, only beginning to streak with gray, was plaited in a thick braid that reached halfway down her back. Joyce has a heart of gold, but she's also a shrewd businesswoman and student of human nature.

"Are those real?" I asked in alarm, pointing to her clear plastic shoes, which appeared to have goldfish imprisoned in the heels.

She looked down, momentarily perplexed, then laughed, "Oh, no Sweetheart! People used to do that, but I would never walk on a little fishy's head! These guys are plastic, just like the shoes!" To prove it, she lifted one foot and rapped on the heel with her knuckles. The fish didn't even blink.

Before I could ponder too deeply this peculiar example of barbarism in the name of style, Joyce asked, "So how is she?"

"Who?" I was still staring at her shoes. "Oh, Sara? Well, you're right. She's pretty upset," I agreed.

Joyce went back to arranging a pyramid of vials containing viscous jewel-toned liquids with elaborately inscribed labels proclaiming "Inner Harmony," "Quiet Reflection," and "Peace."

I picked up one of the small bright containers. "Hmph. About time they bottled some of this stuff. How well do you know her?"

"Who?" I could tell by the squint that Joyce was in the throes of some critical decision. "Oh, Sara! Not well. She comes in here fairly regularly, usually with Faye, but she's not real gregarious, you know? But just as sweet as she can be. She works for her mother as a sort of personal assistant."

"Really?" I was amusing myself by pulling the cork tops out of the little bottles to see what "Inner Harmony" and "Peace" smelled like in distilled form.

"Yeah. They've come in to buy for a lotta movies Faye designed. One trip, they bought more than three thousand bucks worth of silver jewelry."

I whistled, impressed. At Joyce's prices, that was a wagonload of trinkets.

"Whaddaya think, Babe," Joyce leaned her head on my shoulder, tired of her task. "Should it be set up with just one color in a section or all mixed in together like this? I've been stacking these suckers for over an hour and it's nothing but a blur to me right now."

"I think it looks great the way you have it," I said truthfully. "What do you know about her mother?"

"Not much, really." Joyce stepped back to survey her handiwork then blessed it with a dismissive flap of her hand. "She knows a lotta famous people. Drops a lotta names, anyway. Seems to work all the time, which in her business is no mean trick."

"What's your impression of her personally?"

"I really don't have a personal relationship with her. Faye's sort of a cold fish. No offense, Babies," she apologized to the plastic carp in her heels. She paused then, thinking it over. Joyce once told me she makes a conscious effort not to judge others. A lot of wasted energy, if you ask me. "It bothers me sometimes, the way she talks to Sara," she finally conceded. "She's very short with her. Orders her around. She's always correcting her. And you can see how timid Sara is. It's like watching a puppy being kicked around the store."

Gail came over to add a pre-packaged gift box to Joyce's display, just in case you wanted to give some lucky friend "Inner Harmony," "Quiet Reflection," and "Peace" all in one shot. "That woman's a bitch," she summarized.

I was still trying to get a feeling for the whole scenario. "So, Joyce, just out of curiosity, if you two aren't that close, why do you think Sara called you for a recommendation?"

"Well, Babe, she said she'd noticed your office next door, and she didn't want to just take potluck out of the yellow pages. I told her you were very talented." Joyce smiled her mother-hen smile that always makes me feel like I'm six years old.

I took it all under advisement, said goodbye, and went back next door where I spent a fun-filled hour on the phone gathering information for a couple of background checks I was doing for a jewelry store in Studio City. They were looking to hire a security guard and just wanted to make sure they didn't end up with a convicted felon or a compulsive gambler. Or both. That chore chored, I locked up for the night and headed out to my '87 Toyota Corolla. One hundred sixty-four thousand miles (and counting), and it still hums like a top. The sunroof does have a tendency to leak when it rains, but, fortunately, in Southern California, that's really only a problem in February, and a few pieces of electrician's tape pretty much does the trick. Not an elegant solution, to be sure, but if I were out to impress anyone, I wouldn't be driving a twelve-year-old Japanese economy import around this mecca of designer car fascism in the first place.

I'm not sentimental when it comes to cars. As far as I'm concerned, they're just one of the necessary evils that go hand-in-hand with living in a city that's smeared itself across four hundred-sixty-some square miles. But that little Corolla has earned my respect. It's a lot more reliable than any man I've ever welcomed into my life (for example). Don't misunderstand: I'm not a man-hater. I'm even still friends with my ex-husband. Well, I would be if we ever saw or spoke to each other. To be fair, I've never been an ideal domestic partner. I'm a solitary creature by inclination and long habit. The exception that proves this rule is my current roommate, a black-and-white cat named Skunky who tends to be ill-tempered and scrappy with everyone except me. I pretend to be alarmed by his bad behavior, but I'm secretly touched by his singular devotion.

My full name is Maggie McGrath — Margaret J. McGrath to American Express. I'm 5'4" (or thereabouts), 120 pounds (or thereabouts) with blue eyes and brown hair that sometimes looks red when I'm out in the sun, heralding my Irish lineage. At thirty-five, I'm a confirmed ex-New Yorker and ex-cop. I was always one of those Manhattan-ites who scoffed at the mere idea of moving to the West Coast. But then came a series of life crises that left me for a crucial period bereft of the capacity for original thought. So I headed for the sun.

I rent an airy one-bedroom duplex that sits atop one of the Silverlake hills on the east side of Los Angeles. Although there are those Angelenos who never venture east of Fairfax Avenue, convinced the frontier beyond is dangerous foreign soil, it's what I choose to think of as more culturally diverse than the west side. Many artists live in this section of town, partly for another of the reasons I prefer it to Santa Monica: it's cheaper. My little house was built in the 1930's, Spanish architecture with hardwood floors and wonderful windows throughout. On a fine day, I can see the Pacific from my balcony. And at night, I'm treated to a dazzling panorama that stretches from Hollywood's crazy-quilt of lights to the jagged, vibrant skyline of downtown.

The light this perch affords me is important for two reasons. I'm one of those photo-sensitive creatures who gets blue on a gloomy day with a tendency to mope around like I've lost my best friend. And I'm a painter — not by trade, but by passion. I've turned my service porch into a studio, and that's where I spend my happiest hours with the sun streaming in from the south and west, blending color and line and generally making a huge mess. The results aren't ever going to set the art world on its ear, but that's not the point anyway.

The Toyota and I crept along in the sluggish traffic inevitably glutting Sunset Boulevard at that hour, the vehicular equivalent of gelatin beginning to set up. I down-shifted to second and wondered if it wouldn't be faster to walk. Finally able to turn left and start the steep climb, I felt a thrill of contentment. Our hill is an oasis set above the chaos of the city, and the late winter rains had left it awash with color. The front of the house across the street from mine was blanketed by brilliant magenta bougainvillea. Down the street, a coral tree flamed with spectacular orange blossoms. Red and yellow hibiscus bushes flourished in many yards, along with flowers and plants that need more coaxing in the arid climate — jonquils, poppies, and roses. I passed my favorite neighbor, a shaggy old granddaddy of a palm tree, the only one on the hill. Like me, it's a transplant from another land and so has become something of a living talisman, encouraging me by example with its decrepit dignity and grace to adapt and thrive.

My landlady lives in the duplex next to mine, a fellow cat-lover named Chris Jameson. A pretty forty-ish blonde, she runs a vegetarian catering business called Amazing Grains that does a brisk trade with the health club crowd, and she's forever whipping up some leafy delight for me to sample. I gotta hand it to her — the woman's a genius when it comes to food. If anyone could make sprouts taste good, it would be Chris. Of course, that's already been proven scientifically impossible. When I pulled up to the curb in front of the house, I was surprised to see her sitting on her tiny front porch, the mirror image of mine except for the fact that hers is a riot of greenery and blossoms. Nothing but the hardiest cactus can survive my horticultural ministrations.

"I can't believe you're home at this hour," I greeted her as I came up the walk. "What's the occasion?"

She gave me a crooked smile and tucked her hair behind her ears, a habit she has when she's nervous. "I'm taking a couple of days off. We don't have anything major happening this week, so Liz and Eric can hold down the fort. I'm waiting for Lenny to pick me up. He's got a gig in Berkeley, so I'm going up with him. I left a message on your voice mail. Do you mind looking in on the girl while I'm gone?"

Lenny was Chris's good-for-nothing-treats-her-like-dirt bass player boyfriend; the girl in question was Chris's completely adorable tabby cat, Lisa.

"You know I'll be happy to visit the girl," I said. "Are you okay?"

"Yeah," Chris lied, scraping at an imaginary spot on the knee of her jeans. "We just need some time together away from the usual routine."

Right.

"Well, have a safe trip and a fun time. And don't worry about Lisa," I said as I retreated into my house so I wouldn't have to trade false pleasantries with Lenny when and if he showed.

The Skunk-man was waiting for his Fancy Feast — only the chicken or turkey — he won't touch the fish or seafood. I popped a potato into the microwave for myself. I much prefer a properly baked potato, but when it's a choice between waiting an hour for the real thing versus ten minutes for a crunchy facsimile, immediate gratification wins out every time. This little potato parable is quite telling. In fact, I suspect if I were to examine it more closely, I might find it's the defining credo of my life. I poured the remainder of my morning pot of coffee over ice and took a quick shower before facing the sartorial decisions awaiting me.

Procrastinating was, of course, no help. My closet yielded little I felt was promising. I was intimidated by the idea of dressing to mingle with a roomful of people whose entire professional focus was clothing. I finally settled on a pair of black crepe pants, a black scoop-necked sweater, black leather belt, black silk jacket, and black Hush Puppies. I guess I have a bit of New York left in me, after all.

I looked up the address of my destination, bid Skunky, who was not at all pleased to see me making tracks again so soon, a fond adieu, and walked out my front door, where I paused a moment on the top step to contemplate the thick brown layer of smog that hung like a shroud over the buildings and palm trees of Hollywood in the early evening sky. I'm convinced that many of the social and behavioral idiosyncrasies particular to the Southern California milieu — so puzzling and bizarre to the rest of the country — are directly related to the environment. It's only logical: oxygen-dependent mammals continually forced to breathe air the color and consistency of pond scum must be in the process of evolving into an entirely different species.

I climbed into the Toyota, headed back down the hill, and took a left on Sunset. I chugged east toward the skyscrapers of downtown, my mouth watering like Pavlov's dog as I passed the bakery at the corner of Sunset and Coronado, where you can get the most delicious orange cake and cafe con leche that will keep you awake for a week. (Food is key to all my geographical reference points throughout the city.)

Twilight was approaching, headlights flicked on, and the city began to paint itself with light. The gathering darkness softened the rough edges and took some of the tarnish off the cityscape. When seen by the light of the unforgiving

Southern California sun, the seedy gauntlet of motels, restaurants, and Latin night clubs strung along that stretch of Sunset in the Echo Park area cast a dingy pall over the neighborhood; but at night their multi-colored neon signs transform the boulevard, and it becomes a festive carnival midway.

Talk about your deceptive appearances.

Three

The Fashion Institute of Design and Merchandising is a school that specializes in training fashion and interior designers, textile artists, and marketing people for the fashion industry. It occupies an entire city block — an imposing if somewhat unlikely 3-D jigsaw of geometric shapes. A clock tower made of burnt-orange concrete embedded with geometric tiles sits out front. Square, diamond, and circular windows in a variety of sizes are randomly scattered over the face of the main building while three enormous upright brick circles loom over a patio cut into the center of the second story. Part of the facade mimics the homey shape of a peaked roof with the hump of a giant dome poking up from behind it. To me, the whole thing just looks like it's trying too hard — but then again, I'm no designer.

I parked at a meter I didn't have to plug since it was after six o'clock. Finding free parking in the city always puts me in a good mood, so I crossed the small oval park that borders the Institute with a buoyant step. I went in through a back entrance that opened into a big round lobby with a floor made of flagstone pavers. A long white cloth-covered table was set up to one side, directly across from a bank of four elevators. Plastic glasses of pre-poured wine and soft drinks were set out for general consumption, all of it undoubtedly as flat and warm as bathwater.

The food situation looked a bit meager. Some little orange blocks of processed cheese and Ritz crackers lay drying out on a large glass platter. A bowl of miniature pretzel twists was the only other solid nourishment in sight. Two young men in white shirts and black bow ties stood behind the table poised to renew the stingy fare at the same rate it disappeared. They weren't exactly doing land-office business.

There was quite a crowd of people collected, all of whom seemed to be acquainted with each another. They'd knotted themselves into sociable clumps, their conversations blending and competing, the volume rising exponentially. And the acoustics being what they were in a room made of cement, the din was awful. The exhibit, I learned, was on the third floor, and after failing to find Sara in the throng, I gave my name to the fellow who was checking invitations as guests passed into the elevators. He found my name on his magic list, and I was allowed to escape upstairs.

I got out on the third floor promenade where another crowd of people milled, visited, drank, and perused the costumes and drawings on display with benign indifference. I noted with a twinge of self-satisfaction that my ensemble was quite compatible with the guidelines of the evening's dress code. Black was overwhelmingly the color of choice for this group, and few of them were more remarkably or ostentatiously dressed than I.

I began to wander, wishing I'd seen more of the movies that were represented. The exhibit was a peculiar hodgepodge organized with no logic that I could perceive, and there were many odd stylistic juxtapositions, such as an 1860's ball gown sandwiched between a tricked-up comic spacesuit and a hockey uniform. I paused briefly in front of the latter, wondering what efforts of design had rendered it unique.

Continuing to amble, I finally spotted Sara at the edge of a tight clutch of people. I waved, but she was too focused on the person at the center of the group to notice me, so I crossed the room to join them. The woman who was the object of their attention was an odd bird-like creature. Her hair was an improbable shade of bluish-red, absolutely straight, and cut in an angular bob with a thick curtain of bangs resting on top of her oversized mauve-tinted glasses. The impression this combination created — could it have been her goal? — was that she'd donned a shiny purple helmet and pink goggles. I guessed her age to be mid-fifties, but she had a youthful body she was obviously happy to show off in skin-tight black satin bell-bottom trousers, black platform boots that added several inches to her tiny stature, and a clingy pink satin shirt. Her hands were weighted with rings, and an expensive manicure had provided her with a formidable set of pink-lacquered talons.

I touched Sara's elbow and startled her.

"I'm sorry. I wasn't trying to sneak up on you."

"Oh, I'm so glad you're here." She smiled, and her pinched expression softened as she took my hand. "Thank you for coming. I told Mother you'd be here. Let me introduce you."

She led me through the knot of people gathered around Faye, raising her voice to be heard above the chatter. "Mother, there's someone here I want you to meet."

"Sara, darling, there's no need to shout. I can hear you perfectly well when you speak at a normal decibel level." Faye affected a clipped mid-Atlantic accent as artificial as her appearance —like a bad actor attempting Shakespeare.

"Mother, this is Maggie McGrath, the woman I spoke to you about earlier. Maggie, Faye Symington," Sara recited without looking at either of us. She'd begun to wring her hands, the same nervous tic I'd observed in my office.

The bird-woman looked me up and down appraisingly through her tinted goggles but did not extend her hand. "This surely isn't your investigator person?" She was all amused, world-weary sophistication.

"Yes, ma'am." (I sometimes become hyper-polite when I'm actually on the verge of making a rude gesture.) "Congratulations on your nomination," I added.

"Oh, yes! Isn't it marvelous!" Faye trilled, suddenly enthusiastic as a schoolgirl.

The digital shrill of a cell phone interrupted us, and she produced a small handset from some pocket, flipping it open with an impatient gesture. "Yes?" she answered edgily. She listened, her lips pursed in annoyance. With a sharp glance in my direction, she turned to take a few brisk strides that put some distance between us.

Just then, there was a commotion at the edge of her cluster of admirers lingering nearby. "Where is that evil cow?" a sodden voice demanded.

I was still watching Faye, who suddenly stood up ramrod straight and stamped one small booted foot. Her voice carried across the room, strident and angry. "I warned you before that simply isn't acceptable! Fix it, Lillian! And I mean now, or I'll find someone who will!" She broke the connection by flinging the phone to the floor.

"Where is she? I'll find her, no matter where she's hiding!" An elfin-looking young man, very drunk, lurched toward us. He toppled into Sara, nearly knocking her down, but he didn't seem to notice. Planting his feet, he tried to steady himself, focusing narrowly on Faye. "This just proves how fucked this business is," he slurred, "when no-talent, back-stabbing trash like you starts getting awards!"

With that, he threw his drink in her face. For a moment, everyone was frozen in shock, too stunned to react, but a second later the tension dissolved into a hubbub of confusion; several pairs of hands gripped the man's arms, and he was led away. Sara had grabbed a handful of napkins and was dabbing hesitantly at Faye, who sputtered with indignation.

"Sara, for heaven's sake, get away from me! Don't poke at me like that!"

"But, Mother! Your blouse! I'm afraid it will be ruined!"

"It already is, you idiot! Mopping at it with a paper napkin certainly won't help!"

Sara turned away, tearful and abashed.

"Don't slink off now to snivel in some corner. Get our coats, and let's get out of here! Now!" Faye ordered, still spitting and hissing like a malignant firecracker.

I looked around. People had scattered like dry leaves, and the only person nearby was a young woman wearing a strategically cropped T-shirt that allowed her to display a number of Technicolor tattoos.

"Who was that guy?" I asked.

"His name's Jeremy Latham," she replied, adjusting her shirt so that an image of Thumper (as in Bambi) was visible on her shoulder. Thumper was making the rude gesture I'd been tempted to offer Faye. "He's a cutter/fitter."

"What's the story there?"

"I don't know the details," she said vaguely. "I guess they must have had some kind of falling-out."

"Oh, you think?" I deadpanned.

The girl rolled her eyes and turned her back with a shrug that pointed Thumper's offending digit my way.

I intercepted Sara on her way back from the coat check. "Are you going to be all right to drive home?"

"I'll be fine, thank you," she smiled wanly. "Can we just keep our appointment tomorrow, as we agreed before?"

"Of course." I reached out to pat her arm. She returned to Faye, who stalked off without a word, trailing a miserable Sara in her wake.

I decided to hang around for awhile to try to get some information that would help me put the incident in context, but everyone I spoke with was just as much in the dark about the scene Jeremy Latham had staged. As I worked the room, it became clear that Faye was not beloved by her peers. I supposed some of the coolness was attributable to professional jealousy, but nobody wanted to gossip too much with an outsider who had nothing juicy to swap — though I did manage to glean some tantalizing snippets of conversation along the way, such as:

"We've been pushed two weeks, for the third time. Beatty's such a megalomaniac, he can't let loose of anything."

"Aren't you grateful, though, for the extra prep time?"

"Not me! I like getting it on camera. More time just means more dicking around making changes with everyone putting in their two cents — which adds up to a small fortune in no time."

And:

"No kidding? Billy Crystal wears a hairpiece?"

"Cross my heart."

"Geez, you'd think he could afford one that looks better than that."

But after a half-hour of this stuff without a bite on the topic that concerned me, I was beginning to get a headache and had just about decided to give up and go home.

"Can you believe she had the nerve to submit that? Quel scandale!" said a voice at my elbow.

I turned to find a man grinning at me. He had amused green eyes and a wavy mane of blonde hair. I looked at him quizzically, and he gave a lilting nod, indicating the hockey uniform I'd puzzled over earlier.

"What do you mean?"

"I mean, dear heart, that the lazy trollop rented this monstrosity just as you see it from a costume house. She didn't design a stitch of it. But the movie was a big hit, so when she sent it over, they went ahead and put the nasty thing on display."

He laughed uproariously. "Actually, it's a perfect send-up of the whole business: the movie made lots of money, so all other considerations are automatically rendered irrelevant. You were staring at it so intently, I thought I'd found someone else who appreciated the irony."

I smiled at him sheepishly. All I'd been thinking about — with great longing, I might add — were my jammies and bed. "I can't pretend to be nearly so astute or well-informed. I'm not a costume designer."

"Neither are most of the people who claim it as their profession!" he snorted.

I guessed he was a little tipsy and glad for an audience. Lucky for me.

"I'm Maggie McGrath."

"Max Whitcomb." He made a satirical half-bow.

"And what is it you do, Max?" I asked lightly.

"I recline on my laurels." He snagged two glasses of wine from a waiter passing with a tray and handed one to me. "I am a former Academy Award nominee," he continued, mockingly imperious, "though at the moment I am doing a sure-to-be-undistinguished little movie that features a clairvoyant talking basset hound in the pivotal role."

I winced.

"Precisely," he agreed, taking a big gulp from his wine glass.

I sipped my own, puckering at the bitterness of the jug varietal. "What do you think of the design nominations this year?" I asked when I got my lips working again.

"I think the main criterion for nomination this year must have been the amount of fabric used on a given project," he said with a wink.

I laughed. "I know so little about your business. What movie was Faye Symington nominated for?"

"Ah, darling, kind-hearted Faye," he mused sardonically. "She was nominated for yet another film adaptation of a nineteenth-century novel. You must have noticed that Hollywood has recently re-cannibalized the better-known works of Jane Austen, Edith Wharton, and the Brontës. And, dear heart, one of the few certainties in this most uncertain business is that if an idea works once and makes money, it will continue to be flogged ad nauseum in an effort to get it to spew more cash." Max was warming to a subject obviously close to his heart. "So some eager producer, spurred more by greed than vision, decided to bring a book of Anne Brontë's — she was the younger sister of Emily and Charlotte — to the screen. And it's for that demi-epic, *The Tenant of Wildfell Hall*, that Madame Symington has been recognized with a nomination by her peers. I have to say Faye's work was creditable, if not inspired. At least it wasn't embarrassing. We've had a few nominations in the past that were positively cringe-fests."

"How did that happen?"

He shrugged. "It's a club. Designers nominate designers, so all kinds of factors come into play. Political considerations that have nothing to do with the quality of the work. Personalities, petty jealousies." He finished his wine and looked around expectantly for another waiter with a tray.

"You're not telling me the Academy Awards are like a junior high popularity contest!" I scoffed.

The green eyes twinkled. "Maybe not entirely. But the two are not without parallel characteristics. Though you can be sure Faye's nomination wasn't based on her personal popularity. That score surely tallies in negative numbers," he smirked. "So, you see, sometimes professional standards win out over personal animosities, after all."

Another illusion shattered. First the Tooth Fairy, now this.

"Ah! Excellent!" As another waiter sailed by, Max traded in his empty glass and slurped at its replacement.

"Do you know Faye well?"

"Only professionally." The penny dropped, and he turned to look at me searchingly. "Why all the interest in La Symington? Are you a journalist of some stripe? Am I going to wake tomorrow morning to find myself quoted in harrowing length and detail in some yellow rag?"

"No, no," I answered quickly. "You have my word I won't repeat any of this, in print or otherwise. But what about Jeremy Latham?" I persisted. "Do you have any idea why he threw the drink at Ms. Symington this evening?"

"I truly haven't a clue." His eyebrows quirked in an elegant arch. "What is all this really about, young Ms. McGrath? It strikes me your fascination with our Faye goes beyond the scope of idle curiosity."

Definitely my cue to exit. I checked my watch. "Uh-oh! I need to go grab my friend. He'll be wondering where I've gotten to. You've been a doll, Max, and I'm glad to have met you. I enjoyed our visit. It was very, um, educational."

His answer was a slow, speculative smile.

By this time, it was after eight o'clock, and I figured I'd learned as much as I was going to, so I left. The night air was brisk, and I hurried to get back to the car. Reviewing the evening as I drove home, I could see how Faye might well inspire little spurts of homicidal fantasy in anyone who crossed her path. Worked for me. Which narrowed our list of potential no-goodniks right down to anyone she'd ever spoken to. An auspicious beginning.

Skunky was delighted to see me, though he contained his excitement admirably. He's far too proud to fawn over me the way a dog would. Still, he deigned to hop up on the bed once I'd settled in with my knitting. I've never liked to sew, but I find it relaxing to work with yarn and needles; the gentle repetitive rhythm lulls me into something like a meditative state, or at least as close as I'm ever likely to get. I stuck an audio book in the tape player beside the bed — tonight it was Henry James' *Turn of the Screw* — and picked up my current project. I was halfway through the sleeve of an angora cardigan I'd meant to be a Christmas present for my mother. Now I was shooting for her birthday in June — the perfect gift for summer, don't you agree?

Four

The next morning the city was covered with a damp gray blanket of haze that made for excellent sleeping-in weather. So it was more of a chore than usual to root myself out of bed at six-thirty. After drinking my first cup of coffee in a nearly catatonic state, I rallied enough to be able to face my free weights. Exercise bores me, but it's the only way I can figure not to spread out and atrophy like a middle-aged lump of petrified fungus. I was a gymnast in my youth — and I have the thighs to prove it — so I try to get to the gym at least once a week to throw myself around the floor for old times' sake. Otherwise, I walk in the hills for my lower body and work out with the weights for my upper body.

I showered and dressed quickly in black jeans, sneakers, and a forest green sweater over a black T-shirt. I have thick, straight hair that I keep in a short wash-and-wear style, so I'm liable to show up at my first destination on any given day with a wet head. Such was the case that morning when I pulled up in front of the Symington house at 8:25. It was an impressively large, if not beautiful, modern beige stucco-and-glass construction set up on a ridge with a sweeping view of the canyon. There were two split-level areas for parking just off the steep driveway that led to the house. I parked on the lower level and hiked up a flight of stone steps.

I rang the bell just as another car careened up the driveway, a little red BMW convertible driven by a young woman. She more or less abandoned the car in the middle of the parking pad nearest the house and started up the steps. She resembled Sara physically — same light brown hair and willowy figure — and canny professional that I am, I shrewdly deduced that I was about to make her sister's acquaintance. She seemed a little unsteady on her feet this morning, and judging by her outfit, she was just getting in from the night before. Unless the body-hugging black lace mini-dress she wore was her idea of casual day-wear.

"Morning," I said.

"Oh, hi," she replied without enthusiasm. "You must be the detective. Jesus." She swept past me and unlocked the door. "You might as well come on in."

She held the door for me, and I stepped into an entryway lit from overhead by a skylight. The house smelled like fresh coffee and toast. I followed her into a large, open combination family room/kitchen area. Three of the walls were mostly glass and overlooked the canyon, which from that vantage was completely undeveloped, a colorful patchwork of trees, wild grasses, and early spring flowers. We might have been in a wilderness retreat, for all that we could see of the city.

"My name's Jeri," she yawned.

"Maggie."

"Whatever. Listen, nothing against you personally. I just think Sara's blowing this thing way out of proportion. Not that that's new behavior."

She kicked off her spike heels and bent over to massage her feet. "Well, I'm beat," she said and gave another jaw-cracking yawn. "I'll leave you kids to it. Have a great time." And with that, she padded off down a hallway.

Left to my own devices, I began to look around and was immediately struck by the room's absence of color and detail. Like a generic still-life with no artistic spark, the broad strokes were laid in with competence and taste, but with no modulation or texture. There were no photographs, no books, no personal objects to reflect individual choices or give any hints about who was living here.

The furnishings were heavy and modern with simple lines in light neutral tones. Two identical sofas faced each other across a blonde mahogany coffee table in a sunken conversation area to the left. An informal round dining table and four chairs sat farther across the room by the windows. A large fieldstone fireplace divided the room in two. The kitchen — light, open, and well-equipped with white appliances — was on the right. Beyond all this was a large wooden deck suspended above the hillside. Huddled in a bulky cardigan sweater, Sara sat out there staring across the canyon, which was still wrapped in a layer of mist. A mourning dove sang its doleful chant; it was very peaceful. A shiver ran up my spine.

"How are you this morning?" I greeted her, breaking the spell.

She looked at me blankly, her daydream interrupted, but summoned up a quick smile. "And how are you, my faithful friend? Would you like some coffee? I've just made some fresh."

I declined, knowing I'd reached the caffeine overload threshold. Any more would be courting a headache and the shakes.

"I just met your sister," I said, pulling a chair near hers and sitting.

Sara's expression turned stony. "So, she finally decided to make an appearance."

"You said she's living here now, too?"

"She's in the middle of her second divorce, so this is a way-station for her at the moment. Mostly, she stops in to change clothes." She sighed in exasperation, combing her hair away from her face with her fingers. "I don't mean to sound so bitchy. But Jeri has never had a responsible thought in her life. She just sails through, doing whatever she likes, whatever feels good at the time."

"I gathered she doesn't take this business with the threats seriously."

"Jeri doesn't take anything seriously. It's a point of pride with her."

I settled back in the chair, trying unsuccessfully to find a comfortable position on the flat iron gridwork of the seat. "I'm surprised she wasn't at the party last night."

"Oh, that sort of thing is hardly Jeri's style." Sara gave a tight ironic smile. "Not if she can't be the center of attention."

Like mother, like daughter, was what I thought. What I said was, "So, getting back to that, what was the whole drink-throwing episode about?"

Sara blushed and glanced away, back out to the canyon. "I really don't know," she replied, her voice now as distant as her gaze.

"You didn't discuss it with your mother on the way home?"

"We didn't speak at all on the way home." She looked at me directly now. "Mother doesn't mean to be unkind. That's just her way of managing an uncomfortable situation."

"What about the phone call that upset her so badly? Do you have any notion what that was about?"

"I'm sorry," she murmured vaguely, shaking her head.

"Well, then, do you know who she might have been talking to? Someone named Lillian."

Sara cleared her throat. "It could well have been her business manager, Lillian Baxter. But really," she stirred with agitation, "I'm afraid you'll need to ask Mother about that."

"Where is she this morning?" I asked, easing up on her.

"At Sony Studios. They were establishing new wardrobe this morning, and she wanted to take a look at everything before they got the first shot."

"Establishing wardrobe?"

"That means clothing that hasn't been on camera yet is being photographed for the first time," she explained.

"I see. What film is she designing?"

"It's called *Deadly Extreme Force.* Sylvester Stallone and Steven Seagal are the stars."

"Mmmm. Interesting." Not.

"Mother feels she needs to start doing action movies, since that's where most of the work is," Sara said matter-of-factly.

Just then, a man in his early thirties came out to the deck. He was barefoot, wearing faded jeans and a gray sweatshirt. He had the sort of coloring my grandmother used to call Black Irish — dark hair, very pale skin, and clear blue eyes. He was attractive but soft-looking — almost effeminately delicate. He carried a steaming mug of coffee.

"This is my husband, Galen." Sara's tone was pleasant, but I thought I saw her flinch when he leaned down to give her a kiss on the cheek.

"Where's Jeri?" he asked, leaning back on a chaise lounge.

"Getting her beauty rest," Sara answered tartly.

"A perfectly sensible thing to be doing at the crack of dawn," he muttered.

Sara ignored him and turned to me. "Where do we start, Boss?" she asked with a lightness I knew she didn't feel.

"Let's divide it up," I said briskly. "I'll canvass your neighbors about the other night. Sara, why don't you call Pacific Bell to request the additional services, and Galen could start putting together a flyer about Snow —"

"Oh, he's a hopeless illiterate when it comes to the computer," she laughed. "I'll take care of the flyer."

"Then what appointed task shall be my portion of this weighty mission?" Galen asked with the barest hint of a sneer.

Sara got up and went back into the house without a word. The tension between them was already making my toes curl up, but I figured this must be their typical M.O. because it didn't seem to bother Galen at all. He winked at me, lifting his coffee cup to salute his wife's retreat. *"Bon chance, mes amis!"* he called. I began to understand why she was so desperate to recruit an ally.

I spent the rest of the morning going from house to house talking to the nearest neighbors. But none of them had an unobstructed view of the Symington house, and no one had noticed anyone or anything out of the ordinary. That didn't really surprise me: the property was much more isolated than I'd expected. But I was puzzled to find that none of them had more than a passing acquaintance with Faye — or anyone else in her household, for that matter — even though the family had lived there for more than ten years.

I met Sara back at the house for a lunch of sandwiches and iced tea on the deck. The morning haze had burned off, and the afternoon was a Southern California classic, sunny and warm.

"What kind of security do you have for the house?" We sat facing each other across a round picnic table made of heavy weathered planking. The rough wooden benches had been warmed for us by the sun. A honey bee hovered nearby, hoping to share our lunch, then darted off to snack on the wildflowers dotting the hillside. It seemed an absurd notion to think that anything bad could ever happen here.

"We have an alarm system." Sara squeezed a lemon wedge into her tea. "It's connected to a private security service hired by the neighborhood association. They send a regular patrol around, too. 'Prevention One' is the name of the company."

I took a bite of my sandwich, which was layers of roasted chicken and watercress spread with a tangy herbed mayonnaise on whole grain bread that smelled like it'd just been baked. Maybe if I did a really good job she'd make me a pile of these as a bonus.

"That's great," I said, sucking watercress out of my teeth. "I think it might also be wise to install motion-sensor lights. They switch on automatically whenever anyone or anything approaches. Makes it harder for someone to get near the house at night without you knowing about it. I know a guy whose company handles that. If it's all right with you, I'll give him a call after lunch."

She tilted her head and looked at me thoughtfully, the corners of her mouth turned up in a sad little smile. "You're the only one who understands, Maggie."

Strands of hair escaping from her ponytail were caught by the soft breeze whiffling up from the canyon, and they played around her face like a wispy halo. She looked terribly young and vulnerable. I found myself wondering about her life: what kind of home did she have here? For a married woman living in the bosom of her family, she seemed very much alone.

I called my friend, and he sent a crew right over. We discussed the place-ment of the lights, which would operate on a timer activating them at dusk. The workmen assured me the installation would be completed the same afternoon, and with that project well on its way, I was satisfied we'd accomplished all we could there for the moment. The time had come to beg an audience with La Symington, as Max Whitcomb had dubbed her the night before. I found Sara at the computer working on her flier. Promising to check in with her later, I set out to corner the lioness in her lair.

I was soon to discover that Sony Studios (formerly Columbia Pictures, and before that, MGM) is a gated professional community occupying several square blocks of prime real estate on the flat lands of Culver City, southwest of Beverly Hills and east of Santa Monica. The studio is home for a number of television series that regularly tape on the lot as well as the itinerant feature films that move in and utilize both office space and sound stages for the duration of their production schedules.

The sound stages, each with its identifying number, are vast, dark, sound-proofed (hence, the name) buildings of raw space. Each film sends its armies of construction people into these essentially empty structures to create a new world from the ground up. In addition to offices and stages, there are buildings on the lot containing editing rooms, screening rooms, costume stock storage (a permanent collection of clothing from various historical periods available for rental), and both men's and women's costume workrooms where clothing for the films and TV shows is made or altered to fit the actors. There is an Electrics Department, a Property Department, a sawmill, and scenery construction shop. One entire building is devoted to paint. All the various crafts and disciplines necessary to support the logistical behemoth that is a feature film in the mak-ing are housed within the gates of the studio.

Very few cars are allowed on the lot. Almost everyone must park in either the underground structure across from the Madison gate or the multi-level garage just inside the Overland gate. Security guards stationed in little booths at each entrance maintain a vigil to make certain that no unauthorized riffraff trespasses on the hallowed ground they have been charged to protect. When people who have never had any discretionary authority get into uniform, they inevitably become officious and self-important. Such was the case of the pudgy young man with the buzz cut and mirrored sunglasses who commanded the Overland gate when I drove in.

"Name, please." His manner was a flawless blend of boredom and disdain; he didn't even bother to glance at me. After all, I was driving a lowly Toyota, for heaven's sake.

"Maggie McGrath."

"Spell the last."

"M-C-G-R-A-T-H"

A pause while he punched some computer keys.

"No, I don't find you," he reported severely. "Did someone call you a drive-on?"

"Excuse me?"

He expelled a breath impatiently, clearly dismayed that one so ignorant as I would be allowed to pilot an automobile or hold U.S. citizenship.

"A drive-on. Drive-on pass," he said in a tone that warned he was not to be trifled with.

"I guess they must have forgotten," I said apologetically, "but I'm here to see Faye Symington, the costume designer for *Deadly Extreme Force*. She's expecting me — we have an appointment. I was told visitors to the studio could park in this garage and walk onto the lot."

That much was true: Sara had given me that bit of information as I was heading out the door.

"Not if I don't know you have a legitimate reason to be here," he said, wagging a chubby forefinger at me.

I suppressed a nearly overwhelming urge to bite it. "I have Sylvester Stallone's costume in my trunk. It's new wardrobe they're establishing this afternoon," I improvised, tossing my brand new vocabulary around with cocky assurance.

I was afraid he'd demand to search my car, but the star's name proved a powerful open sesame he couldn't afford to ignore. "In that case, you'd better drive on," he said grudgingly. "They're on Stage 23. But don't stay! Go in, drop the clothing, and come right out again."

I was tempted to ask him if we should synchronize our watches, but since I'd already gotten my way, I only gave him one of those wide, blank grins — all teeth and no heart. "Right. Thanks."

He reached in and stuck a handwritten pass on my windshield giving me permission to navigate the narrow alleyways that bisect the studio. The Toyota putt-putted along in second gear while I looked for the painted numbers on the buildings and dodged pedestrians, bicycles, and the ubiquitous golf carts that are a favorite form of on-the-lot transportation. As I edged through a four-way intersection, I was nearly rammed by one of those pint-sized vehicles. Loaded with bodies, it came barreling around the corner of a sound stage on two wheels without even slowing for the stop sign. I slammed on my brakes with an oath and leaned out the window to offer the driver a curt suggestion, but my tongue tied itself in a knot when I saw one of the passengers was Harrison Ford, clinging for dear life to the jumpseat. He smiled at me and rolled his eyes, mouthing "Sorry" as the cart sped away. I'm not normally the type who gets star-struck, but — trust me on this — the man is worth ogling.

And so, whistling happily to myself, I pulled up beside Stage 23 and squeezed the car as close to the building as possible. To my left was a door marked "Stage Entrance" with a flashing red light mounted above it. A man stood outside lounging against a wooden railing, smoking a cigarette, and I was forced to check him out pretty carefully because he was gorgeous. On the far side of forty, but not by much. Tall. Blonde. Chiseled. Built. He wore jeans that he filled out quite nicely with a medium blue T-shirt that matched his eyes exactly. His clothing was covered with paint spatters.

"Hi there."

"Hi."

"Do you work on the show? I haven't met you yet." He had an easy, warm smile and a natural sensuality he radiated like a seismic pulse. At least from where I stood. Forget Harrison Ford: this day was getting better by the minute.

"No," I gulped. "I'm here to see the costume designer."

Clever banter, Maggie.

The red light stopped flashing, and he opened the door for me. "Well, let's go in and find her."

We walked through a small entryway and yet another door into a blast of icy air that felt like a slap in the face. It took a minute for my eyes to adjust to the darkness cloaking most of the cavernous space, though at the far side of the stage a relatively small area was flooded with light by tiers of enormous bulbs arranged on metal stands like strings of high wattage cabochons. A free-form network of thick black cables virtually carpeted the floor; coiled in piles and snaking across the stage, they formed an obstacle course for the unwary. A spindly forest of wooden folding chairs with cloth seats and backs was clumped around two video monitors.

The air fairly hummed with the suppressed energy of seventy-five people scurrying around like a platoon of worker ants performing every activity in silence. Some of them wore headsets that allowed them to communicate quietly and efficiently while they worked. And they'd each claimed a bit of floor space as personal territory, setting up little camps with equipment, tools, and supplies — whatever they needed to access in order to most quickly perform their jobs.

"We're going again!" some guy with a headset and walkie-talkie shouted.

A bell shrilled, and all movement ceased as the stage got very quiet.

"Settle, please!" called a man wearing a pair of earphones. I put him in his late thirties with dark brown hair curling around his collar and thinning at the crown. He had a bookish look about him — horn-rimmed glasses, a bit thick through the middle. His gaze was riveted to one of the video monitors. "A-a-a-n-n-d action!"

It was then I saw Sylvester Stallone suspended in mid-air by some sort of body harness in front of an immense blue backdrop. Poised above him on a scaffold masked by the drop was a coltish young woman wearing an impossibly short, tight skirt and a bustier top that barely contained an impressive pair of store-bought breasts. She was balanced precariously on four-inch heels, wielding a submachine gun.

"What are they doing?" I asked Mr. Gorgeous.

"It's a blue-screen shot," he whispered close to my ear. "They photograph Stallone against this blue drop and matte in the real background later. He'll be hanging off the side of a building when you see this on the big screen in the theater."

"Wow!" It would almost be worth sitting through a Sylvester Stallone movie to see how this shot worked. Almost.

The girl struck a vampy pose with the gun pointed in Stallone's general direction, a stance more comical than threatening.

"Cut!" shouted the guy with the earphones. "Evangelina, what the hell are you doing with that gun? You look like a majorette waving a baton up there!"

The actress shaded her eyes, submachine akimbo. "Burton, since we've stopped anyway, can we discuss the dialogue in this scene?"

The fellow removed his earphones and replied with elaborate patience, "There is no dialogue, Sweetheart. It's an action sequence. You're trying to kill our hero, but sadly, the scene ends with you falling to your death. Have you forgotten that since we rehearsed it fifteen minutes ago?"

"No," she pouted, "but I've been thinking we should add something here to let the audience in on what's really happening. Maybe a, whaddaya-call-it, monologue!" She brightened at the thought. "I could be sitting in front of the mirror, combing my hair — Oh! I know, even better!" she squealed. "Standing in front of a full-length mirror, nude, thinking about this horrible thing I'm about to do." She closed her eyes and stretched out a hand as if to invite him to share her vision of the scene. "My perfect body a perfect contrast to the blackness in my heart."

At this point, one of the crew members gave an audible groan.

Her eyes snapped open. "I'm just trying to get clear on this, Burton. If I don't understand it, the audience sure as hell isn't going to!" She flipped a swath of dark curls over her shoulder and thrust out her most obvious assets defiantly. "Like, what's my motivation? It doesn't make any sense. I had sex with this guy last night, and now I'm trying to kill him? I mean, I just wouldn't ever do that!"

The beleaguered director jumped up and strode over to the base of the scaffold. "It's called acting, Evangelina. You should try it, preferably at some point when you're on camera. You're not playing yourself. You're a spy, a double agent. This man is your enemy. You slept with him to obtain information, and now you want to get rid of him. Jesus! Didn't you even glance at the script?"

"Now that you mention it," she whined petulantly, "my acting coach says it's no wonder I'm having trouble finding my character's center when the writing is so weak."

"That's it! Take a break everybody! Evangelina, I want to see you in my trailer!"

He stalked off toward the stage door. She tossed her head and gingerly tottered over to a set of wooden stairs leading down from her perch. Stallone, who hadn't uttered a sound throughout the exchange, was lowered to the ground and immediately engulfed by a retinue of people handing him towels, bottled water, a cell phone, and generally dancing attendance.

I gave a low whistle. "Well, that was exciting!"

"Lovers' spat. That's how they get their kicks," my new friend chuckled.

"Now they'll go make up in his trailer for an hour or so while the rest of the company cools its heels. On the clock, of course. It's no wonder we're so far behind schedule."

"You're kidding!"

"Dead serious."

"Hunh. Nice work if you can get it."

"I'm Rick Yeats," he said, holding out his hand to me.

"Maggie McGrath. What's your job on the movie?" I asked, feeling like I was back at Career Day in high school.

"I'm the paint foreman. I work with the production designer to realize his vision of each set, using paint to create the proper effects."

I squinched up my face in confusion and he laughed. "Come on over here, and I'll show you what I'm talking about." He motioned me to follow him across the stage to a twenty-foot- long free-standing masonite tunnel where two painters were working inside by the glare of a huge work light. Now I knew why they kept the stages so cold. Inside the wooden chamber, the heat from the light was stifling.

"This is going to be a marble hallway when these guys get done with it," Rick explained. "Rob and Moe, this is Maggie."

The painters nodded to me over their shoulders, never pausing as they swirled their narrow-headed brushes in a complex pattern over the masonite surface.

"It's a multi-step process, but it's a helluva lot cheaper than building a hall-way out of real marble." Rick pointed to the wall. "After we get the base coat on, we mix the colors we're going to use for the marble pattern in oil-base lacquers called japans. That's what the guys are doing now, laying on the colors to simulate the depth and texture you see in a piece of marble. Can't stop in the middle, though," he winked at me, "or you'll lose your rhythm."

Could it be my imagination or was that a double entendre? I raised my eyebrows in what I hoped was a knowing way. Just in case.

He pointed across the floor to another set, two rooms that looked to be the worse for wear, complete with stained wallpaper and flaking paint. "That's supposed to be a run-down apartment. After the carpenters built it, we hung paper and painted it to look like new, then aged it all, using materials and processes to give the illusion it's an older place." He spread his arms in a gesture that included all the work happening on the stage around us. "It's not just about putting paint on a wall; it's about physically defining a particular environment."

Clearly, this guy loved his job.

"I appreciate the tutorial. It sounds . . . conceptually challenging," I groped, trying to be appropriate in his lexicon. "And, uh, creative." Even to me, I sounded like a simp.

"Keeps me off the streets," he replied breezily.

He pointed out the set costumer, a tall, slender woman with jet black hair named Diane, who was part of Faye's crew. "That young lady can tell you what you need to know. I hope I see you again sometime. Come by, and I'll take you out for coffee."

He grinned, and I suddenly felt like I was melting from the inside out.

"I'd like that."

He waved. "Don't be a stranger."

Yikes.

I forced my attention back to Diane, who was in the middle of some urgent task, muttering to herself and chewing fiercely on a huge wad of gum as she aimed a blow dryer at a damp shirt hanging from a clothes rack. I had to shout to be heard over the noise.

"Hi! I'm looking for Faye Symington."

She didn't switch off the dryer or look up from her work. "She was here earlier, but she's gone back to our office in the Garbo Building. If you want to leave a resume, I'll be sure she gets it. Or you can drop it off yourself," she shrugged, still working with equal intensity on the shirt and her gum.

"Thanks. I'd like to talk to her."

"Suit yourself."

I inferred from her tone that seeking Faye in person would not have been Diane's first choice.

"Can you tell me how to get to the Garbo Building?"

She gave me directions: it was an easy hike from Stage 23.

"Our office is down in the Snake Pit," she added.

Snake Pit?

Five

No architectural credit to its glamorous eponym, the whimsically named Garbo Building was a squat bunker-like structure of beige concrete block. The reception desk was helmed by a vacant-looking older woman with a tightly teased bubble hairstyle last popular in the mid-sixties. Another fashion victim frozen in time.

"Wipe your feet!" she snapped as I came in the front door.

I looked at her and smiled. It wasn't raining, so I thought maybe this was her idea of repartee, a bit of madcap receptionist humor. No such luck, and there was no mistaking her meaning when she repeated testily, "I said, wipe your feet, young lady, before you step another foot in here."

I guessed all that back-combing had played havoc with the blood circulation to her brain. It wasn't like this was such a showplace. The reception area was hardly more than a cubicle with indifferent blue-gray carpeting and laminated furniture. But I did as she said and told her I was looking for Faye's office.

"It's in the Snake Pit," she sniffed, still put out with me and my untidy habits.

"And that would be someplace downstairs, I'm assuming?" I said pleasantly.

"Oh, for heaven's sake!" she grumbled, "through the door and down the hall."

Of course — silly me. The hallway she'd alluded to was lined on one side by a row of offices. The other side opened onto a large workroom packed with cutting tables piled high with fabrics and heavy industrial sewing machines that produced a mechanical cacophony drowning all other sound. Dress forms draped with partial garments were scattered around the room like so many headless, half-dressed beauty contestants.

At the end of the hall was a stairway leading to the basement, a stark utilitarian space with low ceilings made to seem even lower by networks of exposed pipes, the whole of it painted a flat mouse-gray that sucked up most of the light that managed to seep down into this catacomb. The glare from fluorescent fixtures didn't do much to penetrate the gloom. Rounding a dark corner, I gave a bleat of alarm at the sight of a shadowy cage heaped with female body parts. It turned out to be a service elevator; the wayward limbs belonged to plaster mannequins. But my heart kept up a panicky little dance as I hurried on down the hall toward the suite of offices known as the Snake Pit. They were, supposedly, not so-called because of the warren-like configuration that made them so claustrophobic and charmless, but rather because in the old MGM days, that spot had been used as a set for the Olivia de Havilland vehicle with that title. Faye was in the largest office, located at the farthest corner of the cul-de-sac where the "pit" ended. I could hear her talking in an agitated voice from halfway down the hall.

"It shouldn't be losing money when we have huge crowds of people lining up to get in every night of the week!"

There was a lengthy pause; she was apparently on the phone. I'm not in the habit of eavesdropping — honestly — but this was no time to interrupt.

"No. NO! Listen to me!"

Another pause. Then her voice went up half an octave. "You've had your chance, Robert! I've been more than patient! I'm not listening to any more excuses or double-talk from you or Lillian! I'm taking the whole damned mess to my own person to sort out. He's going to tell me once and for all what's what!" Her pitch dropped to a menacing growl. "And if I find out you've been fucking with me, believe me when I say there won't be a corner of the world that'll be safe for you! I'll turn up the heat until you pop like a roasted pig! You know I can, and I'll do it with pleasure!"

Brief pause.

"Oh, no? Well, you just watch me!"

She slammed the receiver down. I waited four long beats, then knocked lightly on the doorjamb.

"Who is it?" More of a snarl than a question.

Taking my life in my hands, I stuck my head in the door. "Faye, Maggie McGrath. Have I caught you at a bad time?"

To my surprise, she pasted on a big, false smile. "Maggie, dear, do come in."

Her office was a shrine to armed force; the walls were fairly plastered with research boards depicting military clothing from all over the world. Swatches of camouflage fabric in every color and pattern imaginable were tacked to pieces of foam core propped up along the baseboards, and two small bookcases overflowed with a collection of books and periodicals devoted to the military and related subjects. The one incongruous note was struck by a poster-size blow-up of a still photograph, beautifully framed and leaning against one of the bookcases, a candid of the two stars, Stallone and Seagal, with their heads bent together in serious conversation. A cartoon dialogue bubble issued from both their mouths: "We are two of the biggest assholes who ever walked the earth." I craned forward to read the scrawl of black magic marker that filled the lower right-hand corner: "When I first came out to Hollywood, they told me, 'Film is a collaborative medium.' What they should have said is, 'Film is a collaborative medium — bend over.'"

Faye's eyes followed my gaze. "A parting gift from the screenwriter," she said casually. "He sent one to all the department heads just before he quit the film. The wimp. Don't worry," she seemed to divine my question, "nobody above-the-line would ever be caught dead down here. And nobody else counts."

She was sitting behind a large wooden desk piled with a chaotic jumble of books, files, sketch pads, glue sticks, scissors, and drawing implements. A lamp with a printed silk scarf draped over its shade gave off a diffuse light but failed to soften the institutional bleakness of the room. Also competing for precious desk space was a statue on a pedestal of a winged being holding a globe in its out-stretched arms, a trophy of some kind.

"I'm so glad you came by," she said cordially.

Faye wore a tailored navy blue jacket trimmed with a crisp outline of white piping and large white pearl buttons. Her purple hair was mostly covered by a navy cloche adorned with a big white silk flower that resembled nothing found in nature. The tinted glasses hung on a beaded chain around her neck, so I could see her face better than I'd been able to the night before. She had hazel eyes like her daughter's that slanted up slightly at the corners and a small nose that had probably benefited from some surgical sculpting. It was not an unattractive face, but the effect was spoiled by a puckery little mouth that gave her a look of constant disapproval, as if she'd just tasted something unpleasant.

"I was going to call you today. I'm afraid we got off on a bad foot last night." She pulled her lips back over her teeth in a terrifying parody of a friendly grin. "Have a seat, my dear. Let's chat and get to know each other better."

Said the spider to the fly.

I sat down uneasily with my inner ear cocked for the hidden agenda and opened the spiral notebook I always carry in my bag. "I think it would be more to the point, Ms. Symington, if we could talk about the matter of the notes and phone calls. I don't want to take any more of your time than necessary."

"I wish you'd call me Faye." A stiff smile, clearly an effort, accompanied this invitation.

"Faye," I agreed. "Can you please tell me when the first note arrived?"

She tugged at the beaded chain on her glasses, her eyes glazed with annoyance. "I thought you went through all that with Sara."

"She told me all she knows," I said carefully, "but you may have information she doesn't, maybe without even realizing it. A different perspective on the same facts can sometimes be a help."

Especially from the target's point of view, I thought.

"I really can't fathom what I might know that Sara doesn't. I'm so bloody sick of the whole business," she sighed peevishly.

I felt myself flush with impatience. Her little passive-aggressive routine was already wearing thin, and we'd only exchanged a few sentences in our two brief meetings. "I can appreciate how you must feel, Faye. But threats made by anyone who is twisted and malicious enough to butcher your pet and leave it at your front door are cause for legitimate concern."

"Yes, poor Snow. He was a stupid creature, but sweet enough," she mused, doodling on one of her sketch pads. She appeared to be absorbed by the random squiggles she was producing, sort of a do-it-yourself Rohrschach that I was betting spoke volumes (not that I'd want to read them, mind you) about her self-involved psyche.

"If we might digress for just a minute," she looked up from her drawing and smiled sweetly, changing tactics, "there is an aspect of this situation that I'd particularly like to discuss with you."

"All right." I hoped that letting her take the lead might prove more productive.

"It's an ill wind that blows nobody good," she continued thoughtfully, "and I think we might be able to turn all this to our advantage."

"How do you mean?" I couldn't imagine where this was going.

"Well, Maggie," she said using her best "just between us girls" tone, "I hired a publicist about a month ago. I knew I was in the running for a nomination, and press does nothing but help in such circumstances. It's true that there is no such thing as bad publicity. I think we may be able to get some mileage out of this — human interest combined with Hollywood celebrity — perfect for stories in *People* and *Us*. You know, 'Oscar Nominee Persecuted By Anonymous Nemesis.' It may even be good enough to land a couple of talk show guest spots. I think Regis and Kathie Lee would jump at it!"

She resumed her doodling with studied nonchalance, a series of elaborately rendered dollar signs. "I'd like to keep you on, Maggie, but with the understanding that you'll cooperate fully with the publicist. I'd like you to be quoted in the articles, offering your professional opinion. It gives the story more dimension." She glanced up, looking for my reaction. This was all a game to her, and I was just another puppet to use as best she could.

"Well, that's just —" I was about to say idiotic — "not a very good plan," I went for something less inflammatory. "If this character is turned on by publicity, it might just encourage him."

She dismissed that notion with a wave of her hand. "When one gets to be a superstar in one's field, one does so at a cost," she replied grandly. "One becomes the object of the malicious envy of those who've not had the same success."

"So you think the harassment is motivated purely by professional rivalry?" I asked, reminding myself that stranger scenarios had proven true. "Do you have any thoughts about who that might be?"

"It could be anyone. Everyone's jealous of me now because of the nomination." She fixed me with a gaze as hard as marble. "To achieve the heights I have, one has to be so focused, so single-minded, that nothing but the goal matters. I can't worry about other people's feelings. So I've stepped on some toes on my way to the top." One tailored shoulder lifted in a delicate shrug. "That's the way this business works." She looked down at the trophy on her desk and fingered it lovingly. "This is the Emmy I won ten years ago. It's the first thing I bring into every new office I set up, to remind myself that high standards reap tangible rewards. And soon there'll be another little gold statue to keep this one company, because this is my Oscar year. I just know it!"

I thought it was time to let some air out of her balloon. "Then tell me about Jeremy Latham. Why did he come after you last night?"

She turned an arctic stare on me. "Jeremy Latham is a pathetic, sick-minded non-entity. He barely exists."

"And I couldn't help but overhear," I pressed her, "both last night and this afternoon, you've had a couple of angry altercations on the phone —"

"I wasn't aware you'd been hired to spy on me!" she interrupted angrily.

Great. So here we go; the gloves are off. "Faye, I'm on your side. But I can't help you if you're not straight with me," I snapped.

We glared at each other, and I took satisfaction when she dropped her eyes first. She began to rearrange her desk, manufacturing activity. "You'll have to excuse me now. I really am crushed with appointments this afternoon."

So much for our "getting to know you" chat.

"We can continue this later," I nodded curtly and got up to leave. "In the meantime, give some thought to what I've said. We shouldn't be fanning the flames of this situation when we have no idea who or what we're dealing with." Then, hoping to appeal to the motherly side of her nature, I paused in the doorway and added, "Sara is very upset and worried about you. I think it might be helpful to her if you're sensitive to her concerns."

That set her off like a rocket.

"My daughter is a neurotic, unstable girl! She doesn't have my strength of will. It's just lucky for her that I've always taken care of her. But sometimes her weakness and dependency are nothing short of suffocating. I don't have the energy or the patience right now to hold her hand through another nervous collapse. This is my time in the spotlight! I've worked hard for it, and I deserve to enjoy it!"

So much for maternal instinct.

I leaned against the doorjamb, studying her. I found the pathology interesting. She worked so hard at maintaining that thin veneer of charm, but despite her efforts, the real Faye kept gurgling through the cracks. "What about Galen? Doesn't he take some of the burden from you?"

"Galen!" she scoffed. "He's an actor!" (As if that explained any number of personal failings.) "Another millstone around my neck. Why I ever permitted that marriage in the first place is now a mystery to me! He's lazy and self-centered — he's as spineless as Sara. No. He's no help to me at all." She sighed, closing her eyes and remarshaling her defenses. "Please, just do as I ask. My publicist's name is Harry Wald. When he calls, be cooperative, and you will have earned your fee."

I was dismissed.

I walked back to my car, thinking maybe I should just bag the whole thing. I certainly had no intention of participating in Faye's self-promotional scheme. Nothing I'd learned so far was of much benefit. My client was a selfish, disagreeable woman who valued notoriety over the well-being of her daughter. Poor Sara. Whichever side of the Nature vs. Nurture question you subscribe to, she got a bad deal. And it was for her sake alone that I decided to stick with it for the time being.

I was troubled by a swarm of questions that buzzed around my brain like annoying insects. Was Faye so arrogant that she couldn't imagine her own vulnerability? If my cat had been fileted and left on my doorstep, I'd have a worry or two about it. Or was she somehow involved? Could it all have been engineered as a bid for cheap publicity? It was an ugly possibility I had to admit. And what about that angry phone call? What was losing money that shouldn't be? A movie? I made a note to check with Sara about what films Faye had in current release and what her financial stake in them was at this point. And about who "Robert" of the recent tongue-lashing might be.

I like to start with the obvious and work my way around to obscure because A) that's easier, and B) sometimes a cigar is, after all, just a cigar. To that end, I stopped at a coffee place on Venice Boulevard for a double latte and a look at the phone book. I jotted down the address that interested me, and I called the number that was listed to see if anyone was home. A man's voice answered on the sixth ring sounding gravelly with sleep even though it was nearly four o'clock in the afternoon. I hung up, picked up my coffee, and was on my way.

Six

Jeremy Latham lived in Silverlake on Berkeley Avenue, a sloping tree-lined street in a pleasant middle-class neighborhood. I pulled up in front of a little white one-story California craftsman bearing the number I'd noted. The yard was artfully landscaped with a variety of drought-resistant plants and was bordered by a low wooden fence, also painted white. I let myself in the gate, climbed three steps to the porch, and rang the doorbell. Bare footsteps shuffled toward the door.

"Who is it?" I recognized Jeremy's reedy voice.

"It's Maggie McGrath. We met last night at the exhibit. I tried to call but got no answer. I came by to see if you're all right."

The door opened a crack, and Jeremy peered out, blinking against the glare of the afternoon sun. A short owlish-looking man, he might have been anywhere from late twenties to early forties. His hair was a downy fringe of brown concentrated mainly around his ears, and he wore rimless glasses that magnified his eyes, giving him a look of perpetual amazement.

"We met last night?" he repeated uncertainly. "I'm sorry, I was in pretty bad shape."

"I know." Practically the first honest thing I'd said to him. "Don't worry about it. I only live a few blocks away, and I was on my way home anyway, so I just decided to stop by. You're okay, then?"

"Yes, thank you," he said primly.

There was an awkward pause, then we both started to speak at once.

"Would you —?"

"May I —"

We both laughed, and Jeremy opened the door for me. "Would you like to come in for some coffee? Or tea?" he offered.

"Coffee sounds great," I said, though I was already buzzing from the latte.

His living room was furnished with pieces from the '30's and '40's. I sat on a gray tweed sofa, and Jeremy excused himself to fix the coffee. The room was comfortable and attractive with a polished wood floor and large windows facing west and south framed by drapes made of vintage fabric, a soft floral print in shades of light gray, green, and coral. A brick fireplace occupied much of the east wall, its mantel crowded with framed photographs.

I crossed the room to get a better look, my predilection to snoop easily overcoming good manners. A number of the pictures appeared to be family snapshots — Jeremy posed with young children (nieces and nephews?) and adults who resembled each other enough to be siblings. Some of the group pictures included a slight auburn-haired young man, and there were also several photos of just Jeremy and him. A single portrait of the young man in a lovely silver frame sat by itself at one end of the mantel with a dried rose lying in front of it and a votive candle to one side.

"That's Scott."

Jeremy was balancing a tray laden with coffee cups, a china coffee pot, cream, sugar, spoons, and napkins, which he set on the bird's-eye maple coffee table in front of the sofa.

"He looks nice."

"He was," Jeremy said fondly. "Do you take cream or sugar?"

"Black, please."

He poured the coffee, which smelled good and strong, and handed me a cup.

"Thanks." I sipped.

I studied him as he drank his like medicine. He was obviously nursing a walloping hangover; his face had that "morning after" puffiness, and his movements were carefully choreographed to spare his head any unnecessary listings to either side. All the bellowing bluster I'd seen from his alter ego the night before had fallen away. Today he seemed a perfectly well-bred, reserved little man, and I had to wonder how often he trotted out the Jekyll and Hyde routine.

"You seemed pretty upset last night," I ventured.

Jeremy looked pained. "Yes, I guess I made a real ass of myself. I don't usually drink." Something told me he needed to talk, so I sipped my coffee, hoping my silence would encourage him to continue. "Yesterday was an anniversary," he finally said. "Scott died exactly one year ago."

"I'm so sorry," I murmured.

"Thanks. We had six great years together. But I still can't help feeling cheated." He smiled ruefully. "Nothing like a little self-pity to get the blood circulating first thing in the afternoon." He took another gulp of coffee. "I guess I just snapped last night," he said, shaking his head. "It was such an emotional day, and I did have way too much wine at dinner. And then, when I saw Faye Symington holding court with everybody slobbering all over her . . . " He sighed, scrubbing one hand roughly over his face. "I'm sorry. The last of my social graces seem to be evaporating. I'm just a little on the 'woe is me' side today — another bit of payback for last night, I expect — but I shouldn't be dumping this on you. You came by to check on me, and you don't know me from Adam. It's very kind of you to be concerned. Kind of you to listen."

At that moment, I felt about two feet tall. I took a deep breath. "Jeremy, I was at the exhibit last night as Sara Landesmann's guest."

He looked puzzled.

"Faye Symington's daughter."

"So, then, why are you really here?" he demanded in a bitchy tone. Not that I blamed him.

My hands went up in surrender. "I can understand why you might be unhappy with me. To tell you the truth, I'm not that thrilled with myself at the moment. But Faye has gotten some personal threats recently, and Sara asked me to look into it. I'm a private investigator," I said, reaching into my bag for my identification. "I'd like to hear your side of the story about what happened last night."

"You've got a lot of nerve. Are you accusing me of something?"

"Not at all. I don't know what to think yet," I replied. "I'm just trying to make some sense of this. Maybe you can help me. That's why I'm here. Really."

He stared at me coldly. I didn't know if he was about to throw me out or do a variation on last night's theme and toss coffee in my lap. Then he stood abruptly and began pacing, his bare feet making soft slapping sounds on the wood floor.

"I don't have to defend myself to you," he said.

"No, you don't," I agreed. "But you seem like a gentle, thoughtful person. To behave the way you did last night, I'm guessing you must have had some reason besides a low tolerance for alcohol."

He whirled to face me again, eyes flashing. I braced myself for a verbal assault when suddenly, almost as if some interior plug were pulled, all the energy drained from his body. He looked exhausted. "I don't know what I believe about life after death," he said slowly, "but if there is such a place as hell, then Faye Symington has earned a seat of honor there."

He padded over to a rocking chair near the hearth and sat in it heavily. He rocked, staring at the ceiling, saying nothing for awhile. The creaking of a warped floorboard marked time as the chair glided back and forth. When he began to speak again, his voice was quiet and even. "Scott was brilliant. He was a gifted draper, much more so than I. Very technically skilled, very creative. He loved working for Faye, I suppose because she gave him so much freedom. She'd come to him with some vague sketch, or sometimes just an idea about the kind of thing she wanted, and he would turn out a beautiful, fully-realized work of art. Which she then took complete credit for, by the way. But that was fine with him. His pleasure was in the doing of the thing. And privately she was very appreciative of his talent."

"Forgive me for interrupting, but what, exactly, does a draper do?" I asked.

I think he almost smiled at me. "Bring your coffee with you." He crossed the room and folded back a set of wooden louvered doors to reveal what had probably once been a dining room, now converted to Jeremy's workroom. A rectangular table with a smooth muslin surface stood near the west-facing windows with an industrial sewing machine snugged up beside it. The table was tall enough for Jeremy to stand and work at it without bending over and was set atop a platform lined with neatly labeled drawers of supplies. The walls were covered with corkboard, and bundles of homemade brown paper patterns skewered by vicious-looking T-pins hung in awkward clumps interspersed with delicate watercolor sketches of women in hoop-skirted dresses.

"I'm working on the clothes for Mimi and Musetta for a regional production of *La Boheme*." Jeremy pulled a dress form half-swathed in a shapeless sea of muslin nearer the table and slid onto a stool beside it. "This is going to be Musetta's Act Two frock — you know, when she sings her famous aria — Daa, daa, da-dee. Dah-da-da-da-da. Dee-dee-dee!"

From my blank expression, Jeremy correctly deduced that I hadn't a clue about what he was singing and broke off, just managing not to roll his eyes, I suspect. "Well, anyway," he soldiered on, "the draper takes the sketch of a costume," he indicated one of the drawings tacked on the wall with a nod, "and creates the pattern used to make it. That often requires a combination of techniques, but the 'draping' refers to taking fabric and molding it on a dress form to achieve the proper shapes for the pattern pieces." He worked quickly as he talked, folding a crisp tuck here with a pin to hold it in place, a pleat there secured with another pin. Before my eyes, the fitted bodice trimmed with ruffles I saw in the sketch began to take shape beneath his fingers.

"It's almost like you're performing some sleight-of-hand magic trick!" I, who am stymied by the act of threading a needle, found the entire procedure extraordinary. I pointed at the dress form. "That's absolutely beautiful!"

This time there was no mistaking his smile. "Next I'll mark all the pieces on the form here to show me where the darts and tucks and seams should be. Then I'll lay it all out flat on the table to true up the lines, and finally I'll cut into the real fabric using these shapes I've developed as a guide."

I frowned as my brain connected the dots. "So, if you don't have somebody very skilled taking care of this part of it —"

"Your ass is basically grass," Jeremy nodded. "It doesn't matter how pretty the drawing is if the pattern used to make the actual garment isn't right. So, I'm sure you can appreciate what an important part of the costuming process this is."

I nodded. "Did Scott work exclusively for Faye?"

His expression clouded. "No, but they did several projects together." He picked up a piece of yellow chalk and hefted it in his hand as if mulling something over, then gave his head a little shake and began making hash marks on the muslin bodice, his movements brisk and efficient. "Until Scott got sick. We'd known he was HIV-positive for three years, but he hadn't been symptomatic." His tone was matter-of-fact. "It became more and more difficult for him to work. He couldn't be certain how well he'd feel from one day to the next, so he wasn't always able to meet his deadlines, which wasn't like Scott at all. It made him frantic, all the more so when people stopped calling him. It was heartbreaking."

The marking completed, he began plucking out the pins holding the bodice together. "And then Faye got another movie — a big period movie — and she called, asking if he could do the female star's clothes. Well, he was ecstatic. He told her, Yes, of course, he'd be delighted! Then reality set in. He knew he didn't have the stamina to drive back and forth to a shop everyday, that he'd need the leeway to be able to work whenever he felt like it, even if that was at three o'clock in the morning. So he called her back. Asked if she could arrange it so he could work at home but still be covered by a union contract so his benefits would be maintained."

He snatched a piece of the bodice from the dress form and began pinning it out on the muslin surface of the cutting table. His hands worked as steadily as before, but his voice betrayed his emotion. "Faye knew he was desperate to work, so she used that to her own advantage. She told him he could work at home, but only for cash under the table, which she buried in the budget somehow."

"I get it," I said. "No health insurance."

"And no set hours, either," he said grimly. "It was a huge project — the one she's nominated for, as a matter of fact. She gave him a huge amount of work, and why not? She was getting top-dollar talent at bargain-basement prices. I tried to get Scott to cut back, to give up some of the work she piled on him, but he was obsessed with proving he could do it. He drove himself beyond the point of exhaustion." He looked up at me, his gaze flat and metallic. "Three months later he was dead."

"And you blame Faye."

He turned to stare out the windows to the west. "I shouldn't have thrown the drink at her," he said softly. "That wasn't worthy of Scott's memory. But if this world is not completely insane — and I often think it is — she'll have to answer for the way she treated him. Someday."

We were both silent for a time. Then he shook his head and went back to his pinning. "Believe what you like. I've made no threats against Faye. I try to keep myself as positively focused as possible. Most of the time. Better for my immune system." His mouth twitched in a humorless smile. "But you'll find no shortage of people who wish her ill, and with cause."

"Would you mind being more specific?"

He shrugged as if to say 'where do I begin?' and reached for a clear plastic ruler he then used to line up two of the hash marks on his muslin pattern. "There's her ex-assistant, Amy Hodges. They parted on very bitter terms, from what I hear. I think Amy may have even left the business because of it." Two quick flicks of a sharpened pencil produced a crisp seam line on the pattern.

"Any idea what the trouble was?"

"Not really." Flick, flick. "I heard some gossip at the time — this would have been a couple of years ago — but Amy and I were never close friends, so no, I couldn't tell you for sure."

"Do you know if Amy still lives in Los Angeles?"

"No, I don't." His pencil continued to dance over the muslin, marking stitch lines. "But you should call the Costume Designers Guild, the film design union. They'll know how to get in touch with her."

"Anybody else?" I prodded.

He sighed a little impatiently. "Not that I can think of right now. She's just alienated a lot of people. It's probably her greatest talent." He leaned back to push a couple of buttons on a small boombox sitting on the windowsill behind him, and the high quavering notes of some coloratura heroine rippled out. "I hope you don't mind." His apology was all form, no content. "I need to have music while I work."

Contrary to popular opinion, I can take a hint. Besides, I'd about run out of questions for him. "Thank you for your time and the information." I held out my hand. "It was nice to meet you, Jeremy. I wish you all the best."

"Thank you," he replied coolly. "Good luck."

I walked out into the intense afternoon sunshine and climbed wearily into the Toyota. Yeah, I'd had just about enough fun for one day. Auntie Em's was only a few blocks west. I drove over there and parked behind the store. I went in by the street entrance to my office which meant I had to contend with a hillock of junk mail on the floor. The mail at my office is delivered through a slot in the lower part of the door. It's kind of an annoying system because everything that's dropped through the slot just goes splat in the middle of the floor. Not only is it messy, but if I happen to be in conference with a client, it can be startling to have a small avalanche of paper suddenly come hurtling through the door.

No messages on the voice mail, so I went next door for the comfort of a friendly face. The interview with Jeremy had left me depressed and vaguely unsettled. I was beginning to get the feeling that Faye had, over the years, sewn the seeds of enmity in many fertile fields.

"There you are!"

Joyce was sitting behind the counter reading one of the romance novels which are her only remaining vice, her feet propped on a small stool she keeps back there for that purpose. It cheered me just to see her outfit. Her vintage circle skirt was decorated with a Spanish motif — a cape-wielding matador and bull outlined in red, green, and silver sequins. With an eye to cross-culturalism, her hair was knotted on top of her head, rakishly speared by a pair of chopsticks with red rhinestone balls dangling from the ends. This festive ensemble was completed by a red silk shirt tied at her waist and a velvet ribbon choker that served as a perch for a small artificial bird nestling daintily at the base of her throat.

"I sent Gail home early. It's slow today, and she had a dentist appointment this morning, so she was feeling kinda crummy." She got up and headed for the tiny kitchenette curtained off from the rest of the store by an Indian bedspread. "Want some herbal tea? I've got some great raspberry leaf — good for cleaning out the toxins," she called.

I hate herbal tea, but I was in the mood to be fussed over, so I accepted gratefully. Joyce re-emerged a minute later and handed me a mug of hot, medicinal-smelling liquid. "So, I've got this great idea." She sat down and clasped her hands in her lap, fixing me with a bright-eyed gaze.

"Okay," I said warily.

"I want to renovate the second floor here. It's just wasted space now. Make it into a coffee bar with, you know, espresso drinks, fat free muffins, biscotti." She made a rolling motion with her hand indicating endless possibilities.

"Yeah, that sounds great," I said with some genuine enthusiasm. *No more of this shitty herbal tea,* thought I.

"And I thought we might make it a kind of mini-gallery. Local artists could bring in their work, and we could feature someone new every month. Whaddaya think?" Joyce clapped her hands in excitement.

"Joyce, when you get jazzed about an idea, you're like a force of nature," I said with a laugh.

"You don't think it's a good idea?" she asked, crestfallen.

"I didn't say that. I think it's a really good idea. Sounds like a lot of work, though."

"Oh, it'll be fun," she said blithely. "And I know who I'd like to feature the first month."

"Who?" I sipped at the awful-tasting tea.

"You!"

I gasped, sucking a mouthful of tea into my lungs and spent the next minute and a half coughing till I was blue in the face while Joyce pounded on my back solicitously.

"I don't think that part of the idea's so great," I managed to choke out as my breath came back.

"Oh, come on, Babe! I love your little forests. You shouldn't be so shy about showing your work."

Most of my paintings are of trees — don't ask me why. Their images are just deeply resonant for me. But the thought of a public show sent me into a tailspin of anxiety.

"I paint because I love it, Joyce. For fun. Putting it on display for strangers to pick apart and criticize would not be fun for me. It would make it all way too serious."

My palms were breaking a sweat just thinking about it.

"Well, give it some more thought before you say no," she said, as though I hadn't already done just that. But Joyce is nothing if not persistent, so I knew I hadn't heard the last of this.

Then we talked companionably awhile about inconsequential things and soon I was feeling better. I thanked Joyce and went back to my office to tackle one last chore for the day. Starting with 213, I began calling Information for the various possible area codes within the greater Los Angeles urban sprawl. I hit it on the third try, in 818. The Costume Designers Guild was in Sherman Oaks.

"May I help you?" It was a woman's voice heavily accented by the familiar cadence of the New York metropolitan area — a fellow refugee.

"I hope so. I'm looking for a telephone number for a woman I believe is a member of your union. Amy Hodges."

"And you are?" she demanded sternly.

"My name is Maggie McGrath. I'm calling for Faye Symington," I added quickly.

"Oh. All right," she said, placated by the prominent name. "I'm going to have to put you on hold."

She was gone a long time, and I was subjected during that interval to some atonal yelping, the broadcast from a self-proclaimed "cutting edge" radio station that made me yearn for good old-fashioned syrupy Muzak. I had almost reached the limits of my endurance when she came back on the line.

"Amy Hodges is no longer an active member. I can give you the number we have for her, but I can't guarantee that it's current."

She gave me another 818 number where a machine answered, "Hi, this is Amy. Leave a message. When I get it, I'll call you back. Couldn't be simpler."

I waited out a series of obnoxious beeps. "Amy, this is Maggie McGrath. I'm a private investigator and would appreciate your help with a couple of questions. Please call me at your earliest convenience." I recited both my numbers and hung up.

One more call; the machine picked up there, as well.

"Sara, it's Maggie. We need to talk, but it can wait till tomorrow. I'll call you in the morning. Take care, and feel free to call me tonight if you need to."

After repeating my home number, I hung up, grabbed my bag, and stopped in to say goodnight to Joyce. I started to drive home, but a loose end was nagging me, so I headed back across town to Nichols Canyon Road. The sun had set by the time I arrived. There were no cars parked outside the Symington house. But as I came up the driveway, two of the new lights came on in sequence, and when I got out of the car and climbed the front steps, two more lights picked out my approach. Satisfied, I returned to the car and finally went home to feed the cats.

I felt so guilty when I let myself into Chris's house. Poor Lisa thought she'd been abandoned. I'd forgotten to feed her that morning, so both her regular food dish and her bowl of crunchy snacks were licked clean. She yeowled reproachfully when I came in the door. I fed her and petted her and told her how beautiful she was, so that by the time I left, harmony was restored. But I had to agree with her: the little house felt lonely without my neighbor.

I went through the same routine at home with Skunky. He usually makes a big drama out of the Return of the Prodigal Owner. To hear him tell it, you'd never guess he's one of the top ten most spoiled cats on the planet.

It was one of those nights I felt too drained to undertake anything creative or useful. I just didn't want to think that hard. I settled for a long hot bath with a liter of Diet Pepsi, a box of Wheat Thins, a trashy mystery, and the Skunkster sitting on the side of the tub keeping me company. A hearty dose of artificial colors and sweeteners, plenty of salt, and disposable reading chemically flogged those pesky neurons of mine into submission, and I was asleep by ten o'clock — a nearly perfect evening to my way of thinking, and I say that with a clear understanding of just how pathetic it makes me sound.

Seven

"Oh Maggie, she's dead!"

I knew then I was probably still asleep.

"Maggie?" A disembodied voice urged me to wake up. Somehow I'd gotten hold of the portable phone by my bed, and it was propped up against my ear. Groping for my powers of coherent thought and speech, "Huh?" was what I managed.

"Maggie?"

"Yeah."

"This is Jeri Collins, Sara's sister." The edge of tears in her voice helped jumpstart my brain.

"What is it? Is Sara all right?'

"Yes. I mean, no, not really. But it's Mother I'm calling about —" Her voice broke. "Oh, Maggie, she's dead!"

"What?" I'd gotten all the individual words but was having trouble stringing them together.

"Someone killed her; she's been murdered!"

"What the hell happened?" Now I was awake — from 0 to 60 in ten seconds flat.

"I'm really not sure yet. The police are on their way over. Oh, my God! I just can't believe it!"

"Just hang on, Jeri," I said, working to keep my own voice steady. "Who's there with you now?"

"No one — I mean, just Sara." She drew a shuddering breath. "Listen, I hate to ask you this, but could you come over here? Now? We're all alone here and Sara's —" Tears threatened to overwhelm her again. "She's been asking for you."

"How is she?" I'd already started pulling on my jeans.

"Basket case," Jeri sobbed. "I gave her two Valium, but she's still hysterical."

"Where's Galen?"

"On his way back from San Diego. He was supposed to have an audition there this morning, so he went down last night and stayed over. I called him just before I called you. He should be on the road by now."

"I'll be right over."

I pulled on leather boots and a sweater, grabbed my jacket, and as I ran out the door I checked the clock. 5:05 A.M. Half an hour later, I turned into the Symington driveway. It was still dark, and the motion-sensor lights winked on to reveal an unmarked Chevrolet sedan parked alongside Sara's Jeep and Jeri's BMW.

I bounded up the steps and rang the bell. Jeri answered the door, looking haggard. Her light brown hair was an unkempt cloud wreathing her face. She wore no make-up and was dressed in leggings and an oversized sweatshirt.

"Two detectives are here. They were just telling us what happened."

"How did you find out about it?" Surely the cops hadn't called ahead with such tidings.

Jeri leaned back to brace herself against the arch of the entryway. "I felt like I was coming down with the flu, so I went to bed early. Mother hadn't come home, but that wasn't unusual. I slept like a rock, but Sara woke up at four o'clock, and Mother still wasn't home. She called the office, and the police answered."

She sighed wearily and covered her eyes with one hand. I patted her shoulder and steered her into the family room where a very pale-looking Sara was sitting with two men in dark suits. As soon as she saw me, she sprang up and flung herself into my arms. "I'm so glad you're here! It's so awful! I don't think I can stand it!"

I held her and let her cry for a bit, then led her back to sit with the two policemen. They introduced themselves as Detectives Donleavy and Ames of LAPD Homicide. Donleavy was a lieutenant and the older of the two, maybe in his mid-fifties. Like a man just rousted out of bed, he needed a shave and his suit could have used a press, but something told me he probably always looked that way. What was left of his thinning hair was salt and pepper. The contours of his face had begun to soften like unbaked dough, drooping into a series of creases. But his eyes were bright and hard and alert as he watched us. His partner was about twenty years his junior, a wiry fellow with sandy hair and a mustache.

Sara introduced me as a family friend. Since I wasn't a blood relation, Lieutenant Donleavy was reluctant to continue the conversation in my presence, but Sara insisted I remain, and in the end, he deferred to her wishes.

Faye's body was discovered in the Snake Pit office at approximately 12:30 A.M. by a studio security guard making his nightly rounds. His curiosity was piqued when he saw doors open and lights still on at the far end of the hallway that was always locked up and dark by the time he came on duty. He'd gone to check on whoever was burning the midnight oil and found Faye lying face down beside her desk with the back of her skull caved in, the brown industrial carpeting around her soaked in blood. The instrument used to accomplish her death was her beloved Emmy statuette, which lay on the floor next to her, covered with blood and gore. Sara and Jeri clung to each other while we listened to the details with Donleavy acting as spokesman.

"Do you know how long she'd been dead when the guard found her?" I asked when he'd finished.

"The ME tech at the scene thought two to three hours, tops. We're going to start interviewing members of her crew, other people who worked near her in the building, and the movie's production staff to determine who had the last verifiable contact with her." All this was volunteered by Detective Ames. Donleavy shot him a warning glance.

Sara sat with her eyes closed and her head bowed. "Did she suffer much pain?" she asked in a strained whisper.

Donleavy grimaced and shifted uncomfortably. "No, Miss, the death was very quick. The first blow probably did it. I doubt she felt anything."

She covered her face with her hands and began to rock back and forth, weeping softly.

Jeri put a protective arm around her sister. "If you'll excuse us, I think I'd better take her to lie down now."

"I don't want to lie down!" Sara shrieked, pushing away from her. The next moment she collapsed again in her sister's arms, burying her head on Jeri's shoulder and almost screaming with agony.

Alarmed by her outburst, I half-rose from my seat, then stood there in a hesitant semi-crouch without a clue as to how to make myself useful. "Maybe we should call a doctor," I suggested anxiously.

"Just give us a minute, will you?" Jeri snapped tearfully, coaxing Sara to her feet. She wound her arms around Sara's waist and guided her down the hallway toward the bedrooms.

I lowered myself back onto the couch, and the detectives and I were left sitting in an awkward silence that was only amplified by the ticking of a wooden clock hanging over the mantel. I knew I had to get it over with, so I plunged ahead. "I don't know how much Jeri and Sara had time to tell you before I got here, but Sara was concerned for her mother's safety because of harassing notes and phone calls she'd received within the past two weeks." They both stared at me in surprise. Donleavy narrowed his eyes, waiting for the other shoe to drop. "I'm actually here this morning because Sara hired me the day before yesterday. I'm a private investigator," I said, steeled for the look of distaste that flashed across his face.

He uttered an impatient grunt and rubbed his eyes. "Why didn't you tell us you were a PI right away?" he demanded.

"Yeah, what are you trying to pull here?" his partner chimed in.

I stiffened but kept a lid on my temper. "When I walked in that door, you were in the middle of telling two young women how their mother had been bludgeoned to death. And for whatever reason, Sara wanted me with her. What was I supposed to do, say, Yoo-hoo! Wait, guys, before you go any farther, you should know I'm a private investigator? What difference does it make?" I asked harshly. "I'm telling you now, and I'll tell you whatever I know. I'm not here to get in anybody's way, so don't get your egos out of joint." I shook my suddenly aching head. "I care about Sara," I added softly. "I just wish I could've helped her more."

"Well, you know what they say about the road to hell," the Lieutenant muttered. But he'd dropped the accusatory tone; now he only sounded tired and cranky. That I could relate to. He stifled a yawn. "Jesus! I'd give my left nu—"

he froze mid-stretch and cut his eyes at me, "knee for a cup of coffee right now."

"That would make two of us," I said dryly.

One corner of his mouth twitched, but he managed to short circuit a grin. "Let's back up now and go over all this from the beginning," he said gruffly.

I pulled out my notebook, referring to it occasionally as I told them about the events of the previous forty-odd hours from my point of view. When I'd finished, Donleavy asked if I still had the last threatening note. I assured him it was in a file I'd started on the case, and I agreed to turn it over to them. Since he and Ames were going to be at the Symington house for awhile getting statements from Jeri, Sara, and Galen, I decided to fetch it from my office right away. I started toward the door, but I couldn't shake off the question that had been needling me for the better part of an hour. I turned around, looking from Donleavy to Ames and back again. I had to ask. "Did the condition of Faye's office suggest there'd been much of a struggle?"

Donleavy gave me a flinty look, his mouth pulled into a hard, thin line. "No. No evidence of any struggle at all," he said shortly.

I accessed the 101 freeway going south at Cahuenga. It was still early enough for traffic to be moving steadily, if not speedily. As I joined the parade of commuters, I started dogging myself with a litany of "if only's" as in "if only Sara had come to see me a few days sooner". . . then what? Did I really think Faye would still be alive? Well, who knew? And that was the trouble. I didn't know much of anything. I'd been on the field such a short time, I still had no idea who most of the players were.

I figured the killer had almost certainly visited Faye's office on some occasion before the murder. As I'd demonstrated to myself, the task of getting onto the lot — even for an outsider — wouldn't be difficult. But the route to the Snake Pit was so complicated you'd have to know the way already or be forced to ask for directions. Just a trifle conspicuous if you're planning to bonk somebody on the head. That was assuming the murder was premeditated rather than a sudden act of unplanned violence. Neither could be ruled out at this point. There was also a third possibility, that Faye's murderer had, indeed, planned the crime, but was not the one who'd staged the recent reign of terror. Only one thing was sure: Faye Symington knew her killer.

I stopped at the office only long enough to run in and grab the file. I was back on Nichols Canyon Road before eight o'clock. Galen had arrived in my absence and was being questioned by the detectives out on the deck while two women I hadn't met were sitting in the family room drinking coffee.

The older-looking of the two had shoulder length gray hair pulled straight back from her face and tied with a scarf at the nape of her neck. Her high forehead and clear hazel eyes reminded me of Sara and Jeri. She wore a simple brown wool skirt that came to just below her knees and a beige sweater set. Her shoes were sturdy sensible oxfords.

The second woman, I realized upon closer examination, was probably not a great deal younger, but she was waging a pitched battle against Father Time. Her crop of expensively tinted blonde curls was carefully moussed and painstakingly tousled. She was quite trim and wore a fitted eggplant-colored suit with a skirt that showed off her shapely legs but was of a length more appropriate for someone a generation younger than she. Even at that early hour her eyes were dramatically lined and shadowed, her lips painted a dark brown-red. She wore make-up like a mask. It didn't enhance so much as re-form her features.

They both looked up in surprise when I came in the door, and I wriggled my fingers in a little wave of greeting. "Hello. My name's Maggie McGrath. I'm a friend of Sara's."

"Claire Harris." The woman with the familiar hazel eyes held out her hand. "I'm Faye's sister. And this is Lillian Baxter." She gestured to the blonde.

Well, well, I thought. *The gang's all here.* I was so distracted by the aging fashion plate that I nearly forgot to offer my condolences to Claire. "I'm very sorry for your loss," I said just a beat late, as if my synapses were misfiring.

"Thank you," she replied, "though I'm afraid Faye and I lost each other long ago."

"Since you mention it, I'm rather surprised to see you here," Lillian said icily. "I didn't think you and Faye had spoken for years."

"We hadn't," Claire agreed. "I'm here for the girls. Jeri called and asked me to come."

She was about to say something more but seemed to think better of it when a beautiful young woman with masses of dark curly hair came in from the hall. "This is my daughter, Gina," she said.

I held out my hand to her. "Maggie."

"Nice to meet you," she murmured.

"How are the girls doing?" Claire asked.

Gina tipped her head to one side, giving it a doubtful shake. "Jeri's asleep now, but Sara's not well at all. I didn't want to leave her, but she insisted." She gave a helpless shrug. "I couldn't think what else to do for her."

"It's all right, dear," her mother soothed. "Come sit with us for awhile."

Just then, Galen and the two detectives came in from the deck. I handed the file to Donleavy.

"We'll probably want to talk to you again," he observed as he leafed through its scanty contents.

"I'll make myself available."

"Is there anything more you need from us now?" Claire asked anxiously.

"Not right now, Mrs. Harris, but I'm sure we'll be in touch again soon."

She started to get up from the sofa, but Donleavy stopped her. "Don't bother, ma'am, we can see ourselves out. Please tell Ms. Landesmann and Ms. Collins we'll keep them informed," he said as he and Ames walked out the door.

Galen wandered over to the kitchen. He seemed pensive and withdrawn; the interview with the policemen had left him shaken. I followed him under the pretext of pouring myself another cup of coffee which was the last thing I needed.

"How're you holding up?" I touched his arm lightly.

"Man, talk about the fucking Inquisition!" he exploded, recoiling as if I'd stung him. "Those guys were all over me about what time exactly did I get to the motel? What time exactly did I order in the pizza? What time exactly did I have to take a leak? Jesus! What do they want, a videotape of me asleep for eight hours in the fucking Ramada Inn?"

He picked up his coffee and stalked out to the deck. I went back into the family room where Gina and Claire were visiting quietly with their heads together while Lillian rummaged through her purse. After much noisy rooting around, she finally pulled out a small silver case from which she extracted a thin brown cigarette.

Claire looked over at her reproachfully. "If you're going to smoke, I'd appreciate it if you went out on the deck."

Lillian gave no acknowledgment and went burrowing in her purse again, coming up this time with a matching silver lighter. With studied nonchalance, she clasped the cigarette firmly between her brown-red lips and lit it, inhaling deeply. Claire stood up and started down the hall with Gina at her heels.

"We'll go sit with the girls for awhile," she said stiffly.

"Good riddance!" Lillian snapped before they were quite out of earshot. She tossed her head angrily, setting her tangle of curls aquiver. "I don't like that woman. I've never trusted her. And neither did Faye. She always said I was more of a sister to her than Claire ever was!"

That observation brought her a fresh awareness of her loss. She pulled a handkerchief from her sleeve and dabbed carefully at the corners of her eyes so as not to ruin her make-up. Her nails were long and curved and were painted the same dried blood shade as her lips, reinforcing a disquieting mental image of some she-creature just come from ripping apart her breakfast.

"Are you in the film industry, too?" I asked, hoping my question sounded like a polite attempt to distract her from her grief.

"Oh, no, no, no." Lillian shook her head and exhaled a cloud of pale smoke. "I'm an investment counselor. I handled all of Faye's financial activities. She was far too busy with her design work to be able to oversee all her interests."

I was delighted to have that door opened so quickly, but I knew I needed to tread carefully here, and I've found that flattery can be a disarmingly useful tool. "Managing money takes such creative vision! I'm completely in awe of anyone who can do that. I'm lucky to be able to balance my checkbook."

"Yes, it's interesting work," she said shortly, perhaps worried I was going to hit her up for free advice.

"Do you belong to an investment firm?" I tried again.

"No, I'm independent. I have a suite of offices attached to my home." She gestured expansively, waving the evil-smelling cigarette in a pungent arc. "I'm able to give my clients a great deal more personal attention than they would ever receive from a large firm."

My built-in bitch-o-meter was pulsing in the red zone. I already had Lillian pegged as a self-serving, self-important, self-obsessed pain in the ass. No wonder she and Faye had been so close. Although, judging by the phone calls I'd overheard, those two best girlfriends were feuding. There was a murmur of voices in the hallway. Sara and Claire came back into the kitchen followed by Jeri and Gina.

Claire patted her niece's arm and said, "I'll make some tea, dear. Why don't you go sit down?"

Sara nodded mutely and came over to sit on the sofa facing Lillian and me while the others busied themselves in the kitchen.

"Maggie, Lillian, tea?" Claire offered.

"No thanks," I called.

Lillian didn't bother to respond.

Sara stared at me, looking hollow-eyed and stricken. "We have to find out who did this," she said so quietly that at first I didn't understand her.

"Sara, the police are jumping on this with both feet," I said.

"But they have so many cases to deal with. Promise me, Maggie, you'll keep working on it."

"I can't interfere in a murder investigation. I'll cooperate with the police, but they're the ones with the resources and authority to handle this."

"But you used to be a police detective," she argued.

I guessed Joyce had told her that, and I wondered how much she'd said.

"And I trust you. Please don't abandon me when I need your help most," she pleaded.

By this time Lillian was staring at me, frankly askance, but I ignored her. "Sara, I would never abandon you, and I'll do whatever I can to help you get through this."

Not satisfied with my equivocation, she got up and turned her back on me, abruptly crossing to the doors that led to the deck.

"And just what is it you do for a living?" Lillian arched her penciled eyebrows disapprovingly.

"I'm a private investigator. Sara hired me to find out who was harassing Faye."

"Too bad you weren't more successful."

"Yes, it is."

I got up without excusing myself and went to join Sara. She seemed rooted to the spot, staring intently out the windows that gave onto the deck and canyon. I followed her gaze to the far end of the deck where Jeri and Galen stood, partially hidden by a huge potted cactus. As we watched, Galen folded Jeri in his arms, kissing her lightly on the forehead. Then she lifted her face, brushing his lips in a lingering kiss.

Oh shit.

I darted a sideways glance at Sara to see how this touching scene of double betrayal was playing with her. She turned quickly from the windows and started for the front door.

"I'm going for a drive," she announced in a flat voice.

Claire and Gina looked up in alarm, and I lunged for her. "You're still sedated — you can't drive!" I clamped a hand on her arm.

"I need to get out for awhile!"

"Well, I'll drive you, then. I'll take you wherever you want," I said stubbornly.

"I need to be alone!" she hissed through clenched teeth. Shaking me off, she flung the door open and dashed down the steps to her Jeep.

"Why didn't you stop her?" Lillian demanded from her seat on the couch.

"Thanks for the assist," I shot back. "What do you think?" I asked urgently, looking to Claire. "Should I go after her? Or should we call the police?"

"She shouldn't be driving," her aunt acknowledged. "But I think sending the police chasing after her would do more harm than good." A sad smile played on her lips as she shook her head. "And woe betide anyone who would try to stop her once she's made up her mind to do something. Sara's much stronger that most people recognize."

"Mother's right," Gina piped up. "We should give her a little breathing space."

"She probably does need some quiet time alone, poor dear," Claire sighed. "There are some complicated feelings she's having to work through right now."

More than you know, I thought, looking back at the deck.

I needed to get out of there, too, to collect my thoughts and regroup. I left business cards with all three women. Claire and Gina promised to stay at the house until Sara came home or checked in, and I asked them to keep me informed. Claire agreed and hugged me reassuringly. I skipped saying goodbye to Jeri and Galen. As I went down the steps to my car, I noticed a gold Mercedes on the upper parking pad with the vanity plates "BIGBUKS." The Lillian-mobile. I hurried to the Toyota. Suddenly, I couldn't get away from there fast enough.

Eight

I was craving the comfort of society without the burden of conversation, and breakfast seemed as good a way as any to put off deciding what to do with the rest of my life, so I headed for my favorite coffee shop, The Crest, just a few blocks from my office at the corner of Sunset and Lucile. It hovers just on the cusp of being a dive, but it reminds me of the Greek coffee shops you can find in almost any part of New York City, its cozy interior a semi-sanitary concoction of fake wood paneling, faded linoleum, cornflower blue vinyl booths, and only slightly sticky white Formica countertops and tables. A blackboard that never changes announces the daily specials. My only caveat would be to stay away from the Italian selections. Other than that, the food is simple, good, and cheap. The waitresses are all middle-aged Hispanic ladies with a hazy grasp of the English language and hearts as big as their hairdos. It's a real neighborhood joint: the same people come in at the same time everyday and order pretty much the same thing. I do, anyway. I guess that's why I'm such a faithful drone: if I find something I like, whether it's a man or a meal, I figure it's gonna be just as good the 165th time I have it as it was the first. Call me crazy: you'll no doubt find yourself in excellent company there.

I ordered my usual — a spinach and feta omelette, dry wheat toast, and coffee, but I didn't allow myself to review the morning until after I'd eaten and was sitting with my second cup of coffee, which was actually more like my sixtieth of the day. Typically, the more I learned, the more questions I had. I surely would have liked to take a closer look at Lillian's business dealings with Faye. She'd testified so vehemently to their mutual affection that it reminded me of the line from *Hamlet:* "The lady doth protest too much, methinks." And there were also Faye's angry references to her on the phone. Methought I smelled a rat. So who was Robert?

I paid my check and pointed my car toward the office. I put on a pot of coffee (yes, I am an addict), sorted the mail into piles of varying degrees of urgency, and checked my voice mail. Nothing. Damn. I'd have to come up with my own agenda.

I knew I could get myself in some serious hot water if the police thought I was interfering, so I felt disinclined, despite Sara's pleas, to continue the investigation. I made a half-hearted stab at straightening up my desk and thought about dusting, but settled for tackling the crossword puzzle in *The New York Times Magazine*, which I hadn't gotten to on Sunday. For me, this is one of the major perks of self-employment, by the by. I can go nose-to-grindstone with the best of them when it's necessary, but the chance to goof off now and then without somebody peering over my shoulder is food for the soul. I was stumped by a six-letter word starting with "e" meaning "to draw artfully by arousing desire" when the phone rang.

"Hello," I answered sullenly.

"Maggie McGrath?"

"Yes."

"This is Amy Hodges returning your call."

"Oh! Well, uh, Amy, thanks for uh, calling back, but the uh, matter I was looking into is in the hands of the uh, police. As of this morning," I stammered.

"Is it something to do with Faye Symington's murder?" she asked breathlessly.

"How did you . . . ?"

But of course, as soon as people began arriving for work at the studio that morning, word would have started to spread.

"You all must have some grapevine."

"You can be sure of that," Amy agreed. "And I'm not even really in the loop anymore. So, what did you want to ask me?"

"Have you spoken with the police yet? I don't want to step on their toes." I also didn't want to mention I'd given them her name and phone number in the course of my debriefing that morning.

"No, but I can't imagine why they'd want to talk to me, anyway," she said lightly. "I haven't seen Faye for almost two years. We weren't even on speaking terms."

I squirmed silently, trying to decide what to say.

"Oh, I see." She laughed at my discomfort. "Someone's been carrying tales. What a surprise. Well, don't worry, that's all very old news. It's true I didn't like Faye, but I wouldn't bother with killing her. Besides, I was at the store last night doing inventory with two other people until almost one o'clock. My boyfriend picked me up there, and I spent the rest of the night at his apartment."

Her tone was off-hand and cheery — no false sentiment or even a hint of regret. I cleared my throat, knowing I should leave this to the police. "Well, you might be able to shed some light on a couple of things that have me especially curious —"

"Listen, I can't talk too long right now," she interrupted. "I'm only on a short break. But if you'd like to meet me later, I'll answer any questions I can."

"What time would be good for you?"

"My lunch break is from three to four. I work at Nordstrom's in the Westside Pavilion. Meet me at the California Crisp concession in the food court on the top level."

"See you at three," I said.

Rationalizations began to blossom the second I hung up. After all, I had a right to satisfy some personal curiosity; no harm in that. The day was going to be a dead loss, anyway. I couldn't concentrate on anything useful. I went back to my puzzle. I still had some time before I needed to plunge into the cross-town traffic to get over to Westwood. I was making good headway and trying not to worry about Sara when there was a knock on the connecting door to Auntie Em's.

"It's open!"

"Why didn't you tell us about this?" Joyce looked every inch the fashionable equestrienne today in a pair of jodhpurs, shiny black boots, and a fitted hip-length jacket. All she lacked was a riding crop even though I know for a fact her closest encounter with a horse came when she rented the video of *The Black Stallion.* Her tone was scolding but she was brimming with excitement as she came in waving a newspaper like a flag.

"It can't be in the paper already!" I was dumbfounded. "Let me see that!"

Joyce spread the paper out on the desk. It was one of those tabloid rags, *The Hollywood Observer,* the kind with lots of out-of-focus color pictures of female celebrities parading around in hideously over-decorated evening gowns. I've always supposed the profusion of photographs was simply a bid to compensate for the lack of any truthful information otherwise contained in these publications.

"I don't see it!" I cried, vainly scanning the page for the article chronicling Faye's murder in luridly descriptive terms.

"Here. Right in front of you." Joyce pointed to a medium-sized headline at the top of the page proclaiming, "Oscar Nominee Stalked By Anonymous Persecutor." "You're quoted all the way through it!" she beamed. "This should be great for your business!"

"Damn her!" I muttered.

I read the article quickly. It was obviously hashed together by Faye's hack publicist and whatever hack writer he'd been able to entice (Aha! I filled in the blanks on my crossword) into slapping his byline on this fanciful yarn. I was characterized as the heroine of the piece, a "stalwart, resourceful gumshoe who was nonetheless baffled" by the "wily culprit" who was "terrorizing" my client. I had evidently been on the case for several weeks with no substantial leads, but I was determined to see the villain brought to justice. Joyce was correct: the story was liberally sprinkled with nonsensical quotes attributed to yours truly. I groaned and buried my head in my arms.

"What's the matter? I think it's great!" Joyce declared.

"You mean, besides the fact that almost none of it is even in the vicinity of accurate?" I mumbled. Sighing heavily, I looked up, my head still on my desk, and asked my dear friend to take a seat. Then I told her all about my morning.

"I told the police I'd only been on the case for a day. That story makes it sound like it's been my entire career!" I moaned.

Then I had a heartening thought: cops were too busy to read that kind of trash. And even in the unlikely event they did get wind of it, they were savvy enough to know it was mostly a bunch of trumped-up lies. Slightly cheered by this hopeful though probably self-deluding logic, I turned my attention back to Joyce, who sat stunned and, for once, speechless.

"I just can't believe it!" she finally managed. "Poor Faye!" And then with a gasp, "Oh! Poor Sara!" She got up, eyes brimming, and went back into the store, shaking her head sadly.

So at least one of my questions from yesterday had been answered: I was pretty certain Faye hadn't orchestrated the harassment scenario as a publicity stunt. I was a little ashamed to find that, unlike Joyce, I had no emotion at all attached to her death. It was simply a fact to be dissected and examined to determine its cause. That was my only interest. And I was sorry to be so unmoved by the loss of another human being. I did feel tremendous compassion for Sara, and mindful of that, I put in a call to Claire.

"I was about to call you," she said. "I just got off the phone with her. She's at the beach house in Malibu — she's going to spend the night there. She said she needs to have some time alone to think."

"Do you believe that's wise right now? How did she sound to you?"

"She's sad, but she'll get through this. She and my sister had a very complex relationship." She hesitated, and I could sense her internal debate, which she tabled for the moment. "Well, someday I'll tell you all about it. Or maybe Sara will. At any rate, I think it's all to the good that she's confronting her demons rather than running from them."

"Would you mind giving me the number out there? I don't want to intrude, but I want her to know I'm thinking about her."

"Of course, dear," she replied kindly.

We agreed to talk soon and said goodbye. A machine answered at the Malibu number; Sara's voice was on the recording. I left a brief message repeating my numbers and urging her to call if she needed to for any reason. Then I tried to concentrate again on the crossword, but I'd lost my momentum. Shifting into work mode in spite of myself, I typed up a summary of the information I'd collected for the owner of the Studio City jewelry store and slipped it in an envelope so I could post it on my way out. And maybe it's true that virtue begets virtue because next I was moved to pick up the bill on top of the most urgent pile of mail, fish my checkbook out of the desk, and diligently send money flying out the window until it was time to go meet Amy.

At a few minutes past two, I locked up again and stepped out into another hot and humid afternoon — strangely extreme weather for that usually moderate time of year. The Toyota felt like an oven preheated to broil, and I soon felt cooked. The air conditioner took its own sweet time getting revved up, so most of the journey was uncomfortable, and the normal antics of L.A. drivers such as split-second-with-only-inches-to-spare-lane-changes-without-benefit-of-signal made me even grumpier than usual.

Nine

Inscrutable lines of independent incorporation divide the cities of West Hollywood, Beverly Hills, Culver City, Westwood, Santa Monica, and Venice. They're all massed together in a solid urban block, all part of the greater Los Angeles metropolitan conglomerate. But they are legally individual fiscal entities. So even though the monster of a multi-level shopping center called the Westside Pavilion is just down Overland Avenue a mile or so from Sony Studios, they are nevertheless in separate communities.

On most weekdays between the hours of 10:00 A.M. and 7:00 P.M., the Santa Monica freeway is basically a parking lot, so I stuck to the surface streets and made decent time across town. When I got to the shopping center, I managed to dodge the gauntlet of aggressive valet parkers and leave the car on the roof, then took the escalator one flight down to the level of shops that included the food court. After stopping at the Coffee Merchant to fortify myself with a double espresso, I drifted out to the common patio shared by all the food vendors and grabbed a place at a table in the corner to people-watch and wait. At about 3:10 I noticed an attractive blonde I guessed to be in her early thirties standing in front of the California Crisp counter. She seemed to be waiting for someone, continually scanning the crowd and studying people as they passed. I got up and went over to meet her, waving a greeting as I approached.

She smiled. "You must be Maggie. You look like a Maggie."

Whatever that means.

"Hi, Amy," I said, shaking her hand. "Thanks for meeting me today."

She had a perfect oval face with wide-set gray eyes and a long, swan-like neck. Her hair was artfully cropped to look like she'd just put her head in a Cuisinart and must have cost her a fortune at some salon in Beverly Hills. "No trouble. Are you hungry?" She was already herding me toward one of the food counters. "I'm starving!"

I decided she'd meant that literally when I saw what she ordered for lunch. She was tall and slender with fine, elegant bones, and I was amazed by the amount of food she could put away in one sitting. As we talked, she worked her way through a tuna salad sandwich with extra mayonnaise, potato chips, cream of broccoli soup, a side of pasta salad, and a huge slab of cornbread dripping butter and grease. With a large Coke.

"How do you stay so thin?" I asked as I forked up a bite of my Chinese chicken salad with low-fat dressing.

"It's my metabolism," she mumbled around a mouthful of tuna. "I have trouble keeping weight on."

This interview was already depressing me.

While we ate, I explained the reason for my phone call, glossing over the fact that Jeremy Latham had singled her out as someone who might harbor a grudge against Faye.

"So somebody was kind of stalking her? That's creepy!" Amy shuddered.

"How did you happen to hear about the murder?"

"One of my friends who's a costumer on a TV show over at Sony called me from work this morning. She was the first, anyway. I've gotten several calls about it since then." The corners of her mouth turned up in a small Mona Lisa smile, and I raised my eyebrows by way of encouragement. "I was just thinking 'good news travels fast.'" She clapped her hands over her mouth like a mischievous child. "I'm sorry. I know that's horrible!" But there was that tiny smile again. I found her unabashed glee a little off-putting under the circumstances, but at least she wasn't a hypocrite. And I had to admit I hadn't been all that fond of Faye myself.

So far I'd done all the talking, priming the pump, as my grandma used to say, in the hope it'd net me something worth listening to in return. "How long did you work for Ms. Symington?"

"Too long," Amy groaned and rolled her eyes. "I did four movies with her. Well, technically, three and three-quarters. She fired me before we finished the fourth one."

"What happened?"

She leaned back in her chair, studying her empty plate regretfully. "We were doing the remake of *Lady Chatterly's Lover* starring Veronica Leaman —"

"I've read she has a reputation for being difficult."

"Oh, Veronica and I got along great! She was no problem at all, which is actually what got me into trouble."

"How so?"

Her face suddenly clouded over. She blew out a breath and looked away from me, shaking her head as if this was one batch of thoughts she'd rather not collect again. "I didn't know until this minute how much it all still bothers me," she said softly.

I chewed my lip, hoping she wasn't going to sandbag me now that I'd hauled myself all the way across town. "Just tell me as much as you're comfortable with."

She looked over at me and nodded, then looked away again. "We shot a lot of the film in New England," she finally said. "I went out for the entire location, but Faye was doing another picture at the same time, so she would come out for a couple of days here and there. She really wasn't around all that much."

"Is that unusual? For the costume designer not to be around for filming?"

"Somewhat unusual on a period film of that size, but not unheard of. We'd fitted most of the actors' costumes in L.A. before we went on location." She flapped her hand in a 'what the hell' gesture. "So, anyway, because I was the one who was there all the time, Veronica got used to me; she sort of came to rely on me." She shrugged. "It's natural. You bond with people on location — it's kind of like being at summer camp."

She absently poked at a pickle with her plastic fork, frowning to herself. "But toward the end of shooting, they added a scene that meant we had to make a new costume for Veronica. Faye flew out with a draper to do the fitting, and I was in on it, too, taking notes. Veronica didn't like the color of the fabric Faye had chosen, and they were trying to decide what to do when Veronica turned to me and asked, 'What color do you think it should be, Amy?' Well, if looks could kill, I'd've been bloody pulp on the floor from the daggers Faye was shooting me. She said, 'Yes, Amy, do give us the benefit of your vast expertise.' I knew I was in real trouble then. After the fitting, Faye sent everybody else out of the wardrobe trailer and ripped me up one side and down the other for being disloyal and 'circumventing her relationship with the star.' And she fired me on the spot. I went home the next day. Veronica stood up for me, and if I'd wanted to push it, she could've made the producers keep me on because she has that kind of star power. But I just wanted to get out of there."

"I have to say that all sounds pretty extreme."

Amy shifted uneasily in her seat. "You wouldn't think so if you knew Faye. She's paranoid. Always suspecting intrigue where there isn't any, always thinking somebody's out to undermine her. She's very high maintenance. And she wasn't satisfied with just getting me off that picture. She bad-mouthed me all over town. She made a point of calling every designer listed in the Guild membership directory to tell them not to hire me. She said I was dishonest and lazy and that I'd do anything to get ahead. I hadn't been working in films very long; I came from the New York theater, which is a completely different world. Faye was the first big-name designer to hire me out here, so I suddenly found I was black-listed. I couldn't get work." As she told her story, she seemed to compress her lanky frame before my eyes: she hunched forward and crossed her long legs, wrapping her right foot around her left calf until she'd knotted herself up like a contortionist. I felt a charley horse coming on just watching her.

"How long had you been working for her at that point?"

"For more than two years." Two spots of high color had risen in her cheeks. "That woman is in a class by herself when it comes to holding a grudge. If you get on her bad side, she's not happy until she's done as much damage to you as she can." She paused and sat staring at a point over my shoulder, lost in the disappointed hopes that still clung to her like a fine mist.

"Why didn't you go back to theater?"

She thought about that briefly. "I'd relocated to Los Angeles to concentrate on film work. And I like it here. I have a boyfriend I care about, and I'm tired of being a gypsy." She smiled ruefully. "And working in theater in Los Angeles is sort of like snow-skiing in Florida: it's not where you go to find the most talented people doing the best work."

"So Faye single-handedly derailed your career."

"It's only a detour," Amy replied coolly. "Nothing is ever wasted."

How incredibly Zen of you, I thought. I was pretty sure I couldn't be so philosophical in the same circumstances.

"She actually did me a favor, even though I couldn't have seen it at the time." Amy relaxed enough to unfold herself and sit back in her chair. "I never did like the film business — it's so different from theater. You make a lot more money, but that's all it's about. Money and power and egos. Especially egos. So much of the time, the work itself gets lost in all the bullshit. At least in theater, costume designers are respected as creative collaborators. In film, more often than not, we're treated like servants."

"That reminds me of something else I wanted to ask you. Do costume designers share in the profits from a film?"

She shook her head. "Usually not. Production designers have a better shot at that than costume designers. Every film is different, of course, and it all depends on the financial structure of the specific deal. Maybe with a low-budget picture where everybody defers payment, meaning nobody takes a salary until the movie shows a profit. But no, other than that, it would be a rare, really almost a unique situation for a designer, especially a costume designer, to have financial participation."

Well, that blew one theory out of the water.

"I know what I'm in the mood for," Amy announced as if the subject had just been under discussion. "Let's get some ice cream." With that, she made a beeline for another food counter leaving me to scoop our garbage onto a tray and toss it in a trash can as I scrambled to catch up with her.

"When you were working for Faye, did you ever meet a woman named Lillian Baxter?" Ten minutes later we'd snagged a bench by the metal railing that looked down onto the lower levels of the mall, and I was nibbling half-heartedly on a cone filled with a frozen treat appropriately called Mississippi Mud. Fat-free, sugar-free, cholesterol-free, and — no surprise here — taste-free.

"Lillian!" Amy's voice dripped with scorn. "What a pain that woman is! That's another weird thing about Faye. She gathers a little group of people around her, mostly employees, and then treats them like friends and confidantes. Except the balance of power is completely skewed in her favor, like a made-to-order dysfunctional family. And when somebody falls out of favor, like me, they get kicked out of the nest by Faye. As you might imagine, there's a fairly high rate of attrition." She dug into her banana split with gusto. "But I guess that's easier for her to handle than real relationships. Less threatening. This way, she gets to maintain absolute control. I was part of that group for more than two years, so yes, I know Lillian Baxter. Better than I ever wanted to."

"You dislike her personally."

"Intensely."

"What do you think of her as a business manager?"

"I don't know enough about the details of Faye's finances to make an informed judgment, but I can tell you that on a gut level, I would never trust Lillian."

"Do you think Faye trusted her?"

"As much as she trusted anybody," Amy shrugged. "That sort of thing was always provisional with Faye."

"Was there someone named Robert in your little group?"

"No. There were never any men who were part of the inner circle. Well, there was one gay guy for awhile, but his name wasn't Robert."

"How about a business associate of Faye's? Someone who also had dealings with Lillian? Maybe an accountant?"

I knew I was grasping at straws, but something had clicked for Amy, and her brow creased with the effort of recollection as she licked chocolate syrup from her spoon. "You know, it's funny you should ask that, because the only fight I remember Lillian and Faye ever having was over a restaurant that Lillian got Faye invested in. In fact, I'm pretty sure Faye owns it, or owns most of it. It's called Fat Farm, low-fat gourmet health food, with a fully stocked bar to round out its appeal, and I guess it's supposed to be about the hottest place in town right now. But it wasn't when Faye bought into it. I got the impression Lillian sort of railroaded her on that one." She waved her spoon to indicate this was all peripheral information. "Anyway, what I remember, because Faye got me involved, is that Lillian hired some guy named Robert Camden to manage it. She brought him in from out of town, even paid for him to re-locate, and all this without consulting Faye because he was supposedly this restaurant genius, according to Lillian."

"Where did he come from?"

She pointed the spoon at me. "Now, that's an interesting tidbit I'll get to in a minute. Faye was furious when she found out about Camden. I remember her screaming at Lillian over the phone that there must be nine thousand guys she could have hired for the job right here in L.A. and why was she having to import some yokel from the sticks to lose money for her? But Lillian wouldn't back down, which was completely out of character because she always kisses Faye's ass."

Amy chuckled, relishing her memory of Lillian's distress. "So, Faye demanded references for the guy. Lillian said she'd get them, but that was the last we heard about it. We were in the middle of a big project, so Faye got side-tracked for awhile, but when things slowed down on the movie, she got on her broom about it again, and Lillian finally came up with the references, which Faye handed over to me to follow up on." She went back to work on her mountain of ice cream. "The thing was, none of them checked out. Nobody had ever heard of Robert Camden at any of the places he'd listed, except for one that was out of business, so there was no one to ask."

"How odd."

"Not to mention incredibly stupid. I guess he just hoped we wouldn't check them. But the thing is, it all worked out for him, anyway, because about that time Fat Farm re-opened and got great reviews in a couple local magazines, so there was beginning to be some buzz about it. And business was good, so Faye let it drop."

"When was all this?"

She drummed her fingers on her lower lip while she calculated. "A little over a year after I started working for Faye, so about three years ago."

I gave a low whistle. It could fit. Faye's harangue on the phone could conceivably have been about a restaurant, an apparently successful restaurant that for some mysterious reason was losing money. I absent-mindedly glanced down at the ice cream cone I'd been clutching this whole time. True to its name, the Mississippi Mud sat glued in place like a hunk of plastic. It wasn't even melting, just sort of sweating on the surface. I grimaced and dropped it in the trash can by our bench.

"Do you know if Faye made all her money in films? Or did she come from a wealthy family? I mean, I'm sure costume designers are well-paid, but the house in the canyon, the beach house in Malibu, the expensive cars, owning a restaurant, and whatever else she's into . . ." I stopped because Amy was looking at me through narrowed eyes with a puzzled expression.

"What?"

"For a detective, you sure don't know much about your own client," she observed pointedly.

"What?" I repeated.

"You seriously don't know who she was married to?"

"Tell me."

"Her late husband was Hugh Forsythe."

"She was married to him?!" I squeaked. Even I had heard of Hugh Forsythe, one of the most successful and prolific film makers of his generation.

"He must have been a lot older than Faye," I said, recovering myself a little.

"Twenty-odd years," Amy said. "And very married when Faye met him. So was she, for that matter, but she didn't let that get in her way. He eventually dumped his wife to marry Faye — after she unloaded her husband. That was really the beginning of her professional success. She's not a great talent, and she probably would've had a mediocre career if she hadn't married a world-famous director. I think the ex-wife still lives someplace in Hollywood — a little crazy, so I've been told. Now, there's someone who really hates Faye's guts!" Amy polished off the last bite of ice cream and got up to throw away her trash. "You feel like walking around a little bit?"

"Sure." I stretched to get rid of a kink between my shoulder blades, and we started ambling past the rows of homogenous mall stores cloned in every shopping center from coast to coast.

"Did you ever meet the first Mrs. Forsythe?" I asked.

Amy shook her head. "No, just heard the tales. Faye said that for years after the divorce, the ex would get roaring drunk every six months or so and show up at their house to stir up some kind of ruckus. They finally got a restraining order."

"What's her name?"

Amy looked sheepish. "I actually don't know. She was only ever referred to as 'Hugh's ex-wife' or something less polite."

"Did you know Mr. Forsythe?"

"No." She shook her head again. "He died the year before I went to work for Faye."

"Was he Sara and Jeri's father?"

"No, that was Faye's first husband. Poor Sara," she murmured.

"Why do you say that?"

"I don't know." She hesitated. "It's not like I knew her all that well, but she just seemed so completely in her mother's thrall. Jeri was the rebellious one — always in some kind of trouble. But I figured she'd be okay once she settled down." A troubled look crossed her face like a shadow. "Sara got stuck in the good girl role — living at home, catering to her mother. It just didn't seem like she'd ever get out and have a life of her own."

"I got the distinct impression Faye considered her a burden."

"Well, of course Faye played the martyr about it — to the hilt. That's one of her favorite poses. But she needs Sara's dependency in order to maintain control. And that's the most important thing in the world to Faye; she's the ultimate control freak. Or I guess I should say was." She fell silent, snared again by her thoughts as we scuffed along the gleaming tile walkway. She came to with a little smile of embarrassment. "I've really talked your ear off. You'll have to send me a bill for the therapy session."

By then we'd reached the Nordstrom entrance. I gave her one of my business cards and asked her to call if anything more occurred to her, then I headed back to the roof, steeling myself for the ordeal of a cross-town sojourn at the worst possible time of day.

By the time I got back to Silverlake, the nightmarish stampede of rush-hour traffic had taken its toll, and I had a mother of a headache. I parked behind Auntie Em's but decided to take a long walk in the hills to clear the cobwebs before re-entering my dusty sanctum. Besides being my favorite way to exercise, the walk is a great way to tune into myself. I try to turn off the frenetic verbal part of my mind and just listen — to nature, to my intuition, to whatever's out there that feels like talking to me.

I like walking best in the evening. For one thing, the sun is gentler late in the day, so it's cooler. For another, sunset over the Pacific seen from the vantage point of the Silverlake Hills is a spectacle of astonishing beauty — if you can forget that the array of colors is largely due to the refraction of light by densely clustered particles of pollution. It's a sight to take your breath away, literally and figuratively. And it always makes me think about what a paradise this land must truly have been before it was overrun by ten million people.

As I huffed and puffed up the hills, the tension of the day began to fall away from me, so that by the time I trotted down the final incline, I was completely relaxed. I felt so refreshed that I decided to go back to the office and type up the notes from Amy's interview to give to Lieutenant Donleavy. Some of that information would surely be useful to him. I'd hand it over in the morning and clear the decks so I could get back to business as usual.

I was rewarded for my industry with a message from Sara on the voice mail: "Maggie, it's Sara. Thank you for your thoughtful message. You really are a dear. I just wanted to let you know I'm fine — really — and I promise I'll be in touch soon. Take care."

And so with my mind considerably eased on that score, I made a pot of coffee and settled in at my desk. Two hours later, my task was completed, and I finally felt okay about signing off on the case. I'd come into that little drama halfway through the third act, too late to be of any material use in changing the outcome. And now the curtain was ringing down — for me, anyway.

It was nearly ten o'clock by the time I pulled into my driveway. Every drop of adrenaline had deserted me, and all I wanted was to put myself to bed. But I knew I still had to face two disgruntled kitties who would need to be appeased. Because of the pitch of the hill, my front door is at street level, but my back door is up a flight of wooden steps. I dragged myself up to the first landing and froze there, a sudden thrill of fear zinging through me like an electric shock. My back door yawned open, the house beyond it utterly dark and silent. Shit. I didn't want to interrupt a burglar — I didn't have anything worth stealing, anyway. I held my breath and waited, listening. Nothing. I scrunched down and crept up the remaining steps. Stopped. Listened. Something — a muffled whimpering. I was on the upper landing just outside the door. My feet crunched on broken glass. The outside light had been smashed. I stepped tentatively into the service porch and peered behind the door. Nothing.

Then I began to take in the destruction around me. My easel had been knocked on its side with one of its spindly legs snapped and hanging crooked like a lame insect. The painting I'd been working on lay face down on the floor, slashed diagonally from corner to corner, and I soon found that all my canvases had suffered a similar fate. All my paintings, all the blanks that had been stretched and stacked in the corner were all ruined. Brushes, jars, and paints were strewn across the floor, pigments bleeding from the ends of flattened tubes.

And now the whimpering was more distinct. I recognized Skunky's plaintive crying. Rage crowded out the fear; if anyone had hurt him, I'd be forced to rip their hearts out. I picked my way through the wreckage into the hallway and past the kitchen. Everything that had been in the refrigerator was now broken, poured, and smeared all over the floor in a hideous melange of slippery glop.

On the dining room table there had been a large antique wooden bowl filled with Mexican witches' balls, colored glass spheres meant to ward off evil spirits. Too bad they didn't have more effect on corporeal malevolence. The bowl was overturned, and the balls were now shards of bright glass glinting like a field of broken stars scattered across the floor.

In the living room books had been ripped from their shelves, pillows slashed and gutted, and a pottery lamp lay in pieces. Several of my cactus plants were uprooted, their pots shattered. All of this took only seconds to comprehend, and it was all beside the point. I needed to find my cat. I stood still and closed my eyes to listen. The mewing was coming from the walk-in closet just off the dining room. I opened the door and yanked the pull-chain for the light — one bit of glass left intact.

He was lying on his side just inside the door. His feet and tail were duct-taped together so that he was bound like a calf in a rodeo roping competition. He looked up and howled for me to get him out of this mess. Thank God he could still howl. I ran to the bathroom — similar destruction there — medicine cabinet emptied, breakables smashed. I grabbed a pair of scissors from the floor and went back to cut him loose.

He protested vigorously as the tape took some of his fur with it. Then I saw the note. It was stuck between his forepaws and secured by the tape. Made with the same meticulous cut-and-paste technique as the specimen I'd handed over to the police that morning, it cautioned: CURIOSITY CAN BE HARMFUL TO CATS AND OTHER LIVING THINGS.

I picked Skunky up and hugged him while he licked the tears from my face. After examining him for cuts and squishing him pretty thoroughly looking for broken bones and sore spots, I carried him next door to check on Lisa. But everything there was in perfect order. I fed them both at Chris's, watching Skunky anxiously for signs of post-traumatic stress. But he seemed none the worse for his adventure, and after his late supper, was happy to stretch out for a nap.

I returned next door to survey the vandalism. If anything, it looked worse than before. The bedroom had been hit, as well — mattress and pillows ripped, the mirror over the dresser cracked, pictures pulled from the walls. The destruction was thorough and systematic; nothing had been spared. Even my mother's half-finished sweater was torn to pieces, unsalvageable.

I thought about calling the police, but what could they do? Take a statement, make a report, keep me up until dawn. I was dead on my feet. I'd go see Donleavy in the morning; that would be more to the point. This wasn't your random home invasion. Although the name was still a question mark, I knew who'd been here. And why. And if he thought this was the way to get me to lay off, he was about three dozen kinds of wrong. I'd been willing to leave the whole mess to the cops before this. But now the asshole had wrecked my house, terrified my cat, and shattered the sense of security I'd always felt about my home. It was no longer a haven. That part of the damage, I knew, was irreparable.

I needed to wait until it got light to examine the place carefully. Besides, I was so numb with exhaustion I just wanted to shut my eyes and come down with amnesia. I decided to spend the remainder of the night at Chris's. When I was locking up, I discovered the intruder had gotten in through the window by the back door. One of its panes had been broken, allowing my new pen pal to reach in and unlatch it. The door had been used only as an exit, the deadbolt disengaged from the inside. I re-secured the door, but I didn't even bother to shore up the gaping hole in the window. I figured things couldn't get much worse that night.

I took a shower before climbing into Chris's bed. Skunky and Lisa jockeyed for position on the pillow beside me. The two cats were normally friendly, but they weren't used to sharing quarters, so there was a good deal of hissing and complaining that continued intermittently throughout the night. I finally fell into a fitful sleep and dreamed a nightmare of being trapped under water so murky and dense with tangled vines and moss that I couldn't see to swim or free myself to get to the surface for a breath of air. I woke with a jolt, gasping and sweating. I didn't need Sigmund Freud to tell me what that was all about.

Ten

You know the old saying, "Everything will look better in the morning"? Well, as the immortal Gershwins so tunefully pointed out, "It ain't necessarily so." The next morning I was forced to make a heart-wrenching decision: I had to send Skunky away for awhile. I was going to continue working on the Symington case, smashed glass and spilled condiments notwithstanding. The break-in had actually pushed me back into the fray because it was personal now — my home had been threatened. Hell. Had been laid waste. And I was perfectly willing to accept responsibility for the consequences of that decision. But I couldn't further endanger an innocent animal who depended on me for his care and protection. I felt one of Skunky's nine lives was already forfeit in exchange for his escape the night before. I knew I wouldn't get another warning.

But my options here were limited. Boarding him at the vet's was out of the question — he'd be miserable locked in a cage, and I still didn't have a wide circle of friends in L.A. Certainly not the kind I could just call up and say, "Would you mind taking care of my spoiled rotten grouchy little cat who hates everybody but me for an indefinite period of time?" No, that's the kind of appeal you can only make to your nearest and dearest, those who, through no fault of their own, are related to you.

I made a pot of coffee, fed the four-legged troops, who had fortunately agreed to an armistice, and put in a call to my brother, Jack, in Chicago. We're twins, though you couldn't know that by looking at us. Jack's a prototypical fair-haired corn-fed Midwestern boy while I tend to be somewhat stubbier and dark. To be perfectly candid, we're very un-twinlike in most respects. He's a lawyer and certified public accountant, a family man with a lovely wife, three great kids, and a big house in the suburbs with a swimming pool and tennis court. He's bright, steady, well-adjusted, successful. One of us was obviously switched at birth.

A singular lapse in judgment happens to concern his regard (or lack thereof) for cats in general, my cat in particular. But I knew Skunky would be well-treated, and the kids would be thrilled, if I could convince Jack to let him come for a visit. The tricky part would be to hit the proper balance when posing my request, sounding urgent enough to gain a positive response without setting off any fraternal alarms. His secretary put me through and after the usual "How're the kids?" "How's the weather?" I got down to it.

"So. I have a huge favor to ask."

"Hmmm." Noncommittal. He's a careful one, that Jack.

"I'm working on something that's gotten kind of complicated, and I need to board Skunky for a short while. I wondered if you could be induced to turn your home into a temporary hostel for a refugee feline."

"What happened? Are you all right?" he demanded, sounding very alarmed. Damn.

"I'm fine, just fine. We had a little problem last night, but everything's under control now —"

"Tell me what happened."

"Well, there was sort of a break-in at the house, and I don't think it's safe for Skunky to stay there." Okay, so he wormed it out of me.

"Not safe for Skunky!" he exploded. "Who cares about the fucking cat?"

"I, for one," I answered calmly. "And I'm really not worried about the situation for myself. I'm working with the police on an investigation. The break-in probably wasn't even related," I back-pedaled. "But I need to be able to concentrate all my energy on the case right now. I may even have to go out of town. Please. It would be such a help. I wouldn't ask you if I didn't need to."

"I wish you'd get out of all that once and for all. I worry about you all the time." I could practically see him shaking his head in dismay.

"I know. I'm sorry. But this is me. It's what I do. Believe me, if I thought I could be somebody different, I'd be happy to give it a try."

"Do you still have your gun?" he asked quietly.

I closed my eyes, clenching my jaw. "Yes."

No need to tell him it was in a box on the upper shelf of the closet.

He sighed. "Go ahead and send the little bastard out," he said mildly. "The kids will be happy to see him, anyway. Does he still hiss whenever an adult male of the human persuasion comes within ten feet of him?"

"I have no idea — my social life has been so dismal. Thanks, Jack. You're a peach."

"Just watch yourself. Please." The hitch in his voice made me wish I could give him a hug.

We hung up, and I got busy with travel plans for the big guy. A plane reservation, another call to Jack to discuss the arrival time, then the excursion next door to extract his carrier from the debris. I tried not to focus on the havoc. First things first. Just keep putting one foot in front of the other. A step at a time. Et cetera. Et cetera.

I had a very teary moment when it was time to stuff him into the carrier. He hates it so much, and he knows how to play me like an instrument. I am the proverbial putty in his masterful paws. We swung by the vet's to pick up a health certificate, which really put the Skunkster in a foul mood. He growls and spits like his life's on the line every time he sees that thermometer coming at him. He settled down for the ride to the airport but renewed his protest after we'd parked the car and I was carrying him into the terminal. I petted him through the mesh of his carrier, told him to be a good boy at his Uncle Jack's, and handed him to the agent who would shepherd him onto the plane. She was a motherly-looking sort in her late forties who cooed at Skunky despite the rude noises he was making and promised me he'd be well cared-for. I bolted for the door before I could change my mind. On the way out, I stopped long enough to stick a check in an envelope addressed to Jack to pay for food and supplies for his houseguest and slipped it in a mail slot. Then I trudged back to the car, feeling as lonely as I could ever remember. In less than twenty-four hours my comfortable little world had been virtually dismantled, and it was really beginning to bug me.

I drove back home and left a note at Chris's about the break-in, warning her to be cautious, promising to fill in the details when we talked. Then I returned to my place and went through each room carefully, looking for anything that might give me a hint about the intruder. Like maybe a hastily dropped photo I.D. with his name and address. After a couple fruitless hours thus occupied, I gave in and began the clean-up, starting with the kitchen — to ward off fermentation of the floor. I also swept up most of the broken glass and patched the window I'd ignored the night before. I always have a few extra clay pots out back left over from plants that have bitten the dust, so I re-potted my poor little cacti.

The studio was the worst for me. Putting it together had been a labor of love, and its destruction was a heartbreak. I got a can of turpentine and some rags to clean up the paint, then began carrying my canvases to the dumpster out back. It took me several trips to clear them out, and all the while I felt like I was throwing away little pieces of myself.

By then it was getting late, and even though the house was still a wreck by any civilized standards, I had to get going. I put on some clean clothes because the next item on my agenda was a talk with Donleavy. After a detour to Kinko's to copy the notes I wanted to give him, I set out for the Hollywood police station, a low brick building on the southeast corner at the intersection of Wilcox and de Longpre, a drab and colorless neighborhood, all its vitality long ago paved over or leached away by poverty and despair. I parked across the street from the station in front of the conveniently located S.O.S. Bailbonds. As I turned the lock on The Club, securing it across the steering wheel of the Toyota, I offered up a little prayer the car would still be there when I got back. Even with the cops across the street, this looked like prime car theft territory to me.

The sidewalk outside the station was inlaid with stars mimicking the Hollywood Walk of Fame, but these concrete testimonials were engraved with the names of policemen who'd been killed in the line of duty. It struck me as funny, sad, and a little macabre. Only in Los Angeles.

I entered the station through a set of glass double doors and was greeted by a banner stretched across the far wall that proclaimed, "Bienvenidos a la Estacion de Hollywood." A raised counter to the right, for general information and reception, was manned by three uniforms. Metal chairs bolted to the floor and a similarly secured wooden bench provided seating in the cramped waiting area. Vending machines stocked with junk food and that horrible ersatz coffee lined one of the walls. The decor was completed by a variety of framed movie posters — *The Little Mermaid, White Fang,* and *The Addams Family.* I was wondering about the guidelines for the poster selection process when I spied a door marked "Detective Reception" to the left. I ducked through it into an even smaller waiting area and was about to announce myself to the receptionist when, as if on cue, Donleavy came in through another door. His eyebrows shot up when he recognized me.

"Hey, Kiddo, what brings you all the way over here?"

Kiddo. Oh, well.

"Hello, Lieutenant. I actually came over hoping to talk to you."

"Yeah?" He frowned, glancing at his watch. "Well, I was just on my way out for a bite, but come on along and I'll buy you a taco."

Now what girl could resist an invitation like that?

He led me out the front entrance and back down the sidewalk of dead policemen. I was happy to see the Toyota still perched by the curb. The day was hot without a breath of breeze this far inland to stir the air. We took a right on Wilcox and hiked up the block to a grubby little diner with windows covered by homemade construction paper signs advertising fish tacos, pollo asado, and menudo. There was a counter inside for ordering and a couple of plastic tables mired in the layer of silty grease that covered the floor. Don't get me wrong: I love little hole-in-the-wall restaurants, and I'm not all that fussy about everything being spic and span, but the ambience of this joint was downright roach-friendly. The little fellow I spotted scuttling along the baseboards looked pretty chipper, anyway. I wasn't surprised we were the only customers.

Donleavy gave his order to a youth with as much gold in his mouth as around his neck then looked over at me expectantly.

"I'll just have iced tea."

"You don't know what you're missing," he insisted.

A gap in my experience I was willing to accept.

His food was handed over in a small paper tray, an aromatic mixture that didn't look all that different from the mess I'd just scraped off my kitchen floor.

"Yum!" Donleavy smacked his lips and headed for one of the tables.

"You're going to eat here?" I tried to keep the note of horror out of my voice.

He glanced around. "Well, yeah." It all looked fine to him.

I had no choice but to take a seat across from him at the gritty little table. And for this I'd put on clean clothes.

"So what did you want to talk to me about?" Donleavy was already happily munching away.

"Two things," I said, trying to make eye contact without actually watching him eat. "Faye Symington's ex-assistant called me yesterday, and I took some notes while we talked. Thought they might be useful to you as background. And there was a break-in at my house last night."

I could tell I had his full attention. He'd even stopped chewing.

"Somebody trashed the place and taped my cat's feet together holding a note that looks a lot like the Symington notes." I laid my summary of the conversation with Amy and a ziploc bag containing the note on the table in front of him.

"Didn't you report this last night?" he asked sharply.

"No," I admitted, suddenly feeling defensive on the subject. "There was nothing anybody could do, and I just couldn't face all the bullshit questions and paperwork. Believe me, I've been over the place. He didn't leave any clues aside from the note."

"What about fingerprints? Did you dust for them, too?" he asked sarcastically.

"Oh, come on! Whoever it was had to wear gloves. Check the note. The others tested negative for prints, and I can almost guarantee you this one will, too. What about Faye's office? Did you find any prints there?"

I knew it sounded lame, but the truth was that having a bunch of cops crawling all over my house in the middle of the night would've just about pushed me over the edge. I surrendered with a wave of my hand. "You're welcome to send a crew over to my place — it's anything but ship-shape yet. Have at it if you think it might help."

He glared at me. "How many people knew you'd been hired by the daughter?"

I squirmed like a bug caught on a pin. "Well, unfortunately, just about anybody might know," I cringed, then told him about the tabloid article I'd hoped he'd never see.

"Stupid bitch!" he muttered.

"I beg your pardon?"

"Not you — Symington. What an idiotic stunt!" He shook his head in disgust and leaned his elbows heavily on the table, pushing the remains of his lunch aside. "Do you live alone?"

I nodded, thinking regretfully of Skunky winging his way to the Midwest.

"I think it might be a good idea for you to stay with a friend for awhile. Or better yet, take a vacation. Get out of the way until we can get a better fix on all this."

I chewed my lip. "Are you anywhere near making an arrest?"

He stared at me for a long minute before answering. "I'm only telling you this because I want you to fully appreciate the seriousness of your situation. No," he said vehemently, "we're no place close to arresting anybody. There's no physical evidence connecting any person to the murder, no witnesses, nada."

"What about Jeremy Latham? Did you guys talk to him?"

"The queer with the dead boyfriend? Yeah. Claims he had a bad case of the blues after your visit. Unplugged his phone, crawled into bed, and pulled the covers over his little head." His mouth sketched a mean smile and he shrugged. "The lady made a habit of pissing people off. Your guess is as good as mine. And that's the trouble; either way, at this point, it's only a guess."

He finished his meal in two giant bites. "But whoever it is evidently sees you as a threat. So do everybody — especially yourself — a favor and get lost for awhile. Be sure to let us know where you'll be so we can contact you if we need to." He pushed his chair back from the table, regarding me sourly. "And I hope I don't have to tell you to keep your nose clean where all this is concerned." Then he got up and walked out the door without so much as a backward glance.

I wasn't far behind him, but I stopped to use the dilapidated pay phone on the street just outside the diner. The machine picked up at Sara's Malibu number, and I left a message saying I needed to talk to her as soon as possible.

Eleven

I arrived at Sony Studios around lunch time, and seizing that bit of serendipity, I decided to experiment. I parked the car on the street, waited for a gaggle of employees returning from lunch on foot, and fell in step behind them. A couple of them waved as we passed the security kiosk, and we all walked onto the lot without a protesting peep from the guards. *So there are any number of ways to skin this particular cat,* I thought, making mental apologies to Skunky for the analogy.

I veered off from my decoy group once we were a few yards inside the gate. The lot was bustling; a steady stream of foot traffic along with vehicles of all shapes and sizes crowded the narrow lanes between the stages. A flatbed truck carrying a foam replica of the Statue of Liberty rattled past me going in the opposite direction, and I heard someone shout, "Hey! Maggie!"

I whirled about-face. Who the hell . . .?

The truck pulled to a halt, its brakes screeching their complaint, and my painter friend from the other day leaned out the passenger's side window and waved.

"It is Maggie, isn't it?'

"Yeah. Hi, Rick."

He got out and said something to the driver, and the truck rumbled on its way.

As I walked over to meet him, I got smacked by that wave of pheromones again. I almost never meet a man who attracts me in that butterflies-in-the-stomach way, and when I do, my defenses automatically go up —with good reason, given my romantic history.

"You come back for that cup of coffee?"

"If you're buying," I said. "Are you on a break?"

He looked at his watch and shrugged. "I worked through lunch. Let's go."

We walked toward the middle of the lot to an open-air cafe with tables shaded by striped umbrellas and ordered iced lattes. Being this much closer to the beach made a big difference; the sun felt warm without being oppressive, and a slight breeze ruffled Rick's blonde hair. I noticed he wore an earring in his left ear, a small diamond chip. No ring on his left hand.

Stop it, Maggie!

"So have things settled down here yet? Or are the cops still nosing around?" I asked, trying to distract myself from the intense blue of his eyes.

"Yeah, they're still talkin' to everybody. Amazing." He shook his head. "That was your friend, right? The woman you came to see the other day?"

"The day it happened, in fact."

"Geez, I'm sorry."

"We weren't close. She hired me to do some work for her. I'd only met her the night before."

"Somehow I got the impression you weren't in the business."

He looked at me speculatively, his head tilted to one side in a way that made it a question.

"That's right, I'm not. I'm a private investigator."

"You mean, like Nancy Drew?" His face crinkled up in surprise.

I had to laugh. "Nancy Drew had a rich father who paid all her bills, a red convertible, and a preppie boyfriend."

"And you don't?"

"None of the above."

"How about a non-preppie boyfriend?" he asked with a grin.

"Not one of those, either. And you?"

"No, I'm between boyfriends, myself."

"Funny."

He gave me a sweet half-smile. "I'm divorced. Almost, anyway."

Danger! Danger! Warning lights and alarms went off in my brain. Run, Maggie, run!

"I'm sorry," it was my turn to say. "I know how rough that can be."

"Yeah, well, it'll all be over soon."

The poor jerk. He actually believed that.

"How did you end up doing that for a living?" He ripped open a packet of sugar and began doctoring his coffee.

"You mean, why didn't I pick a job from the girls' list," I said (I admit) a little snappishly. "Secretary, teacher, wet-nurse, that kind of thing?"

"No," he answered mildly. "I mean I'm interested in you, so I'm interested in the kind of work you do and why you chose to do it."

"Oh." I winced, embarrassed by my politically correct rudeness. "Well, I used to be a police detective, back when I lived in New York."

"You were a police detective in New York City?"

"Yup."

"Now, don't take offense — I'm just being nosy." He ducked sideways in his chair as though dodging my imaginary blows. "What got you interested in police work?"

"Following in my daddy's footsteps," I smiled. His clowning struck me as cute, which in itself worried me.

"Ahhh," he nodded approvingly. "That must've made him proud."

"I'd like to think so." I felt my eyes misting over and looked away, unexpectedly tweaked by the old pain, like a pinch around my heart. "He died when I was four."

"Hey, I'm sorry," he said gently.

My throat felt tight and I swallowed hard to clear it. "Yeah, thanks."

"So . . . a police detective in New York City. That must have been a tough job," he offered gamely.

"Some days it was," I nodded, grateful for his tact. "Most days, really. But I loved it. I felt like I was part of something important, working with a lot of other people to make the city a better place to live." And that much was certainly true, as far as it went.

"Well, I'm impressed."

"Yeah, well, so was I at the time, if you want to know the truth. That's the other side of it," I said wryly. I clasped my hands behind my head and leaned back in my chair, closing my eyes against the early afternoon sun. "I really thought I had the world by the tail. I was married then to a real up-and-comer; he had family connections and money. And there I was, only twenty-six years old and already a detective third grade. Hmph," I laughed at that other me. "I was climbing the ladder for all I was worth, and all that stuff seemed pretty important. Some hotshot."

I fell silent, and we sat quietly for a bit, but I could feel he was waiting for me to say something more.

"So why aren't you still a police detective?" he finally asked.

I opened my eyes to find him watching me with a gaze as clear and guileless as a summer sky. "That's a conversation that'll have to wait until we know each other better."

"I'm in no rush," he replied easily.

"Your turn." I scooted my chair a few inches to the right to catch the retreating shade of the umbrella. "What drew you to painting — no pun intended."

He laughed. "I actually went to art school, believe it or not, at Cal Arts and studied portraiture. Signed up for an exchange program to spend a year in Florence and fell in love with Italy, so I made up my mind to go back after I graduated. I'd inherited some money from an uncle, so I helled around Europe, painting and partying for as long as it lasted, which was about two years."

"I envy you that experience. I'll bet you had a great time."

"I did," he grinned, wiggling his eyebrows á la Groucho Marx. "And I learned two very important things about myself." He held up a forefinger. "Even if I had the talent, I don't have the discipline or the temperament to work alone all the time. I'm like you: I like being part of something, working with other people for a common goal." He held up a second finger. "And I like to eat too well and too regularly to try to make my living as a fine artist."

He shrugged. "So, when the money ran out, I came back to L.A. A friend of mine had a job painting on a non-union movie, and he asked me to work on his crew. I didn't know a thing about the business, but I needed a job, so I figured, why not? The first week I was on it, the movie got busted by the union, we all had to join, and voilà! Twenty years later, here I am. I've been running my own shows for the past fifteen. And I love it. I've never been bored, and I still learn something new almost every day. It's the perfect job for me."

"We're lucky people, you and I."

"As far as work goes, anyway," he said with that lop-sided smile again. He cocked his head, studying me with a look of total absorption. I love observing other people, but it's not so much fun for me being the scrutinee, and I found myself worrying about stuff like stray nose hairs flapping in the breeze. "I'd like to paint you sometime."

I burst out laughing; I swear I couldn't help it. "Boy, does that ever sound like a line! Are we talking matte finish or semi-gloss?"

"Hey! Hey! Hey!" he blustered with mock indignation. "I have nothing but friendly intentions. I'm just trying to create an opportunity for us to get better acquainted. Work with me a little, here!"

I felt myself drawn to his infectious good humor. He seemed like such a nice guy, and there was that animal magnetism thing going on . . .

But his ring finger still has a tan line, for the love of Pete!

"This place must be buzzing," I said, steering us back to neutral ground. "It's almost like he chose to kill her here for the shock value. If he planned it ahead of time, that is."

He allowed me to beat a retreat. "Yeah, the blood-letting around here is usually at the corporate level."

"Did you know Faye?"

He pulled a pack of Camels out of his shirt pocket and tapped one loose. "Nope. Never even really met the lady. Saw her around some." Half-turning in his chair, he struck a match and cupped his hands to shield it as he lit the cigarette. "But she wasn't real friendly. Didn't mix much with the crew. And she seemed kinda hard on her people, sort of a yappy little gal."

A fitting eulogy, if I ever heard one.

"So what's the gossip? Does anybody have any theories that you've heard?""

He shrugged and blew two streams of smoke through his nostrils. "Everybody's talking, but nobody knows anything. Seems like the costume supervisor was the last one to see her. Except for whoever killed her."

"Who's the costume supervisor?"

"Her name's Poppie. Poppie something-or-other. I don't know her last name."

"Is she here today?"

"Yeah. I saw her earlier, anyway. She's probably in the wardrobe trailer over by the stage."

"Would you mind telling me how to get there?"

"I'll show you. We're shooting on Stage 25 today. I need to head over there to check on a couple of things, anyway." He stubbed out the cigarette and stood up. "I'll tell you, though; if you want to pick up the scuttlebutt, you should hang out at the catering truck around lunch time. That's Gossip Central. The shooting company didn't come in until eight this morning, so they'll break at two for the meal."

As we walked over to the stage, our conversation lapsed into uneasy fits and starts. It galled me to find myself hamstrung by my hormones like some hapless teenager. He led me to the back of a huge white semi-trailer. The back end of the truck had been replaced by a sliding glass door, and I could see clothing hanging inside. The metal tailgate was lowered, and a set of wooden steps provided easy access to the door.

"This is my jumping-off point." He hesitated, and I could see he felt as awkward as I did. "What would happen if I gave you a call sometime?"

I looked up into those gorgeous blue eyes. Damn the lousy, horrible, rotten, crummy timing. "I don't think that's probably a terrific idea right now, do you?"

"Probably not," he agreed. "But how about if I need to talk to a private investigator?"

He gave me that sweet half-smile.

"Then I'm in the book." I tried to smile back, but it didn't quite work. "Give me a call after the ink on the final decree has had a few months to dry. If you still feel like it."

"You gotta deal." He waved as he walked off. "See ya."

"Yeah. See ya."

I wanted to lie down right there on the ground, kick my heels, and throw a tantrum. Instead, I took a deep breath, marched up the steps to the truck's back door, and knocked purposefully like the iron-willed, single-minded, hard-bitten professional sleuth I might someday be.

A round mop-topped little woman slid the door open in response. She was about 5'2" and should definitely not have been wearing those elastic-waisted royal blue stretch pants that accentuated every bulge and ripple of her generous figure. She'd compounded her error with a horizontally striped overblouse that cupped her hindquarters in an unfortunate way. Her indifferently styled hair was a dull gray-blonde, her skin roughened by age, weather, and excessive drink. She had an overbite like a cartoon squirrel and small dark eyes hooded by prominent brows. Because of this fluke of biology, she appeared furtive and shifty-looking.

"Yes? May I help you?"

"Poppie?"

"Yes."

"Maggie McGrath." I held out one of my cards. "Faye was a client of mine, and I'm continuing to work for her daughter. I wonder if I could ask you a few questions."

Poppie examined the business card with unusual care, or maybe she was just a slow reader. She pondered it awhile before answering. "I guess so. What do you want to know?"

I stepped past her bulky form into the truck. The air conditioner must have been set on "stun"; it was as cold as a meat locker inside. Double-tiered stationary pipes bolted along the length of each side of the truck provided hanging

space for costumes, and those pipes were so packed with clothing, it was a wonder that anything could ever be found, or freed from the tangle once it was
located. Boxes of shoes, hats, towels, and supplies spilled out of the storage bins
built into the floor under the hanging pipes. A counter at the far end of the
truck offered the only flat work space, but it was piled with stacks of papers,
office supplies, loose hangers, and general refuse, including a discarded
McDonald's drink cup stuffed with a Big Mac wrapper. The air was perfumed
by the aroma of old socks.

There was not a centimeter of uncluttered space except for a barely navi-
gable path down the center of the truck. Poppie led as we gingerly picked our
way along that route to the other end where two stools piled with T-shirts and
long underwear stood beside the trash heap that had once been a counter. She
cleared the seats by unceremoniously dumping the laundry onto the floor. We
sat, and I pulled out my notebook.

Poppie gazed at me blankly, and I found myself wondering why Faye had
chosen this troglodyte to be one of her lieutenants. She might be a whiz at her
job, but judging by the condition of her workplace, I doubted that. Rick had
said Faye didn't seem all that easy to work for, which pretty much summed up
my impression, based on my own brief foray into those troubled waters. Maybe
my client had earned a reputation that made it difficult for her to attract a crew
of top-notch people.

"How long have you been working for Faye?" I asked.

"About four months."

She spoke with an odd sibilant mannerism, her s's hissing slightly. The
result, I supposed, of the overbite.

"Then this is your first movie with her?"

"Yes."

"And what is your job, Poppie?"

"I'm the costume supervisor."

"I've never worked on a movie, so please bear with me. What are your
responsibilities?"

Poppie strained to cross one plump knee over the other and leaned back
against the edge of the counter. "I keep track of the budget, supervise the set
costumers, and help the designer prep whatever's coming up on the schedule."

"So you worked closely with Faye?"

She hesitated, her brow furrowing as if she were afraid this might be a trick
question. "Faye didn't like anybody to get too close, if you know what I mean,
but yes, I spent a lot of time with her."

"Did you know about the threats she'd been getting recently?"

"No, she didn't mention them," Poppie replied, evidently uncurious about
the subject.

"Was she having trouble with anyone in particular that you were
aware of? Or feuding with someone? Did she ever complain about anybody to you?"

Poppie shrugged uncomfortably, her small eyes evasive. "Faye was always mad at somebody. She complained about everybody."

Poor Poppie. Faye had probably tortured her mercilessly with the same delight a cruel youngster pulls the wings off a fly. She wouldn't have chosen to confide in her.

"Were you in the office on the evening of the night she was killed?"

"Not very much. I went over there a couple of times, but I was mostly on the set or here on the trailer."

"But Faye spent most of the evening in the office?"

"As far as I know. She was there every time I went over. She didn't come to the set."

"You must have been working fairly late."

"Yes, we've been shooting really long days — fifteen, sixteen hours. We're way behind. We shot until almost midnight that night."

"And then did you go back to the office in the Garbo Building?"

"No, I checked in over there about ten o'clock. I wanted Faye to know we were on the last set-up. But I didn't go over there again after we wrapped." Poppie shook her head regretfully. "That was the last time I saw her."

"Did she mention if she was expecting anyone?"

"No. She said she was going home."

"How about before that? Do you know if anybody came by to see her earlier in the evening?"

Her heavy brow creased again with the effort of concentration, nearly obscuring her eyes. "Her business manager was here around seven-thirty."

"Lillian Baxter?"

Poppie nodded.

"You've met her . . . she's been here before?"

"Curly blonde hair, skinny, wears too much make-up," she said, confirming that we were, indeed, talking about the same person. "She comes by every once in awhile. But she was really upset the other night when she left. I passed her in the hall, and she pretended she was looking for something in her purse, but I could tell she was crying."

"You're sure about the time?"

"Yes, because I came over to tell Faye we were breaking for the second meal."

"Do you have any idea what that was all about? Did you happen to ask Faye?"

But I knew the answer already.

"And get my head snapped off? Nunh-uh!" Poppie shook her shaggy head emphatically.

"Did you tell this to the police?"

"You know, I really can't remember." She seemed genuinely bewildered. "They got me so flustered with all their questions. I don't like cops — they make me nervous."

"Swell," I muttered under my breath as I leaned an elbow on the counter. It hadn't seemed like a dangerous maneuver, but the delicate balance of the junkpile was disrupted, and a heap of it went crashing to the floor.

"Oh, my God!" Poppie cried, springing from her stool with surprising energy and snatching up a small leather-bound book from the rubble.

"What's that?"

"Faye was looking all over for this!"

You would have thought Faye had better sense than to set anything down in this pig-sty.

"What is it?" I repeated.

"It's her address and appointment book. She called it her Bible. She was so mad when she couldn't find it! She stomped around here for days!"

"May I see it, Poppie?" I asked lightly, my fingers itching to pry the book from her grasp.

"I guess so," she frowned, making no move to hand it over.

"I think I should take it to the police," I urged.

And I would, too. After I'd taken a good hard look at it.

"Okay. Yes, that's a good idea," she nodded.

It was about the size of a paperback novel and made of beautifully tooled dark green leather. The initials "F.S." were part of the elaborately inscribed design — it was definitely a custom piece. I tucked the book into my bag.

"Poppie, thanks for all your help. Please call me if you think of anything else."

She looked at me quizzically, as if she couldn't imagine such circumstances ever arising. There was another door at the end of the truck where we'd had our chat, so at least I didn't have to stumble back through the clutter in order to get out.

"By the way, Poppie," I paused on the top step outside the door, ready to make a note in my book, "what's your last name?"

"Fields," she lisped.

You gotta love that.

Twelve

Feeling like I'd just stepped out of a smelly old refrigerator, I reveled in the warmth of the afternoon sun as I made my way over to talk to the production people. *Deadly Extreme Force* had taken a suite of offices on the upper floor of a two-story cinder block building not far from the stages. A series of hand-lettered signs led me from the entryway around a corner and up a flight of steep, wide stairs just as a UPS deliveryman laden with packages was struggling to make it through the door at the top of the stairway. I trotted up the remaining steps and held it open for him.

"Hey, thanks," he panted.

A plump young woman with brilliant turquoise hair rushed up behind him, gasping, "You'll be back for the rest of it, right? I mean, there're a ton more boxes to go!"

"Yeah, I know, but in case you haven't noticed, I've only got two hands and you geniuses rented space without an elevator, so I can't use the dolly," he grumbled.

"All right, then," she nodded officiously. "Just so you don't forget." She turned on her heel, and I danced around the UPS guy to catch her.

"Excuse me, do you work on *Deadly Extreme Force*?" I followed her into a short hallway.

"Yeah." Her dye job was growing out, and three sprouting inches of dark brown roots made her look like she was wearing a yarmulke.

"I'm looking for your office manager."

"Office manager?" she echoed blankly. "Well, I guess you could talk to Allura . . .. yeah, she'd be the one," she decided.

"Could you point her out, please?"

"Oh, just ask anybody in there." She waved toward a doorway on my left and made her getaway through another one marked "Ladies."

I pushed through the door she'd indicated into a large office sparsely furnished with three desks, a fax machine, and a long table covered with neatly organized stacks of paperwork. Opening off this central hub was a network of half a dozen or so smaller offices buzzing with frantic activity. People darted in and out of doorways at the breakneck speeds of a cartoon on fast forward, their urgent pantomimes underscored by the mechanical percussion of a Xerox machine and phones ringing non-stop.

I zeroed in on a rabbity young woman sitting at the first desk. "I'm looking for a person named Allura. I was told she's the office manager," I said with a perky smile that usually wins them over.

Rabbit Girl licked her thin lips nervously and without saying a word darted her eyes down the line to the woman at the next desk. Evidently Allura. Personally, I think it's a cruel trick to saddle a kid with a name like that. Why not just tattoo a bull's-eye on her and be done with it? No loving parent would think of sending a child out to face the torments of an adolescence spent so christened. Maybe that's why this girl had that Gibraltar-sized chip on her shoulder.

Allura was on the telephone, and because there was no place to sit, I stood in front of her desk while she pointedly ignored me. She was probably twenty-five or twenty-six years old with long, wavy dishwater blonde hair, her slightly orange complexion courtesy of some self-tanning product. Slender and well-muscled, she obviously spent a lot of time at the gym trying to live up to her Christian name. After I'd hovered for several minutes casting a long shadow and staring fixedly at her trying for a mind-meld — or at least eye contact — to no avail, I wandered over to check out the stacks of paperwork on the table.

There was a map to the next day's shooting location, an extras breakdown listing the numbers and types of background people required for each scene, a shooting schedule, something called a "day-out-of-days," which listed the days each member of the cast was scheduled to work during the course of filming, and (Eureka!) a crew list with names, addresses, and phone numbers for all the off-camera people working on the movie, from the director to the caterer. I picked one up; it was several pages long. This would come in handy.

"May I help you?" demanded a voice behind me in a tone that really meant, What the hell are you doing?

I folded the list and stuck it in one of the outside pockets of my bag as I turned and greeted her pleasantly. "Oh, hello!"

Allura still held the phone to her ear, and she glared at me as I gave her my card.

"I'll have to call you back," she muttered into the receiver and hung up without saying goodbye. "What do you want?" she demanded crossly.

"Faye Symington hired me just before she was murdered because of a series of threats she'd received, and her daughter has asked me to continue that investigation. I'd like to ask you a few —"

"Oh, no you don't! You're not going to barge in here and disrupt our whole office! We're very busy!" She'd gone all red in the face, viciously jabbing the air with a forefinger. The chick definitely had some issues. "We had to talk to the cops, but we don't have to give you the time of day. So get out!"

"You're absolutely right!" I smacked my forehead with the heel of my hand as if smitten by a sudden insight. "How could I be presumptuous enough to think that your co-worker's death could possibly be of equal importance to a Sylvester Stallone movie? Please, don't let me interrupt for a moment. And God bless you for the important work you're doing here, you unpleasant little bitch."

Never let it be said that I lack people skills.

By then it was just after 2:00. Bloodied but unbowed, I stalked back over to Stage 25 in search of the catering truck. It wasn't hard to spot: it was a little white vehicle that looked a lot like an old-fashioned Mr. Softee ice cream truck, complete with a side panel that dropped down to reveal a window where orders were placed and delivered. Most of the cooking was done in its tiny kitchen on wheels, but a portable grill had been set up outside where hamburgers and chicken parts were being barbecued to a fare-thee-well. A handwritten menu was posted on an easel nearby. And there were about a hundred people in line.

I spotted Diane, the costumer I'd spoken with on my previous visit. I was sure she noticed me, too, and a flicker of recognition sparked in her eyes. But she quickly extinguished it and told me with her body language she preferred to ignore me. So, of course I greeted her at once.

"Diane!" I cried with perverse heartiness. "Maggie McGrath. We met the other day."

She regarded me coolly with a mixture of curiosity and unease. Something was different about her that I couldn't put my finger on at first. But then it came to me — today she wasn't chomping on a big cud of gum.

"I'm a private investigator working for Faye's daughter, Sara Landesmann."

"I remember you," she replied stiffly.

"I was wondering if we could talk while you're eating."

She shrugged and stepped up to give her order. "I've already told the police everything I know," she said, brushing her dull black hair away from her face. "Which isn't much. I'm on the set all the time, and I try not to pay attention to much of anything else that goes on around here."

She picked up her lunch from the server at the window and made a dash for the door of another sound stage, with me tagging right along.

"So, you wouldn't have any idea how Faye interacted with the other members of the company?"

"She didn't," Diane said curtly, finally grasping the fact that I wasn't easily discouraged. "At least, not if she could help it."

"I can't see how that would be practical. She'd need to talk to her collaborators. The director, the actors —"

"Only when she absolutely had to."

We entered another overly-cool dim stage where banquet tables had been set up to accommodate the company's lunch.

"You might as well come and sit down," she said grudgingly. "You can ask the others about Faye."

I figured this was more a diversionary tactic than an effort to help, but I followed her to a table where a group of women clustered at one end automatically made room for us. They turned out to be her usual group of dining companions, and they were a little more forthcoming.

"Oh! I know I shouldn't speak ill of the dead, but she was the rudest woman I've ever met in my life!" screeched Jackie, the hair stylist, whose cascade of over-processed ringlets was not a sight that would inspire me to entrust my tresses to her care. "She hardly ever came to the set. And she hardly spoke to anyone when she was there. I had a question about Evangelina's hair one day, and she blew me off like I was some stupid pest. Honestly, I just avoided her after the first week of shooting," she sniffed.

"You could tell she thought she was a cut above the rest of the crew. Always with her nose in the air," said Carolina, the make-up artist. A woman of around fifty, she had a thick accent of some Slavic ilk and the drawn look that comes from one too many face lifts. "I've been on three movies with her, but I can't say we've ever had a real conversation. She was a cold person. Very aloof, distant."

My stomach rumbled, reminding me I'd skipped lunch. "I find it hard to believe it's possible to work with such a large group of people every day and still remain so isolated," I said, eyeing a plump chicken thigh on Carolina's plate. In another minute, I'd be drooling on myself.

"Oh, it's possible, all right. But most people seem to enjoy the social aspect of the job. You're here so many hours of the day, it's often the only social life you have while you're on a project. But Faye was a loner," said Jessica, the script supervisor, a thin young woman with keen dark eyes.

"Well, I still say it was a professional hit!"

I looked up in astonishment. The person attached to this outlandish suggestion was a pit-bull of a fellow, bristling with aggression. I had to give him this — he had the courage of his delusions. He was nearly bald but wore the few strands of hair remaining to him in a scraggly braid.

"I'm Kenny, the key grip," he further enlightened me. Whatever that was.

"Kenny," I said gently, "I think it's unlikely a professional killer would rely on a found object to use for a weapon."

Kenny retreated sullenly, muttering to himself. It was then I glanced around to discover we'd begun to draw a crowd. The murder was certainly the hot topic of the day, and everyone had an opinion. I suddenly found myself cast in the role of moderator for a lively group discussion, and it was fascinating. Instead of having to wheedle and pry for information like I usually do, I was beset by people who were falling all over themselves to be heard — kind of a cross between *The Jerry Springer Show* and an old-fashioned town meeting. I carpe diemed by asking what they thought of the idea that the murderer might be one of their own company.

"Hell, we didn't any of us know her well enough to hate her that bad," said one of the teamsters, his lower lip protruding sagely as he shook his head.

"Let's put it this way," added an assistant camera operator, "one of the benefits to this kind of work is that you're not trapped with the same bunch of jerks for years on end. You sign on for six months or so, and then it's over. You can put up with just about anybody for that long. Except Jim Cameron," he added as an afterthought. "Not enough money in the world to get me to work for that son of a bitch again."

Interesting point. His observation met with general approval; heads bobbed in agreement, many murmured their assent.

A middle-aged man with stooped shoulders and a graying cap of red curls who'd been watching quietly on the fringe of our gathering stepped forward. "I'm Mitchell Haines, the first assistant director. As we told the police when they questioned us officially," he said pointedly, "no one was missing from the set for any length of time that evening. And we wrapped just about the time her body was discovered."

I nodded, trying on the knowing Sphinx-like look I've seen Oprah use to such good effect. Whoever killed Faye would have been bloodied and needed to change clothes.

"Okay, everybody, we're back!" called Mitchell, and our discussion group reluctantly disbanded to return to the serious business of manufacturing entertainment-in-a-can. I handed my cards around liberally as the company trickled from the stage.

They'd given me plenty of food for thought. One thing I've learned in my business is that people love to talk. About other people. If there was gossip, a rivalry, feud, or scandal involving Faye and anyone in the movie company, I was fairly certain it would already have surfaced, at least obliquely. Bludgeoning someone to death is an ugly, personal way to kill. That kind of malice isn't easy to hide. So, for now I was inclined to move on, covering as much ground as I could while looking for obvious red flags before circling back to glean the more esoteric bits of information. But I knew the key was there somewhere, woven into the fabric of Faye's life. I just had to keep pulling at all the threads until I found the right one. I trekked back out the Overland gate, waving cheerily to the guards as I passed. They waved back with equal heartiness. I guess they figured they should recognize me. Or maybe they did by now.

Thirteen

Next stop was the Academy of Motion Picture Arts and Sciences Library on La Cienega Boulevard. After checking my bag in a locker, leaving my driver's license hostage, and promising to return and hand over my firstborn child, I went upstairs to the picture collection and printed out a request to look at the photographic files on Hugh Forsythe.

The librarian handed me a pair of the white cotton gloves that are standard issue for anyone handling photographs and two fat files. I took them over to a table and sat looking through random moments recorded and collected from the life of a man I would never meet. My own mortality whispered in my ear as I studied the images of someone once so celebrated and so much in the world who was now so completely absent. Most of the pictures were posed publicity shots. Some included a younger, less purple-haired Faye, but older photos showed Forsythe with a cherubic-looking blonde who had a winsome smile and a curvy figure. She clung to her husband's arm as they walked along a red carpet (I'm assuming, as it was a black-and-white print) at the entrance to a movie premiere. She was young and lovely and looked up at him with absolute adoration. He gazed down at her benevolently, equally besotted — for that moment, at any rate. The captions most often referred to her as "Mrs. Hugh Forsythe." But one picture, which showed them at a casual pool-side charity luncheon, identified her as "Sylvia (Mrs. Hugh) Forsythe." Sylvia Forsythe.

I returned the files and the gloves, made a request for copies of the luncheon picture and two others, then headed for a pay phone and the white pages for Hollywood. There was an S. Forsythe listed on Marathon Street, and I committed the address and phone number to my spiral notebook. Then I picked up my copies, ransomed the Toyota from the parking garage, and set an eastern course. I'd check it out: if this wasn't my Sylvia, I'd just continue over to the office and begin blazing the paper trail that would lead me to her. It occurred to me that Sara might even have some idea where to find her stepfather's ex.

The part of Marathon Street corresponding to the address I'd found was on the sun-baked flats of Hollywood just a few blocks from Paramount Studios. A neighborhood formerly inhabited by studio employees, it still clung by its fingernails to middle-class status, but over the past twenty years the area had suffered a steady decline. The narrow streets were lined with small bungalows in various stages of disrepair squatting on barren postage stamp-sized yards of anemic grass with hardly a tree in sight to provide anything in the way of shade.

S. Forsythe's house seemed even a bit more careworn than its neighbors. The roof needed to be reshingled, and the pale yellow paint was flaking badly. A cracked cement walk led to a set of crumbling front steps and a door that had been white once upon a time, a long time ago. I rapped firmly, and the door gave way, its creaking hinges protesting faintly as it opened. I grabbed the handle and pulled it closed, but when there was no answer to my second, more forceful knock, I allowed it to swing open.

"Anybody home?"

A television blaring in another room was the only sound. I hesitated for a moment, then stepped over the threshold into the dingy foyer where I was greeted by a sour smell, something like old cooked cabbage mixed with old wet dog. The carpet was matted and stained, its original color overpowered by layers of ground-in dirt. Coronas of grime ringed the light switches, and a thick layer of dust had settled over the odds and ends cluttering the wooden side table with a broken leg that stood against one wall.

Straight ahead of me was the kitchen, the source of much of the rank odor. Dirty dishes filled the small sink, and every available surface — countertop, stove, and the rickety table situated under the only window in the room. The stove was covered with grease and spilled food, and the floor didn't look any more appetizing. To my right, the foyer joined a short hallway, no more than fifteen feet long. The sound of the television was coming from one of the two rooms opening off the other end.

I called out again, then started down the hall, following the manic noise of a game show in progress. The first door on my right was the bathroom. I didn't even want to look in there. At the end of the hall was a small bedroom, a nest of tangled sheets on the unmade bed and discarded clothing littering the floor. To the left of the bedroom was another tiny room furnished with a metal daybed, a wicker chair with a torn cushion, and a laminated coffee table covered with a collection of domestic debris that included plates crusted with food, two glasses with an inch or so of liquid in them, magazines, a half-empty bottle of cheap vodka, and a saucer overflowing with cigarette butts. I wrinkled my nose in distaste at the stale bouquet of eau de ashtray.

The TV sat in one corner facing the daybed. On top of it was a picture in a dimestore frame of a woman who looked like the Sylvia Forsythe in the Hollywood luncheon photograph. In this picture she was kneeling with her arms wrapped around a small boy who had his cheek pressed against hers. They were both grinning happily for the camera. The same lovely young woman smiled down from dozens of other photographs hanging on the wall behind the television. A gallery of Sylvias played tennis, posed on a diving board, winked through an armful of roses, blew a kiss at the camera.

I was fighting the urge to start straightening up when I caught sight of a woman in a big straw hat out back of the house. I trotted back out the front door and around the side yard to the tiny patio in the rear. The woman was bent over a pot of wan-looking geraniums, picking off the dead blossoms, which outnumbered the live ones three-to-one. Besides the sunhat, she was wearing a ruffled nightgown and wrapper set made of filmy peach nylon that could have done with a trip to the laundry. She looked up when I came around the corner but didn't seem surprised to find me there.

"It's a shame I can't put them out front," she complained, pointing to the flowers, "but someone'll just steal them or the neighbor kids'll break up the pots. To them, that's fun." She squinted at me, then straightened up and smiled fuzzily. "How nice of you to drop by. It's good to see you again."

I smiled back at her. "Actually, I don't think we know each other, but I did come by today hoping to meet you. My name's Maggie McGrath." I held out my hand, and she cupped her frail, bony fingers around mine. Long gray curls trailed to her shoulders from beneath the hat, framing a face that looked like a piece of withered fruit, deeply etched by an intricate network of lines. I studied her features, vainly seeking some vestige of the woman in the photographs.

"You look so familiar. Maybe we were friends in another life," she suggested with a wave of her hand. "Do you believe in reincarnation?" She leaned toward me, and I caught a pungent whiff of alcohol along with the musky odor of unwashed flesh.

"I guess the jury's still out for me on that one," I replied. "I don't necessarily disbelieve, but it's just not an issue that's showed up yet on my 'need to know' list."

She chuckled. "I like you."

"Well, that's good because I'm hoping you'll take some time to talk with me."

Her eyes widened in surprise and one tentative hand came up to touch her cheek. "Oh my, I haven't given an interview for years." Then she smiled coyly. "You naughty girl, you should have called first. I must look a fright." She clutched the front of her wrapper self-consciously.

"You look just fine," I lied.

"Oh my, you've got me all excited now. Well then, come in, come in." She ushered me through a back entrance into a small pantry that opened into the kitchen and left her hat on a peg by the door. "Let's go into the living room and sit down. Oh! But can I offer you something to drink first?"

"No, thank you." I couldn't imagine eating or drinking from any dish or cup lying around that kitchen.

She pulled a glass off the top of the pile in the sink and winked at me cheerfully. "Well, I'm having a little something, so you just let me know if you change your mind." Then, chirping exclamations of delight and dismay over my unexpected visit, she led me back down the hall to the living room where the TV was still blasting away and settled herself on the daybed, indicating I should take the wicker chair.

"Mind if I turn that off?" I asked, pointing to the TV screen, where a large woman in a polyester pantsuit wept copiously as she was handed the keys to a brand new Cadillac.

"Oh, sure," she shrugged, pouring a healthy slug from the vodka bottle into her glass. I noticed her hands shook. "I just have it on for company."

I crossed to the television and switched it off. Merciful silence. "Is this your son?" I picked up the photograph on top of the TV to look at it more closely.

"Yes, that's my baby." She'd gotten a cigarette out of a package on the coffee table and was trying to light up. Her hands were shaking badly now, so it was an act of will requiring her total concentration, and still the lit match wobbled away from its target as if it had a mind of its own.

Finally I couldn't stand it. "May I get that for you?"

She cut her eyes at me and dropped the match. It fell beside the daybed, glowing briefly against the carpet before it decided to go out. I reached down to put it in the ash tray with its other little friends and took the book of matches from Sylvia. I struck one and held it to the end of her cigarette while she drew on it deeply.

"Aren't you the Sylvia Forsythe who was married to Hugh Forsythe, the director?"

Her eyes turned cold for just a moment, then she tipped her head back and laughed. "I thought we were going to talk about me." She took another deep drag of her cigarette, watching me. "You're a writer, aren't you? And you're here to do an article on me . . . isn't that what you told me?"

"I don't believe I did. As a matter of fact, I'm a private investigator," I said, pulling out my identification. "I'm working for Sara Landesmann, Faye Symington's daughter. Did you know Faye was murdered the night before last?"

Something flickered in her eyes, but she shook her head, still watching me. "How terrible," she said softly, still smiling. And then she began to laugh again, quietly at first, but gathering energy until she was convulsed in hysterics, clutching her sides as the tears streamed down her wrinkled cheeks. Suddenly she was overcome by a fit of coughing, a deep, brutal hacking that sounded as if her lungs were coming up. But the spasm passed as quickly as it had come, leaving her gasping with exhaustion.

I bent over her. "Can I get you anything — some water, maybe?"

But she waved me away. "No, no, I'm fine." Then off my skeptical look, "Really, it's just this awful cold that's been hanging on for weeks now."

She sat up again and patted herself down, because now she'd lost her cigarette. It was lying on the daybed next to her, slightly bent at the end. Grunting with satisfaction, she snatched it up and smoothed out the bent part before she stuck it back in her mouth. Then she looked at me expectantly.

"You shouldn't be smoking with a cough like that!" I scolded.

But when she reached for the book of matches, I opted for the lesser evil and did as she wanted.

"Now where were we?" She leaned back, stretching like an arthritic old cat. She saw my eyes straying to the wall of photographs, trying once again to reconcile the past with the present. "Did you know I was an actress?"

"Films?" I looked back at her.

"Films, TV — I did a lot of live commercials. I had a contract at Warner's in 1958. I'll bet you've even seen some of the movies I was in."

"Is that where you met Mr. Forsythe?"

She rolled her eyes. "Well, naturally," she said drolly and took a gulp of her cocktail. "And it's all his fault."

I waited for her to elaborate, but when she offered nothing further, I asked, "What was all his fault?"

"Everything," she replied in a tone that wondered at my vacuity.

Ah. Well, that explained it.

A sly smile spread across her face. "But I got even." She leaned toward me, lowering her voice. "I hexed him when he left."

"Hexed him?"

"Hexed them both." She nodded triumphantly. "Took a while, but I got them."

Alrighty then.

"So that's what killed them, you think?"

"I know it."

I crossed my arms, studying her. "How'd you do it, Sylvia?" After all, you never know when a good spell might come in handy.

But she pressed her lips together and shook her head, going cagey on me. "For all I know, you could be one of them."

"One of whom?"

"Oh, no you don't." She wagged a gnarled finger at me.

I gave it up as pointless. "Where does your son live, Sylvia? He must be grown by now."

Her eyes narrowed in suspicion. "Why do you want to know?"

"I'd just like to talk to him."

Her eyes flew open, wild and panicked. "Get out! Get out! GET OUT!" she shrieked.

After that, it all happened so fast I barely had time to react. She launched into another horrible fit of coughing, but this time it didn't subside as it had before. The spasms continued to build, shaking her entire frame until I feared her heart would give out. I scanned the little room urgently looking for the phone while her face took on the alarming hue of sliced beets as she helplessly fought for air. Lying on the floor on the other side of the daybed, I found a small green tank with a mask attached to it by a rubber hose. I grabbed it up and held the mask to her face, turning the valve to release the oxygen. She gulped and choked like a drowning victim, but as her ruined lungs began to get some relief, she relaxed and her breathing finally became more normal.

"I think I should call an ambulance," I said gently, smoothing her hair away from her face.

She looked up at me and managed something close to a weary smile. "Really not much point, is there? It'll do me more good to rest now." She seemed more tuned in than before. "Leave my boy alone," she said quietly.

"He's got nothing to tell you. His father was my first husband — died early on in Viet Nam. Hugh barely even acknowledged him — sent him off to boarding school and that's mainly where he stayed." Tears leaked from her eyes. "He robbed me of those years, robbed us both. And after all that, to take up with that little wardrobe girl," she spat contemptuously. She closed her eyes and took a deep, rasping breath, calming herself. "So I hexed them." She looked up at me again, searching my face. "Can you blame me?"

"No." I patted her hand. "No, I can't."

I sat with her awhile, but when her eyelids began to droop with exhaustion I got up quietly, and after adding my home number, I slipped a couple of my business cards under the photograph on top of the television.

"I'd like to talk with you again sometime, Sylvia, and just in case you'd like to call me, I've left you my numbers."

"Oh, goody," she said in a little girl voice without a trace of irony. She started to struggle to her feet. "It was so nice to see you again. Marsha, was it?"

"Please, just rest there," I said. "I'll let myself out."

She sank back, smiling contentedly. "Come visit anytime. I like having young people around."

As I made my way back down the hall, I thought I heard her humming softly to herself. It sounded like "Ding, dong, the witch is dead."

But I might have been wrong about that.

Fourteen

As I trundled on toward the office, I puzzled over my bizarre chat with Sylvia. It was obvious the woman had trouble sorting fact from fiction, but I had no way of telling how much of her ditziness was authentic. Once an actress, always an actress: maybe her thespian talents were more formidable than I imagined. Certainly her antics had made her a slippery subject; I hadn't even been able to pry her son's name out of her, and that was one hole I really needed to shore up. I had to wonder why the idea of my talking to him had caused her such distress. But there was no help for that: I'd have to make tracking him down a priority, regardless.

Something else was bothering me, but it wasn't until I was back at the office putting a pot of coffee on to brew that it surfaced as conscious thought. I had a flashback to Sara sitting across from me on the loveseat describing the crank calls, "that awful breathing — almost a mechanical sound." I wondered if it was anything like the faint hissing of Sylvia's oxygen tank.

I punched in the code for my voice mail and let out an involuntary yelp when the little voice mail message fairy said, "You have twenty-seven new messages." Even though Faye was a below-the-liner, and therefore not a player in terms of the Hollywood power structure, a murder on a studio lot was big news, especially in this town that worships at the altar of the Make-Believe-For-Profit industry. And I was now publicly linked to the case. *The Hollywood Observer* evidently enjoyed a wide readership because I had calls from *The Los Angeles Times*, *The National Enquirer*, *The Star*, the networks, four local TV stations, three radio stations, two people I went to college with, a woman I'd met in a life drawing class, my brother, my mother, my aunts in New Jersey, and one guy who said he'd like to hire me to investigate various parts of his anatomy. But he didn't leave a number.

"Nice work, Ms. Symington," I muttered as I hit the "erase" button. I leaned back in my chair and closed my eyes. Without a doubt, Faye had been an unpleasant woman. Aw, why mince words? She was a solid gold-plated bitch-on-wheels, and everybody knew it. But you mostly don't get killed for that — especially in L.A. where our ranks would be thinned considerably if we weeded out the population on that basis.

I tended to discount a crime of passion: the killer had been too careful and too thorough. He'd left no sign behind either at Faye's office or my house, and he'd slipped in and out of both places without anyone catching a glimpse of him. I was dealing with a thinker and a planner. I was even willing to bet his weapon of choice had some ironic significance, so he also had a twisted sense of humor. Or maybe it was arrogance, the ritualistic flourish of the matador as he dispatches the bull. The thought made me shudder. What motivates a person, a thoughtful person, a careful person, to kill another person? I sighed and rubbed my eyes. It would be a mistake to look too hard now for the answer staring me in the face. And it was important to keep an open mind. But Faye was dead for a reason. I just had to keep absorbing information, following the plodding process that would enable me to develop a context for her murder. Then, with any luck, the reason would become apparent.

I let my mind go blank and sat for several minutes just staring at the Simon Silva print called "Dos Mujeres" I have hanging on my wall. It's a joyful scene of two women bent over a washtub shampooing their hair in the middle of a field of sunflowers. At that moment I wanted nothing more than to be one of those women, happily rinsing my hair with beautiful warm colors. Not sitting in a stuffy little office feeling sorry for myself with a caffeine hangover, a case with no clues, a smashed-up house, and an exiled cat. I splashed my face with some water from the Sparkletts cooler and dried off with a paper towel. Then I popped in next door to see Joyce and Gail.

It was just after closing time, and Gail was locking the bars across the front door. I was in no mood for levity, but I did almost laugh out loud when I caught sight of Joyce. She was wearing some sheer, floaty dress from the thirties and she'd swathed her upper body in complementary vintage scarves, but her enthusiasm for the concept had carried her away and she looked for all the world like a chiffon mummy.

Gail applauded my entrance.

"How's our celebrity detective today?" Joyce asked with a sly grin. "You're going to have to hire a secretary pretty soon. You're phone's been ringing off the hook all day."

"So I gathered," I said glumly.

"What's the matter, Babe?" she asked, catching wind of my not-so-subtle sulk. "How's it all going?"

"I'm exactly nowhere. And I get the distinct impression the police are keeping me company there. Plus, my house got trashed last night. Whoever did it trussed Skunky up like a prize cow. I sent him off to Jack's this morning until this is over."

"Why didn't you call me?" Joyce scolded. "I would have taken Skunky! You both should just come and stay with me for awhile!"

"Joyce, you're allergic," I said reasonably. Which is true: her eyes swell shut, and she can barely breathe after an hour in my house, tops. "And Gail has Merle and Xavier," I said, anticipating her next thought. "Skunky is a miserable houseguest if there are other animals in residence."

"What makes you so sure it's all connected? Couldn't it just be some weird burglar who has a thing about cats?" Gail asked.

So I told them about the note.

"Oh, my God! What have I gotten you into?" Joyce moaned.

"Joyce, please. This is not your doing. You referred a client. That's a good thing. You didn't choose my line of work for me."

"Now what do we do?" Gail asked.

"Well, I wouldn't presume to speak for you ladies, but I'm going home to finish cleaning up my house." I made a wry face. "And then I need to get hold of Sara."

"Don't you think you should just drop the whole thing now?" Joyce said anxiously.

I shook my head slowly. "Can't. But I could use a favor. Do you know anyone in the Costume Designers Guild who was close to Faye and would be willing to talk to me about her? I'd like to get another designer's perspective."

Joyce was already scribbling on a Post-it. "Call Carol Marlen. She and Faye were pretty friendly, I think. Carol's a straight-shooter and a good customer here. Just tell her I told you to call."

"Thanks." I pocketed the paper.

"And now we'll go home with you and help you get the house picked up," she said resolutely.

The thought of Joyce fluttering around in her cocoon of scarves with a dust rag and broom almost made me smile again. "You're the best, both of you. But I need to do this myself. I may even decide to reorganize things while I'm at it." Since approximately half of my possessions had been destroyed, that was a given.

But Joyce wasn't going to give up. "Why don't you come stay at my house, just for tonight? We'll have a pajama party. I'll fix you a nice dinner, you can get a good night's sleep, and then you can do the cleaning tomorrow when you're rested."

"Joyce, I'm fine. I need to be home tonight. I just need things to feel as normal as possible."

"Then let one of us stay with you. I'm worried about you being alone there."

"Joyce, I'm fine," I repeated with more of an edge than I intended. "And I'll be fine tonight. Please don't worry."

"That's like asking the sun to please not come up in the morning," Gail said dryly.

"You two have a good evening," I said as I got up to go. "I'll see you tomorrow."

"Just be careful," Joyce pleaded, and I was startled by the tears in her eyes.

I went back and gave her a quick hug. "Stop that. Everything's going to be okay."

"You promise?" she sniffed.

"Promise," I said with a great deal more conviction than I felt.

Despite my bravado, I dreaded going home to my ruined empty house, so I was relieved for more than one reason to find a note tacked to the front door: I'M HOME. COME TALK TO ME.

Chris was back. She and Lisa came to the door together in answer to my knock.

"Welcome back," I said, hugging her. "How was your trip?"

"Just what you might expect," she replied shortly. "More importantly, how are you? What's going on?"

She gestured for me to follow her back to the kitchen. Without asking, she poured me a cup of her excellent coffee and pulled out a chair by the kitchen table, where she'd already set out a plate of the homemade lemon bars she knows are my favorites.

"It's bad. I mean, seriously bad," I began.

Between bites, I filled her in on everything that had happened in her absence, the unabridged version in Technicolor detail because she deserved to know exactly what was going on. Because of me, Chris, her cat, and her property had been placed squarely in harm's way, and it wasn't over, not by a long shot.

"I'll take you next door so you can inspect the damage. I don't think there's much that happened to the house itself besides the broken window, but it's still a wreck." I took a deep breath. "I've been thinking all day, Chris," I said, avoiding her eyes, "and I think I should move out. This isn't fair to you. And I don't think I could ever forgive myself if something happened to you or Lisa in the wake of this mess."

Chris put up a hand like a traffic cop to silence me. "You and Skunky are family. You don't toss your family out on the street just because the going gets a little rough. We're all in this together, and we'll get through it together."

I felt my eyes fill with tears, and she handed me a napkin. "Come on, let's go next door. Let's get your place cleaned up."

Two brooms are definitely better than one: within a couple of hours we'd restored some semblance of order, and Chris invited me back to her place for a nightcap since the only beverage I had in the house was tap water. I told her I'd be over as soon as I'd gotten a report on my travelling cat. It was after eleven in Chicago, but Jack picked up on the first ring.

"How's my little guy?" I asked after we'd said our hellos.

"He's in rare form."

"Ah, hissing at everybody, huh?"

"Oh, yeah. In fact, he got himself so worked up earlier, I thought he might just keel over from lack of oxygen."

"Is he eating?"

"Not a problem. His appetite's just fine. But he is an ungrateful little bastard. Completely ready to bite the hand that feeds him. Literally."

In spite of everything, I had to laugh. "Thanks, Jack. And tell Annie thanks, too. I really appreciate it."

"How're you holding up? Sounds like quite a case you've got going."

"Yeah, it's keepin' me guessin'."

"The paper said the woman who was killed was the costume designer on a new Stallone movie."

"That's right, she was."

"So, have you met him yet?"

"Who?"

"Sylvester Stallone."

"Jack!" My tone was scornful.

"What?" He sounded defensive.

"What do you care about Sylvester Stallone?"

"Well, he is a big star."

"And ten to one he's an even bigger jerk. Besides, he makes terrible movies."

"I don't know — I really liked *Rocky*."

I held the receiver away from my ear and stared at it in exasperation. I couldn't believe I was having this surreal conversation with my highly intelligent sibling whose opinions and judgment I had always respected.

"So, is he really short?"

"I don't know, Jack! The only time I ever saw him, he was hanging from a rope. I can't believe you're interested in that stuff. He's just a guy. A greasy little guy with a crooked lip. How can you buy into all that phony Hollywood hype? It's disgusting!"

"You're right," he said contritely. "So, how about Steven Seagal?"

"Jack!"

"Just kidding. Hey, lighten up."

I thanked him again for giving my monster refuge, and we said goodnight. I could tell I was losing ground emotionally. My sense of humor was all but gone, and even more worrisome, my perspective on the case had become claustrophobic. Instead of looking at the facts with some objective detachment, I was feeling swallowed by the situation. Not good, not good at all. I sat grasping the receiver irresolutely, then decided, what the hell, it couldn't hurt, and punched in Jen's number.

I met Jennifer Tolan several years ago at one of Joyce's parties. She's a transplanted teabag, a native Londoner who now makes her home in San Francisco. Jen's also a psychic, though she prefers to call herself an "intuitive." Whatever the label, she's the real deal and has been quietly instrumental to police investigations on both sides of the Atlantic — always on a pro bono basis — her charity work, as she calls it.

I hadn't really wanted to go to the party that night, and I was rather unsociably lurking in a corner sloshing through a glass of bad red wine when I felt someone's eyes on me. I turned to find Jennifer watching me intently, then she smiled and nodded, crooking her finger to invite me to join her. We talked for a long time that evening, and I finally asked her why she'd singled me out.

"It's your energy, Luv. It's really quite remarkable. First off, you're a natural healer."

I rolled my eyes. "Yeah, right."

"I'm just telling you what the energy shows me. And you have intuitive powers, as well."

"Jennifer, half the time I can't even remember where I put my keys. If I'm so intuitive, how come I just don't — Poof! — know where they are?"

She laid a hand on my arm then, but it was her eyes that held me. "Because you're not listening, you think you don't have the power to hear. There's a difference, Maggie. And I assure you, if you ever decide to get out of your own way, you'll be able to tap into a powerful energy source."

With her hand still on my arm, she leaned in close, her voice low and soothing. "I wasn't going to say anything about this to you now, but they're telling me I must. There's a spirit that is trying very hard to contact you. He says he was a young man in this last incarnation, and although he didn't know you in this life, you were instrumental to his journey."

The hair stood up on the back of my neck. Jennifer stared at me, searching for a reaction, but I felt as if I'd turned to stone.

"He says you must forgive yourself, Maggie; he forgave you long ago. He says he was weak while he was here, but now he is at peace. And he wants you to find peace, as well."

The muscles in my throat tightened painfully, and I pressed my lips together, fighting back tears.

She squeezed my arm. "You know this spirit?"

I nodded, still unable to speak.

"Then, Luv, you must do as he asks. Let go of this sorrow you carry and allow yourself to move on."

I wanted desperately to believe what she'd told me, but all I know for sure is that I made a new friend that night. As for any burgeoning psychic powers on the home front, there's nothing to report so far; and I find the whole idea a bit unnerving, I have to admit.

A thriving practice of private consultations to clients who are literally all over the world supports Jen in a very comfortable style. As I listened to the soprano bleat of the call going through, I pictured her in the parlor of her Victorian row house surrounded by her herd of cats and sipping a tot of sherry. I was disappointed by the mechanical click of a recording.

"Hi, all. Jennifer Tolan here. Oh, but I'm not really. I'm on holiday and off to London till the fifteenth, lucky me. You can leave a message or call me then."

I held the receiver in a death-grip, trying to decide what to say, then sighed in frustration and hit the "off" button.

"I'm going to put alarm systems in both our places," Chris announced. It was a little later that evening, and we were sitting in her living room with our feet up, listening to an Etta James CD. "And how would you feel about security bars on the windows?"

"Like I was living in prison," I yawned, hunkering deeper into the cushions of her overstuffed sofa.

"Yeah, me too," she admitted.

I took a gulp of hot chocolate and rolled a fat marshmallow around my mouth, savoring the gooey sweetness. Etta was wailing away about love gone wrong, and now that she'd taken care of me, I felt Chris sinking inside herself to brood.

"Do you feel like talking about what happened up north?" I asked quietly.

She shook her head and leaned forward to prop her elbows on her knees. "When am I ever going to get a clue?" she sighed. "I caught Lenny with a groupie — some teenager — in his dressing room. I think he must have set it up, at least subconsciously. I think he wanted me to walk in on them."

"Oh, Chris," I murmured.

"But it's really over this time," she said firmly. "I'm declaring a personal moratorium on sex."

"I think sex has declared a moratorium on me," I said ruefully. "I just wish I'd gotten the chance to vote on it."

"Men," she snorted. "The trouble is, our generation got sold a bill of goods about the whole sexual equality thing. That Venus and Mars guy wasn't far off when you get right down to it, even though his book triggered my gag reflex. Men and women might as well be from two alien planets, for all our basic natures have in common. I mean, how can we be equal when we're so completely different? It's apples and oranges."

"Well, yeah, I can sort of see your point —"

"It's like a cruel joke of nature that we're bound to them sexually. Just think how free you'd feel if you never had to worry about having sex with a man ever again."

I nodded. "Free and very depressed."

In the interest of self-preservation, I decided to change the subject. Any more of this cheerful chatter after the day I'd just had, and I was a goner for sure. "Would you happen to know anything about a restaurant here in town called Fat Farm?" I segued.

"Sure I do. It's a very chi-chi kind of place. Very hot right now, and very expensive."

"Ever hear of a guy named Robert Camden? I think he's the manager there."

"The name sounds familiar, but I don't know him."

"What would you think if you heard a place like that was losing money?"

"Really?" She perked up and scooted forward in her chair. "You're kidding! Does this have something to do with your case?"

"I don't really know yet. Maybe."

"Well, I couldn't say for sure without looking at the books and watching their set-up firsthand, but a place that busy — I'd say if they're consistently losing money, it would almost have to be a matter of mismanagement or fraud. Or both."

"I want to take a look at it. Would you be willing to go with me some night? My treat, of course — business expense. I'd like your professional observations. You can be my consultant."

"Sure, that sounds terrific. But you'll definitely need to make reservations, and I'd say well before the day we're planning to go. I hear they have quite the waiting list." She leaned back again and propped her feet on the coffee table.

"I'll call tomorrow. How does your schedule look this week?"

"For that, I'll keep myself available. At this point, I have no social plans for the rest of the decade."

"Do you think you could do me a favor in the meantime?" I drained the dregs of melted marshmallow and chocolate puddled in the bottom of my cup.

"I can try."

"Would you call your friends in the business and see what the buzz is about Robert Camden? I'd be especially interested to find out where he comes from and where he's worked in the past."

"No problem. I can make some calls tomorrow."

"That'd be great. And do you think you can ask without giving out the real reason you want to know? I'd rather Camden didn't hear I'm checking around about him just yet."

I stood in the shower that night letting the hot water pound me until it ran cold. Then I crawled into bed with the green leather appointment book for company. We'd turned the mattress so the ripped side rested against the boxsprings. I'd have to get a new one before long, but it felt fine for the time being. But as good as it was to be in my own bed again, I missed having a little cat purring on my shoulder.

I began to study Faye's Bible, starting with her calendar for March. She had a standing appointment at a salon in Beverly Hills for a manicure, pedicure, and facial every Saturday morning at nine o'clock. Several dinners were noted with partners designated by first names only: "Ryan/ 8:00 Patina/ Farrah?" must have been an interesting evening. Or maybe not. Damn, I was as bad as Jack.

There were costume fittings for the movie, specifically indicated as such, and a smattering of ambiguous appointments. On March 10: "Shutters/ 11:00 A.M." for example. Did that refer to the hotel and restaurant in Santa Monica, or was she having shutters installed at one of her homes or businesses? But the entry that interested me most was for March 13 at 10:30 A.M., which had been just that morning. It said "Adolphe re: Fat Farm." I flipped back to the "A's" in the address portion of the book. At the very end of the section, actually squeezed in at the top of the first "B" page, was a hastily scrawled notation in red "Lawrence Adolphe" linked by a sharply inked arrow to a 310 phone number. No address. I'd have to call Mr. Adolphe in the morning to learn what his business with Faye re: Fat Farm had been.

By then my eyes felt like the Sandman had emptied his bag on my head, so I gave up and turned out my reading light. A full moon was rising, and its rays streamed through my bedroom windows, casting long cool shadows across the hardwood floor. A bizarre serenade floated into me on a light nocturnal breeze: birds excited by the brightness of the moon sang at full voice until well past midnight accompanied by the throbbing bass-line cadence of police helicopters hovering over Elysian Park, watching for drug deals going down. I was only dimly aware of the active night, but my sleep was light and easily disturbed until almost dawn, when I finally settled into a deep and blessedly dreamless stupor.

Fifteen

When the phone rang at 8:30 the next morning I dragged it into the pile of blankets I'd burrowed under to block out the morning sun. My tongue felt as if it had swollen overnight to twice its normal size, and I had some trouble wrapping it around "hello."

"Maggie, I'm so sorry. I woke you, didn't I?" Sara apologized.

"I'm glad you did," I croaked. "I should've been up hours ago." I glanced blearily at the clock. "Hour ago, anyway. How are you?"

"I'm well, thanks. I got your message."

"Right." I pushed the blankets aside. I'd forgotten to turn the heat down the night before, and the bedroom felt hot and stuffy. "I wanted to let you know I'm going to keep on with the investigation."

"Oh, Maggie, that's wonderful! You couldn't have said anything that would make me happier!"

"I'd like to talk to you in person. Today sometime, if possible."

"Fine. But would you mind terribly coming out here? I know it's a bit of a haul, but it's lovely and quite private. We can have a good, long talk."

"Okay. How about if I come out a little later this morning, maybe around ten-thirty?"

"Perfect."

She gave me the address and directions to the house, and we said goodbye. Wrestling with the urge to flop back on the bed for about twelve hours, I got up to make coffee, the whole rhythm of my morning thrown off by the lateness of the hour and the fact that no one was there waiting for his Fancy Feast. By the time I'd showered, dressed, and consumed enough caffeine to make life worth living, it was nine-fifteen. I dialed Lawrence Adolphe's number, and a woman answered, her tone business-like but serene and unhurried, her voice a mixture of butter and honey.

"Good morning. Adolphe Associates."

I did my best to match her silky delivery. "This is Maggie McGrath. May I please speak to Lawrence Adolphe?"

"Just a moment, please." She was gone a very short time. "I'm sorry, but Mr. Adolphe is presently in conference. May I please take a message and have him call you back?"

"You know," I said pleasantly, "it's my fault for not mentioning this to begin with, but I'm calling on behalf of Faye Symington. You'd better tell him that. He may prefer to talk with me now."

He came on the line almost immediately. "This is Lawrence Adolphe. How may I help you?"

"Mr. Adolphe, my name is Maggie McGrath. Faye Symington was a client of mine. I expect you've already heard that she was murdered."

"I had."

"I know she had an appointment scheduled with you yesterday —"

"Forgive me. I'm unclear as to the nature of your relationship with Ms. Symington."

"I was hired by Ms. Symington and her daughter, Sara Landesmann, because of a series of anonymous threats Faye received shortly before her death," I said, intentionally hedging a job title. "I'm continuing to work for Ms. Landesmann."

"You're now representing Ms. Symington's daughter?"

"That's right," I agreed. "I know Faye's meeting with you concerned the business at Fat Farm, and that's what I'd like to discuss with you."

"Yes, I've been trying to decide what to do about that since I heard the news," he said fretfully.

"About what?"

He didn't answer, and at first I thought he'd broken the connection. "Are you still there, Mr. Adolphe?"

"We can't discuss this on the phone. Ms. Landesmann should come to my office," he said crisply. "I'll explain the situation to her, and then she can decide what action should be taken on behalf of her mother's estate."

"That's all very cryptic, Mr. Adolphe."

"That's all I can say right now," he replied firmly.

"All right, then, would you like to see her this afternoon?"

"I'm afraid that's impossible. Tomorrow morning is the first chance I'll have. Shall we say nine-thirty?"

"If that's the best you can do. And I'll need to confirm the time with Ms. Landesmann."

He gave me an address on Wilshire Boulevard. I thanked him and hung up. I waited a few minutes, then dialed the number again. The same honey-voiced woman answered. She was wasting her talent answering phones — she could have made a fortune doing commercial voice-overs.

Shooting for a breathy Southern accent, I twittered, "Oh my, Ah'm not sure Ah called the correct numbah. Are y'all in the pest control bizniss?"

"No, this is an accounting firm, ma'am," she said in her measured, patient tone.

"Oh! Ah see! Thank yew."

Well, that made a glimmer of sense.

Next I called Joyce's designer friend, Carol Marlen. I got an answering machine, and a youthful high-pitched voice recited:

"At work I am buried.

It's fast-paced and harried.

Once the show's all costumed,

I'll then be exhumed.

But for now, work's where I'll be.

So call me there: (818) 555-3123."

Hmmmm. Another one of Joyce's loopy creative friends who probably believed her horoscope and named her car. (I'd known one ex-boyfriend and I would never be soulmates when he introduced me to "Sidney," his Chevy Nova.) Dutifully, I punched in the work number.

"Costumes. This is Mindy," sang a nasal voice.

"Mindy, this is Maggie McGrath. Is Carol Marlen available?"

She dropped the phone with a clunk and bellowed, "Caarool! Telephone!"

A moment later, the abandoned receiver was picked up. "Hi, this is Carol. Sorry about that. Mindy's new." A beat. "And I'm not sure she's trainable."

I chuckled. "That's okay, Carol. My name's Maggie McGrath. I'm a friend of Joyce Emmett's, and she suggested I call you."

"Any friend of Joycie's a friend of mine," she replied. "Are you looking for work?"

"I'm a private detective, Carol, and I'm working for Sara Landesmann, looking into the circumstances surrounding Faye Symington's death. Joyce tells me you and Faye were friends. I wonder if you'd mind talking with me about her?"

"How's Sara?" The fact that she'd avoided my request wasn't lost on me, nor was the formality that had crept into her tone.

"She's very upset, naturally. But I think she's hanging in there."

"Please give her my condolences, will you?"

"Of course."

My question still hung unanswered in the awkward pause I allowed to stretch out between us. Carol finally cleared her throat. "I don't know that I can be of much real help to you," she said doubtfully. "Joyce was putting the most positive possible spin on things when she told you Faye and I were friendly. We were acquainted certainly, and we weren't uncordial. But friendly?" A skeptical shrug was implied.

"Even so, you work in the same arena. Your insight as a peer with shared professional experience will be valuable to an outsider like me regardless of your personal relationship with Faye," I persisted.

There were several beats of silence while she thought that one over. "Well, I'm going to be stuck all day at Western Costumes pulling clothes, anyway. It's way up in North Hollywood at the corner of Vineland and Vanowen — you can't miss it. Come by, and I'll take a break and talk with you for awhile."

"Is there a particular time that would be good for you?"

"No, one time's as good or bad as another," she said cheerfully.

"All right, then. It'll probably be around twelve-thirty."

"Great. See you then."

The day was glorious, but it was lost on me as I swam through a sea of brake lights at the interchange of the Harbor and Santa Monica freeways. I was so busy congratulating myself that I wasn't even perturbed by the bonehead maneuvers pulled by the usual crop of lousy drivers on the road with me that morning. Like the guy in the Carrera who was so busy talking on his cell phone that he didn't realize he was about to share the lane he was merging into with a bus. You'd think someone driving a sixty thousand dollar deathtrap made to be flattened like a soup can on impact with anything larger than a bicycle going thirty miles an hour would be a little more watchful. But I guess that's just me.

I'd scored with the call to Adolphe, and I was impatient to see how many points I'd racked up. It was a better than fair guess that Faye had consulted him about the financial situation at Fat Farm, judging by her calendar entry, and there was interesting information to be communicated on that subject, judging by my enigmatic conversation with the accountant.

I wondered what Faye's suspicions had been, and how vocal she'd been about them. She wasn't pulling any punches the day I heard her on the phone with the person I now believed was almost certainly Robert Camden. Had she also confronted Lillian? Is that why she'd seemed so upset the evening of the murder when Poppie saw her leaving Faye's office? I wanted to have another talk with the business manager, but not before I'd heard what Adolphe had to say. I chafed again at the delay; right now all I had were questions and speculations.

I rounded the bend where the westbound Santa Monica freeway becomes the Pacific Coast Highway and continued north along the fragile artery of a road that is threatened every year by the elements, which can be savage here on an epic scale. I've heard it said there are no seasons in Southern California, but that isn't so. You just have to know what to look for. Instead of brilliant leaves and running sap, autumn here means fire. It's an annual cycle of destruction that begins with the bare-earth scorching of the hillsides flanking the highway. The winter rains that follow turn the ravaged slopes into a heavy sea of mud that finally gives way under its own weight, plunging down on the road below. People who live in the opulent homes along the ocean have no optional route: PCH is it. But they're willing to put up with the vagaries of nature in order to enjoy their ringside seats on one of her grandest spectacles — the Pacific Ocean. Personally, I wouldn't deal with it all if somebody deeded me a property outright. But they're a breed apart, those folks with more money than sense.

I turned left on Malibu Colony Road, right on Malibu Colony Drive, and found that the number I was seeking belonged to an ordinary-looking smallish, squarish shell-pink stucco house. I parked in a shallow gravel turnaround by the mailbox. Bet they didn't see many dusty little '87 Toyota Corollas in this 'hood.

Sara opened the door before I could ring the bell. She looked pale and thin, but she held out her arms to me, smiling happily. "Oh, it's so good to see you! It seems like it's been a long time!"

She wore khaki cotton slacks and an ice-blue pullover sweater with a pink heart knitted into the pattern of the right sleeve. Her hair was pulled back again in the ponytail that made her look like a schoolgirl. I followed her into a living room that was furnished quite simply, with a large woven Mexican rug in deep warm hues providing most of the visual interest, aside from an extraordinary view. The entire west wall was a sheet of glass looking out onto the ocean and the waves of the surf breaking just a few yards away.

"Can I get you something to drink?" she asked.

"No. Thanks." I felt myself drawn to that wall of glass by the hypnotic synchronicity of the sea washing rhythmically and endlessly against the land.

"I love this house. It's the only place I feel I'm really home." Sara was beside me.

"It's quite a spot."

"It's small, but that's part of what I love about it," she said dreamily. "It feels cozy to me. And peaceful. I used to come here often with my stepfather. He loved it as much as I do. Mother never really liked it. Being so close to the ocean made her nervous."

We stood together gazing at the surf.

"Have you ever seen a picture of him?"

"Who?"

"My stepfather."

"No," I replied, simply because it felt like the easiest thing to say. I'd tell her about my talk with Sylvia at some point, but I didn't want to get into it just yet. Sara still seemed emotionally brittle, and aside from not wanting to upset her further, there were some specific questions I wanted asked and answered that morning in a clearheaded way.

She disappeared into the next room and returned with a framed 8x10 photograph of a graying but handsome Hugh Forsythe holding the hand of a girl who was maybe eleven years old and unmistakably Sara. They grinned at each other, sharing a private joke. She was looking up at him; he inclined his head toward her. There was something about the picture that was oddly familiar to me, but the knowledge only flickered at the edge of my awareness; I couldn't quite grab hold of it.

"He was a lovely man. Very kind. Very warm. He was always good to me." Sara's eyes were brimming with tears. "Strange. Mother's death has made me miss him again so much."

"That's quite natural," I said softly. "A traumatic event often recalls older traumas." I put my arm around her shoulders. "You shouldn't be brooding here all alone. Come back to town for awhile. Or have your Aunt Claire or Gina come stay with you here."

"No, I need to be alone now," Sara said, wiping her eyes with the back of her hand. "I'm sorry. I didn't meant to get all weepy on you."

"You mustn't apologize for showing your feelings — you need to get that stuff out. It's the only healthy way to work through something like this. I'm just worried for you. You need your support system around you now."

"Yeah, some great supporters I have on my team," she said sarcastically.

I bit my lip. "Have you spoken with Galen?"

"Oh, Galen." She waved her hand dismissively and turned away from me, back toward the ocean. "Galen's gone. Gone with the wind," she chanted softly.

"What do you mean?"

"I mean, he's gone. Flown the coop. Struck out for greener pastures. Whatever." All this without turning from the window.

"Where has he gone?"

"Dunno. And don't care," she said staunchly.

"Maybe he just decided to take a break, although I have to say, his timing's pretty rotten. Maybe he's off visiting family until things settle down," I suggested, playing devil's advocate even as I was thinking *Galen, you consummate asshole.*

Sara shook her head. "He doesn't have any family. Not close family, anyway. Galen was an only child, and his parents both died when he was a boy. I've often thought that was a lot of his trouble." She hiked her shoulders in an apathetic shrug. "I've never met any of his relatives."

"But how can you be so sure . . . ?"

Finally she looked at me. "Because he's cleaned out our joint accounts. Cashed in the CD's and stock certificates. He took it all, and he left." Her eyes darted off again. "I think Jeri's with him."

"Oh, shit," I murmured.

She rushed on, "I wanted to divorce him, anyway. This just speeds up the timetable. But the whole thing is so sordid." She shuddered with distaste. "I'll just be grateful when it's over."

You could have knocked me over with a feather. Literally. These people really worked every angle of the whole dysfunctional gestalt. "Do the police know he's gone?"

"I have no idea," she sighed, crossing to sit on a rough wooden bench that stood in for a sofa. Clearly an expensive piece, it still looked like the sort of thing that might leave splinters in your rear. "I certainly haven't called them to sound the alarm."

I trailed after her. "Don't you think the timing is suspicious, Sara? Why would Galen suddenly decide to clear out now? What was his relationship with Faye?"

She blinked at me in surprise. "They didn't particularly care for each other, but I can't believe Galen would have undertaken anything so daring — or so extreme. For all his philandering — and believe me, my sweet little sister wasn't the first, nor will she be the last — Galen is essentially passionless. He just doesn't give a shit about anything. Not really. Now sit down, Maggie. You're pacing."

"But he could have done it. Logistically," I said, perching on an ottoman that looked more forgiving than the bench. "San Diego is only a couple of hours away. I wonder if there's anybody who can vouch for his presence in that motel all night. I'd be willing to bet not, from what he said right after he talked to the cops. Not that that proves anything but opportunity."

"Jeri was at the house with me, or I'd suggest her as a likely candidate," Sara observed dryly.

I didn't like it at all — Galen's disappearance on the heels of Faye's murder.

But then again, why would he kill her? Not for the money. He hadn't waited for any kind of inheritance to come through. The money he'd taken he could have gotten his hands on at any time without physically harming anyone. Why, then? Because they'd traded insults at the breakfast table? It didn't make any sense. I let it go for the moment, but I knew I'd have to call Donleavy. I went back to the business that had brought me out there.

"How much do you know about your mother's financial and business dealings?"

"Very little, I'm afraid. Lillian handles all that."

"Faye owned a restaurant called Fat Farm, didn't she?"

"Yes, that's right."

"Who runs it for her?"

"A man named Robert Camden."

"How well do you know him?"

"Hardly at all. He seems pleasant enough." She shrugged, smiling slightly. "A little on the oily side, but I suppose that goes with the territory."

"How long has he been running the place?"

"Since Mother bought it. About three years ago, I think."

"Is he good at his job?"

"Oh, well, I think so. I'm afraid I'm not the best person to ask. As I said, I simply don't know much about it. But he does seem to have made quite a success of the place."

"Do you know where he comes from?"

"He's a find of Lillian's. I think she met him in Tahoe," she said, looking at me curiously.

"Do you know where in Tahoe? Was he working someplace up there?"

"I have no idea. What are you driving at, Maggie?"

So I told her what I'd overheard of Faye's irate phone call, about my discovery of her appointment with Lawrence Adolphe, and about my conversation with the accountant that morning.

"You have a meeting scheduled with him tomorrow morning at nine-thirty. He'll explain then what's going on, I hope."

"You think Lillian's been stealing from Mother? But they were like sisters!" she protested.

I almost made some pungent observation about the dark side of sisterhood, but I just couldn't go that low. "Maybe she's not in on the scam. On the other hand, it might just be a case of incompetent management. Or maybe, God forbid, I'm jumping to conclusions. Unfortunately, we just won't know anything for sure until your meeting tomorrow."

"Oh, but please! You have to come with me, Maggie. I want you to hear firsthand whatever he has to say."

"I think having an attorney with you tomorrow would be more to the point."

"No." She shook her head firmly. "There'll be time enough for attorneys later. I'm sure they'll take a big chunk of whatever's left. Tomorrow I want you there to help me decide what to do. Please. I'm asking you now as a friend."

She didn't have to twist my arm too hard, and we agreed to meet in the lobby of Adolphe's building the next morning at nine-fifteen. Then she showed me the rest of the house which was, as she'd observed, quite compact. The upper level comprised the living room, a small kitchen, a study, a miniature laundry room, and a half bath. Downstairs were two good-sized bedrooms that shared a connecting bathroom and a covered patio. It was a comfortable little house, with a price tag that would easily exceed a million dollars. Afterward, we stood on the patio soaking up the sun while we watched the gulls playing in the surf. I could understand Sara's affection for the place and would have been quite happy to hang out there for the rest of the day, but I had too many other fish to fry. Which brought the subject of lunch to mind. Sara was still looking a little peaked, and I thought an outing might perk her up.

"All at once I'm starving," I said. "Why don't we go up the road and get something to eat at that funky little place on the pier?"

"No, thanks. I'm not hungry," Sara demurred. "And I'm still not in the mood to get out and see a lot of people."

"Come on! It'll do you good to get out of here for awhile," I urged. "Give yourself a change of scene."

But I couldn't convince her, so I left. I sometimes wonder if I'd stayed and talked with her that afternoon — really talked with her at length and in depth — if I might have learned something that would have tipped me off. Something that might have changed the outcome.

Then again, I'm probably just flattering myself.

Sixteen

I stopped at a Brazilian fast food place (fried plantains to go in a paper sack — one of my personal definitions of ecstasy), then headed over the hill in search of Western Costume. The San Fernando Valley is invariably the hottest spot on the map of the L.A. metropolitan area. I mean that in meteorological terms. And by this point in the day the cool that always comes over the desert at night, a boon that usually lingers through mid-morning, had given way to another round of very un-March-like swelter. Up in North Hollywood, the noon-time heat radiated from the pavement in shimmering waves.

Driving north on Vineland, I was running over my mental list of questions for Carol and so for awhile joined the ranks of the only group of people I revile without apology — inattentive drivers. Which is how I lost track of where I was and zipped right through the light at Vanowen without noticing. Suddenly on my left, I caught a glimpse of a sign that read "Western Costume Co. Pick-ups and Deliveries" with an arrow. I braked sharply enough to draw an angry honk from the car behind me, then followed the arrow into a driveway that led to a large paved parking lot in back of a dingy two-story warehouse. I wasn't sure what I'd been expecting, but this wasn't it.

I pulled up near a loading dock. Beside it an enormous door to the warehouse stood open. A fellow with a long-handled broom shifted a pile of grit from one side of the entryway to the other while he surveyed the smog-cloaked San Gabriel mountain range to the north and me as I approached. I nodded, smiling at him as I passed; he leaned on his broom and favored me with a gaptoothed leer in return.

The interior of the building near the loading dock was quite barren and open, but straight ahead was a sort of hallway created by make-shift walls of chain-link fencing. At the end of the corridor sat a large bespectacled woman presiding from an even larger desk. As I started down the hall, I could see that the fencing partitioned areas on both sides into cubicles fitted out with desks and chairs, like mini-offices. There were a number of people working in the cramped enclosures, typing on computers and talking on phones. The overall effect was distinctly prison-like. I advanced toward the imposing female at the desk (I'd already started to think of her as the matron on duty) and told her I was looking for Carol Marlen. She regarded me with a blank stare of consternation.

"She's a costume designer," I added.

"Well, that sure narrows things down," she said sarcastically. She had a mole on the side of her chin sprouting a curly thicket of hairs that jumped around when she spoke.

"She said she'd be here all day."

"Sorry, it's not my day to watch her." She gestured vaguely. "Try looking back in stock," she said, making the fuzzy spot on her chin hop cheerfully. It really was the nicest thing about her.

"Could you maybe point me in the right direction?"

"Around the corner." Again with the waffly wave that told me nothing.

There was another row of offices to my left, though these were sturdier affairs made of unpainted plywood. They sure didn't waste money on frills at good ole Western Costume Co. Just beyond the shantytown of offices, I saw a large open doorway that led to a room filled by multi-tiered racks crammed with vast amounts of clothing. Stock. No doubt about it.

I headed toward that room and passed another door on my right that opened on a similarly arranged, equally enormous storage area. The air back there was thick with an indescribable stew of odors blending dust, mildew, dry rot, old sweat, and just plain filthy dirt. And I'd thought designing costumes for movies was such a glamorous job. Go figure.

I began to wander among the countless racks, which were organized so well that even a clothing numskull like me could make sense of them. One entire room was filled with all kinds of military uniforms. Various periods in history, various countries, various branches of service. The next room was roughly the size of an airplane hangar, and I began to wonder how I'd ever manage to find a woman I'd never met in this jungle of garments.

"Could that be Maggie?" asked a voice behind me.

I whirled to see a solid yet sprightly middle-aged woman with an unruly thatch of gray hair and an irrepressible grin.

"Carol?" I must have looked shell-shocked because she burst out laughing. "You poor thing! Shame on Virginia for not paging me! How are you?" She held out her hand, noticed it was gray with dirt, and withdrew it, making a face. "Sorry. I'd shake your hand, but I've been pulling their grimy costumes all morning. I don't want to pass along anything contagious. Come on up front, and I'll buy you a cup of coffee."

I followed her along an incomprehensible route through the maze of clothing until we came to a bare-bones workroom set up with tables and sewing machines. The room appeared to be deserted except for a mannequin cloaked in a long white robe that was doing the shimmy beside one of the cutting tables, a steady stream of muttered profanity issuing from a hump on the floor beneath its skirts. Something that looked like a big fur rug with a monkey face lay in a heap to one side.

Carol strode over to the mannequin calling, "How's it going, Honey?"

A mop of strawberry blonde curls framing a very red face poked out from under the tent of white fabric. "Oh, good! Can you please hold this blasted thing up as high as it will go while I screw it into place?" The young woman glanced ruefully at the pile of fur on the floor beside her. "But I don't know what we're going to do about Chewbacca. We might just have to wait for the fitting to figure out how you want to tart him up."

"Whatever you say, Boss," Carol said, smiling at her. "This is Maggie." Then to me, "This is Valerie, my professional better half. Welcome to our nightmare." She held the top of the mannequin steady while Valerie dove back under the cloak. "We usually work out of Universal Studios," Carol said, "but we've set up a kind of guerilla operation here this week because our boy-genius writers have come up with an episode with all our actors dressing up as characters from *Star Wars,* and all the paraphenalia we need is here."

"Mmm." I nodded as though it all seemed perfectly logical to me. "What's the —"

"Don't even ask." Carol cut me off with a wave of her hand. "It's the dopiest thing I've ever read, and that's saying something. Even if I tried to explain it, it wouldn't make any sense."

"It's a sitcom." Valerie's voice was muffled by layers of fabric. "It's not supposed to make sense." She emerged again, mission accomplished, and caught Carol's eye.

"I love my job," they chorused in a flat monotone.

"Listen, Val," Carol said, "I'm going to take Maggie on up to one of the conference rooms to talk for a bit. Can you manage without me?"

"Oh sure." She hopped to her feet. "How about if I round us up some lunch?"

"That would be spectacular!" Carol hooked her thumb over her shoulder, and we set off down a narrow hallway decked out with Astroturf and plastic paneling. It was lined with a series of small windowless rooms, each so completely filled by a rectangular table and chairs that I had to wonder if they'd first placed the furniture, then slapped up a set of pasteboard walls around it, or tweezed it all in a stick at a time like a ship-in-a-bottle.

She ushered me into one of the open doorways. "I'm going to wash my hands and get us coffee. How do you take it?"

"Black, please."

I took a seat by the table. A single fluorescent fixture that was about to give up the ghost flickered and buzzed overhead, casting a slightly greenish glare. Carol returned shortly with two styrofoam cups filled with a thick tepid brew and sat at the end of the table nearest me. She was a pleasant-looking person who apparently cared little for artifice. Her heart-shaped face was free of make-up; her matching rayon pants and top looked as comfy as a pair of pajamas. She had obviously chosen not to dye her hair, and her nails were well-tended but short and unpolished. She seemed altogether decidedly un-loopy.

"I called Joyce after we spoke," she said. "I hope you're not offended. I just needed to be sure I understood the situation correctly."

"I would have done the same thing in your position," I assured her.

"Good." She relaxed and settled back in her chair. "Joyce says you're terrific, by the way. So, what can I tell you?"

"You said on the phone that Joyce over-estimated the extent of your friendship with Faye. How well did you actually know her?"

"Not well at all, personally. We had a slight acquaintance because we both served on the membership committee for the union one year." She frowned, and I suspected she was trying to decide just how much she wanted to say. "I always had the feeling that Faye was one of those women who generally dislike other women, see them as competition. And she was quite a snob. It amused me when you said we worked in the same arena because she would never have acknowledged me as a peer. I'm a TV designer for the most part; I do three-camera situation comedies. Faye was strictly a feature film designer. From her perspective, I was quite far beneath her."

"Really?"

Carol smiled. "You seem so surprised. Hollywood is built on an elaborately layered social system that makes the caste stratification in India look simple by comparison."

"How so?"

She pursed her lips and thought for a moment before answering. "The business as a whole is really more feudal in structure. You have the people who control all the money, and therefore have all the power, at the top. That would include your producer and studio executive types and any directors or actors who have enough pull at the box office to get a project green-lit."

"Green-lit?" I was beginning to sound like a feeble-minded magpie.

"There are people who can attract enough money to a project, simply by virtue of their involvement, to get a movie capitalized and into production. It's not all that unusual for a studio to have a script that's been lying around for years gathering dust when some box office heavy-hitter suddenly takes an interest, and then, Honey, stand back and just watch the rivers of cash start to flow. It's strictly a business, Maggie, and driven strictly by money. Nothing else really matters. So you have a relatively small but very powerful group of people at the top, the lords of the land. And everybody else is scrambling around to serve them: we're the serfs." She gave a comic little shrug. "But within our various serf sub-groupings, we also have our pecking orders. Like I said, people who work on features have a more prestigious place in the hierarchy than those of us who labor in the world of television. We're also paid appreciably less than the film types."

Her tone was light and ironic, but it didn't completely mask her resentment.

Valerie stuck her head in the door just then, looking frantic. "Oh, thank God! Carol!" she hissed and thrust a cell phone at the designer. "It's Charles!"

Carol took the phone and a deep breath, then waited a beat. "Oh hi, Charles." She infused her greeting with such an abundance of goodwill that it had to be bogus. She leaned back in her chair and closed her eyes, listening with the phone clamped to her ear and inserting a thoughtful "Uh-huh, uh-huh" every now and then. After about a minute the guy on the other end apparently stopped to catch his breath.

"Well, I can understand why you're upset, Charles." Carol rolled her eyes and made a stroking motion with one hand as if she were jerking off a giant penis. "But what I can tell you? That's what it's going to cost to produce what is required by the script within our time constraints. And the more time we waste debating that, the higher the price is going to go. Good, fast, cheap, Charles — you can pick two."

She paused again, then, "No, you're not listening, Charles —" She held the receiver away from her ear, and we could hear the guy venting. She brought the mouthpiece close enough to her face to announce, "I'm hanging up now, Charles." Which is what she did.

"What a dick," Valerie groaned.

"Yes, and he's our dick," Carol sighed. "One of the many producers on our show," she said to me. "Too bad I wasted all those years in graduate school taking art and design classes when I could have been studying something useful like accounting."

"It gets worse every year," Valerie said glumly.

"Yup," Carol nodded. "Val and I did a little feature last year just before we did the pilot for this show. For this 'low budget,'" she made quotation marks with her fingers, "independent movie we had five — count'em — five producers and a star who drew a fifteen-million-dollar salary. By the time they got finished paying those guys there was hardly anything left to make the movie. And it's the same with a studio picture, only on an even more bloated scale. It makes me so furious when I hear those above-the-line types saying it's the unions' fault that movie-making has become so horrendously expensive. That's such a crock."

"Carol," Valerie sing-songed, raising her eyebrows, "You're on your soap-box again and time's a-wastin'."

"You're right, you're right," she chuckled at herself. "Just give us another minute, okay? I haven't really given Maggie a chance here."

Val tapped the face of her watch. "I'll be back in fifteen with sandwiches, then we gotta get serious."

Carol looked after her fondly. "I couldn't function without her."

"She's your partner?"

"She's the costume supervisor for the show, but, in fact, we do operate as partners. We complement each other so we make a great team. But she's right. I do have to get back pretty soon, so what else do you want to ask me?"

"Do you find there's a lot of professional rivalry among costume designers?"

"Well, it's a very competitive business, if that's what you're asking."

"Partially. Right around the time the Oscar nominations were announced, Faye became the target of a pretty nasty campaign — heavy-breather phone calls, anonymous notes. That's why I was hired. She told me herself she was convinced the harassment was coming from another designer who was jealous of her."

"Wow. I really don't know what to say about that. I suppose it's possible. Anything's possible. But frankly, I'd be surprised if that's what was going on."

"Why?"

"Well, she was nominated this year," Carol tipped her head to one side, her face puckered up in thought, "but I think everybody feels that was a fluke. Faye wasn't all that close to the top of the heap. She was always more of a middle-range feature designer. Oh, she did have a couple of big-budget, high-profile projects, but she got those because of her husband. You know about that, right?"

I nodded.

"So," she shrugged, "since he died, she's continued to work, but not in a very spectacular way. She just wasn't a talent that was ever going to set the world on fire. There are any number of designers who are more successful. Work more, make more money, do the big movies. And Faye was fighting the age factor. Big time. Films are most definitely a youth-oriented industry, and the age prejudice isn't just in front of the camera. When you get to be Faye's age, it starts to get harder and harder to find work, especially if you have the reputation for being a bit difficult. And she did."

That part didn't surprise me. But I suddenly saw Faye's studied efforts to project a more youthful image in a new light.

"She was her own worst enemy," Carol continued. "Temperamental, easily offended. She was always in the middle of some political stew, falling out with her director or star or producer. She never steered a happy ship, if you know what I mean."

I did.

She wrinkled her nose. "There's another thing that just doesn't ring true for me. All of us designers are such self-absorbed creatures. Sure, professional jealousy and gossip circulate like water. But to become so fixated on another designer . . ." She shook her head. "Well, that would have to be a very sick puppy, wouldn't it? Not that we aren't all a little tweaked," she grinned impishly.

I nodded and scratched away at my notes. What she said made sense to me and reinforced what I already tended to believe — that the professional rival bent on her destruction was only a figment of Faye's self-important imagination.

"Thank you for taking the time to talk with me," I said as I stood up. "Good luck with your show." I felt myself redden. "What a jerk — I haven't even asked you which show you do."

Carol made a wry face. "It's called *The Beat Goes On*, but don't look for any hidden meaning. It's just the network's lame attempt to sound hip."

"When's it on?"

"Wednesdays at nine. This week, anyway. They keep moving us around on the schedule, so it's hard for whatever audience we might have to keep track of us."

"Well, I'll be watching," I lied stoutly.

I stepped back out into the suffocating afternoon, retrieved the car, and escaped from the Valley, making tracks for Silverlake and the office. I walked in the door and got on the phone before I'd even put my bag down.

"Donleavy."

"Lieutenant, Maggie McGrath. I spoke with Sara Landesmann a little earlier today. Her husband, Galen, cleaned out their joint accounts and left town."

"Shit! When?"

"Had to be late Wednesday or yesterday."

He gave a sigh of weary aggravation. "Hell, he could be anywhere by now. Over the border. South America. Any fuckin' where at all."

"I know." I cradled the receiver between my chin and shoulder as I bent down to gather up the mail.

There was a short pause.

"You haven't had any more trouble out your way, have you?" he asked.

"No, Lieutenant."

"Okay, Kiddo," he said brusquely. "We'll be talking again soon, I'm sure."

"You're welcome, Lieutenant," I said to the dial tone. I hung up feeling vaguely irritated and checked the phone book before I made my next call.

"Fat Farm. May I help you?" It was a woman with a lilting French accent.

"I'd like to make a dinner reservation for two."

"Bon. What night is your pleasure?"

"How about tonight?"

"Hmmmm." She managed to make that sound both discouraging and disapproving. But then, brightly, "Oui. You are very lucky, Mademoiselle. There was a cancellation. I have one available seating for two at nine o'clock."

"Nine o'clock?" I whined. (I hate eating that late.) "Nothing earlier?"

"No," she replied severely. "To obtain an earlier reservation, you would have to wait until next Thursday." The way she pronounced "reservation" gave it five syllables.

"Next Thursday!" Chris hadn't been kidding.

"Oui. Our reservation list is always quite full," she replied smugly.

"All right," I sighed, resigning myself to late night indigestion. "Two for tonight. Nine o'clock." I gave her my name and telephone number, then put in a call to Chris at work.

"Are you up for a late-ish dinner tonight?" I asked when she came on the line. "I made a reservation at Fat Farm for us at nine."

"Cool! And guess what? One of my friends put me in touch with a sous-chef who used to live with Camden. He brought her to town with him when he moved here."

"Chris, that's fantastic! Did you actually talk to her?"

"Yeah, for just a minute to make sure I had the right person. Her name's Robin Mallory, and she's plenty pissed off at the guy."

"Do you think she'll talk to me?"

"Yeah, I do. I told her I had a friend who was looking into Camden's background because of a business deal. I didn't know how you'd want to approach it, so I kept everything kind of vague. Like I said, she's steamed about something. I think she'd be happy to rag on the guy."

She gave me Robin's number. I thanked her profusely and hung up.

"Yes?" The woman's voice was brittle and challenging.

"My name is Maggie McGrath. Are you Robin Mallory?"

"Yes." The voice was wary now.

"I got your number from my friend, Chris Jameson." I decided the mostly-honest approach was best. "I'm working for the owner of a restaurant called Fat Farm, looking into Robert Camden's background. I understand you know him quite well."

She gave a humorless snort. "Unfortunately."

"Would you be willing to talk with me about him, informally and off-the-record?"

"Are you a lawyer?"

"No, I'm a private investigator."

"Is Bob in some kind of trouble?"

"I honestly don't know at this point. Possibly."

"Why do you want to know about him?"

"The references he gave when he went to work at Fat Farm were fabrications. I want to find out where he came from and why he felt it was necessary to lie about his past employment."

"Why the sudden interest? Bob's been running the place for years now."

"My client suspects his management may not support her best interests."

"Oh."

There was a protracted silence.

"This would be completely off-the-record?"

"Completely."

"All right. The bastard deserves a little heat," she said bitterly. "But I don't want to talk any more on the phone. We'll meet someplace public. And I'll want to see some identification."

"No problem. You tell me where and when."

"The lake at Echo Park. By the boat rentals. Now, before I change my mind."

"I can be there in fifteen minutes."

I grabbed my bag and sprinted out to the car.

Seventeen

Echo Park is a patch of green just off the 101 freeway that has lent its name to the predominantly Hispanic neighborhood surrounding it. The centerpiece of the park is a tiny lake that features three artificial geysers shooting streams of water hundreds of feet into the air. Bordered by a row of shaggy palm trees, the lake is a refuge for a permanent population of ducks and geese who make their home on a small island connected to the rest of the park by a bright orange wooden footbridge. But a black-barred metal gate on the mainland side is generally kept locked. Even the birds in Los Angeles live behind security doors.

It was a straight shot down Sunset with a jog to the right at Echo Park Avenue, and I got there in less than ten minutes. I left the car at the top of the park and walked down to the boathouse where four-seater paddle boats made of sparkly magenta and turquoise fiberglass were lined up waiting to be rented. On weekend days, the lake was often dotted with the small bright vessels, but there were none on the water that day.

I stationed myself on a blue metal bench beside the boathouse but felt too antsy to sit still, so I got up to stroll along the narrow path by the water. An older gentleman in a kelly green T-shirt and a straw hat was sitting in a lounge chair reading a newspaper. Two fishing poles with their lines trailing in the water were propped on the grassy bank beside him.

"Are there really fish in there?" I asked.

"Well, Honey, you tell me," he replied cheerfully. He got up and went to the edge of the water, where he hauled up a mesh bag that held a half-dozen two- to three-pound catfish. He grinned. "That makes a mighty good dinner."

I couldn't help but wonder what those bottom feeders had been munching, but I smiled and made admiring sounds about his catch. He waved, and I turned back toward the boathouse. A woman with flaming red hair stood beside a wooden planter near the bench where I'd been sitting. She was dressed simply in tight jeans and a cropped sweater that showed her exquisite figure to perfect advantage. She watched me as I walked toward her, and her mouth became set in a line that was not quite a smile. I held out my hand to her.

"I'm Maggie."

"Robin."

She took my hand briefly, barely brushing it with hers, as if the touch were repugnant.

"Shall we take a walk around the lake?" I suggested.

"I want to see your license," she said sternly. Her skin was that creamy white that only redheads get to have and was absolutely flawless.

"Oh, sure." I dug in my bag for the leather folder with my photo ID and handed it to her. "That's my license number. I'm registered with the Department of Consumer Affairs. You can call them to check me out if it'll make you feel better."

She peered at it, then squinted at me, still suspicious. "How do I know you're not working for those guys in Vegas?" she asked.

"What are you talking about?" was all I could think to say.

She waved a hand dismissively. "You're right," she said as though I'd posed an irrefutable argument. "They'd never hire someone like you."

It occurred to me that I might be justified in taking offense at this observation, but no matter. My credibility with her had apparently received a boost.

"How long have you known Mr. Camden?"

She glanced at me sideways. We had begun meandering along the path beside the lake. "About four years."

"Where did you meet him?"

"At a club in Lake Tahoe. It started out pretty casually, but we ended up living together."

"Was he working there at the time?"

"Yeah, at some crummy little inn where he was a desk clerk. He really hated it."

"What was the name of the place?"

"The Moose Head Lodge. You can just imagine. The name says it all. It's actually in Truckee, about twenty minutes north of Tahoe. Like I said, it's a real dump."

"Where were you working?"

"I was an assistant chef at the CalNeva Lodge. Right on the lake, the place Frank Sinatra used to own? I should've stayed there," she said grimly.

We walked along for awhile in prickly silence. I watched an old lady feeding stale doughnuts to a throng of happy ducks. Pigeons hopped across the path in front of us then scattered in panic as two junior delinquents-in-training came whizzing past on their bikes. If I'd veered a hairs-breadth to my right I'd've been history. None of it registered with Robin: her thoughts had turned inward, and she seemed to have all but forgotten I was even there.

"So when Camden got the job at Fat Farm, you came with him?" I prompted.

"Yeah." A shiver ran through her, and she crossed her arms, hugging herself protectively. "He said he needed me with him to make it. It was a real break for me, or so I thought. I came in as the head chef. And I worked like a dog, by the way. I put that kitchen together, and I ran it like a machine. I made that place what it is today," she said defiantly.

"What happened?"

"I found out he was screwing that hag who put the deal together for him!" She cut an anxious look at me. She wasn't nearly as tough as she pretended, and I read the vulnerability in her eyes, the worry that I'd think her as big a fool as she did herself. "It's not that I wasn't suspicious when he first started talking about it. I mean, why was this chick from L.A. so interested in recruiting him? It's not like he had any cash to kick in. It was just too good to be true, you know? But then he made it sound like he was doing it —" She bit her lip. "Like it was such a great opportunity for both of us."

On the verge of tears, she shook her head sharply, willing them away. "I finally figured out that's the reason he didn't want to live together down here. He was almost always over at my place, but he said with us working so closely together, it was better for our relationship." She made a harsh sound that was somewhere between a laugh and a sob. "Relationship! What a joke that was. His idea of a good relationship is plenty of sex with no strings and no questions asked. When I found out about that bitch, Lillian, I told him it was either her or me." Her mouth began to tremble. "That's when the sonofabitch fired me. I tell you, it really fucked me up. For months, I couldn't even stand to leave the apartment. I went through all my savings."

Her voice caught, and she turned away from me toward the lake to pull herself together. "It wasn't just because of him. I finally got the chance to do what I'd always wanted to do, you know? And I did a great job." She closed her eyes and sighed. "But that wasn't enough. I did the best I could do, and it still wasn't enough."

"Oh, come on, Robin!" I said impatiently. "That's not what it was about at all. You got taken by a con man. He used you, and that really sucks. But it doesn't mean you failed."

"Easy for you to say," she shot back.

"Besides, you're still a beautiful, talented woman. You've had a tough break, but it's not the end of the world."

"Whatever."

It was pointless to debate with her: she obviously didn't want a cheerleader. So I shelved the lecture on life lessons and forged ahead. "Do you know anything about the financial situation over at Fat Farm?"

She shook her head. "I had my hands full running the kitchen."

I decided to backtrack. "Why did you ask me if I was working for some guys from Las Vegas? Has Camden had trouble with gambling debts?"

She shifted her eyes away from me again and stood silently staring out at the lake for a long minute. When she looked back at me, her gaze was hard. Evaluating. I watched as the wheels turned behind her eyes, then locked into a decision.

"Robert Camden isn't Bob's real name," she finally said. "I don't know all the in's and out's, but he was mixed up with the mob in Las Vegas before I met him. He got crosswise with the guys he was working for, and he had to split. That's how he ended up in Tahoe. The old man who owns the inn where he was working is his uncle."

I whistled softly. "Do you know what his real name is?"

"Raymond Cicelli. I think."

"But you have no idea what the trouble in Vegas was?"

"He wouldn't ever talk about it," she shrugged. "And I guess I really didn't want to know."

"What's his uncle's name?"

"Ben Hudson."

Then I asked her for Camden's L.A. address and phone number, along with a physical description. He lived in Brentwood. Her assessment of his person was a terse "medium height and build, olive skin, dark brown hair, small dick." We'd completed our circuit of the lake.

I handed her one of my cards, and as we parted she said, "You know, it's funny, but I actually feel better now. I've never told all of this to anyone before." The corners of her mouth twitched in a chilly smirk. "And I like the idea that he might finally be held accountable for some of the shit he's pulled." She turned on her heel and crossed Echo Park Avenue, heading north toward Sunset and drawing appreciative looks from all the men she passed.

"Well, Babe," I murmured as I watched her go, "you just hold that thought."

Eighteen

Chris knocked on my door at eight-thirty that evening looking glamorous and sexy in a slinky dark green knit dress. Her hair was swept up into some sort of fancy twisted braid secured by a carved jade comb.

"Wow! You look spectacular!" I said, ushering her in.

I was still struggling with my toilette. I'd managed to take a short nap in anticipation of the late night ahead, and when I woke, my hair was plastered against my head on one side and sticking out at gravity-defying angles on the other. That was pretty much how I felt, too. Instead of being refreshed, I was logy and out-of-sorts. Dressing for dinner seemed like a chore: I'd much rather have donned a ratty old T-shirt and furry slippers to eat a frozen burrito in front of the TV. And I wonder why my social life is sluggish. But this was business, so I had to buck up.

I had recycled the black ensemble I'd worn to the costume exhibit. While I was dressing, I noticed the jacket had a stain on the left lapel, but I figured the restaurant would be dark, anyway. Adopting the same attitude toward my ungovernable hair, I abandoned further effort.

The night was cool, and Chris and I were as giddy as a couple of teenagers on a field trip as we climbed into the Toyota. I realized belatedly that I should have taken it through the car wash that afternoon — nothing is so tiresome as the hauteur of valet parkers at expensive restaurants. Not that a bath would have effectively shielded my car from their scorn.

Fat Farm was located on a little-traveled side street near the Sunset-Gower Studios. It wasn't a tremendously desirable area, but the restaurant was insulated from the unsavory neighborhood, barricaded behind a high cement wall encrusted with a rainbow mosaic made up of fragments of colored glass and broken tile. The street in front of the place buzzed with activity as a parade of Mercedeses, Porsches, and Jaguars pulled up to disgorge passengers who'd made the pilgrimage to Hollywood for a meal. We left the car with the inevitable valet and stepped through a door nearly disguised by the wall's variegated surface.

The dimly lit corridor we entered was decorated with the same broken glass mosaic glittering faintly in the darkness. I felt like Alice down the rabbit hole as we inched our way toward an eerie pink glow at the other end of the tunnel. When we emerged from the passage, I stopped short in the doorway, transfixed by the hullabaloo that confronted us.

The restaurant was one large room with a remarkably high ceiling and a transparent floor that looked down into a vast aquarium where all sorts of fish and eel-like creatures floated around looking thoroughly bored. An upper gallery bordering three sides of the dining room was punctuated at random intervals by platforms affording the opportunity to dine with a bird's-eye view, for those who craved an element of risk to sharpen their appetites. The back wall was a rear projection screen with images of a fey young man playing peek-a-boo alternating with a disembodied fish mouth opening and closing in noiseless gulps. Pseudo-cubistic canvases depicting people — or maybe they were fish — in poses I guessed were meant to be provocative filled the remaining wall space. Columns stuck here and there slathered with the glass-and-tile mosaic provided some decorative continuity. In lieu of flowers, each table was ornamented by an individually conceived seaweed sculpture. And everything was bathed in the peculiarly vivid pink light so that we all looked like we'd been thrust under the chicken warmer at KFC.

"This place is amazing!" Chris said, clutching my elbow.

"Yep. This Pablo Picasso-meets-Jules Verne thing they've got going is nothing if not original," I agreed.

Fat Farm was filled to capacity, its tables occupied either by customers who could easily afford the average one hundred dollar-per-person tab or by those who were splurging in the hope of buying a special experience and possibly catching a glimpse of some famous faces in the bargain. I gave my name to the maitre d'. Maybe I was being paranoid, but I thought he cast a disapproving sidelong glance at my lumpy hair as he led us to a table, which, mercifully, was on the first level. I knew I'd never be able to swallow comfortably perched on one of those hanging platforms.

"Did you see Clint Eastwood over there?" Chris bubbled. She leaned toward me using her menu as a shield and pointed across the room. "Now, that is a sexy man! And how about the bald spot on Woody Harrelson? I tried not to stare when we walked past his table, but he's really getting thin on top."

"You must have some kind of built-in celebrity radar," I said, feeling observationally challenged. I hadn't noticed anyone familiar— famous or otherwise.

We ordered cocktails — a vodka martini with three olives for Chris and a frozen daiquiri that made my sinuses ache. Those negotiations completed, we tackled the menu. Chris opened the leather-bound tome and began to study it carefully with a critical eye. My eye, on the other hand, was only hungry. I wanted food. Lots of it. And soon. Not the best frame of mind for an evening of gracious dining. The fare sounded as exotic as it was expensive and was most plentiful in the fish and seafood category. I only hoped we weren't expected to troll for our own dinners. "Sweet and sour halibut with lemon rice," "salmon with mint cous-cous," and a "fluffy fish frittata" were only a few of the dubiously mouth-watering offerings. I decided to begin with the fish-and-spinach chowder followed by the fruit-stuffed turkey breast; Chris opted for the wild rice and wall-eye salad as her first course and the yellowfin tuna with pear salsa for her entree.

Our waiter was a pleasant, well-scrubbed young man who told us his name was Evan. He noted our selections with a deferential minimum of chit-chat, then wafted off to the kitchen. I was about to start gnawing on the seaweed sculpture when a busboy with the face of an angel brought a large basket of warm breads and muffins. I fell on them like a starving mongrel. As my blood sugar began to climb toward a normal level, I sat back to behold the spectacle, trying to imagine such an experiential nonsequitur springing up in any other city. But the effort failed.

"Only in L.A.," I muttered. Well, maybe Las Vegas. Only there, they'd make the waiters wear merman costumes. Upon such reflection, I had to admire Fat Farm's restraint. But whatever my personal reservations were about the decor, whoever put it all together had obviously struck a significant chord with the dining-out crowd in town. It was nearly ten o'clock, and the restaurant was packed.

"So, what is it you want me to be watching for?" Chris asked as she buttered a piece of lemon-blueberry muffin.

"I'm not really sure. I just wanted to see this place. You know, get a feel for it? And try to get a look at Robert Camden, if he's around. Just keep your eyes open for anything that strikes you as odd — you know this territory so much better than I do. Other than that, eat a lot. Drink. Have a good time."

"I can do that," she said cheerfully.

Evan reappeared with our first courses. I left the choice of our dinner wine to Chris, and she agonized over the list, finally selecting the Santa Margherita pinot grigio, one of my personal favorites. The food surprised me: it was delicious — original combinations of delicately seasoned flavors, and all of it perfectly prepared. Not that I was persuaded to revise my opinion of Fat Farm as the sort of place only a pretentious asshole with bad taste could love, which went a long way toward explaining its widespread appeal in my adopted city. Nevertheless, we had a pleasant meal. Chris regaled me with tales from her catering misadventures, and we swapped cat stories.

As we were finishing our entrees, I noticed a man in an expensively tailored suit standing at the edge of the dining area, observing the scene with a proprietary air. His eyes traveled deliberately over the crowd like the pit boss of a casino calculating the evening's take. He was attractive in a heavily pomaded Mediterranean way. Not my type, though: I don't care for men who wear more jewelry than I do, and this fellow was majorly be-ringed and braceleted. He oiled his way across the floor, nodding occasionally to regular patrons along his route, then oozed to a stop beside a table of three gorgeous young women. He rested his hand on the bare shoulder of the girl who had her back to me, stroking her lightly while he visited with all three. I gathered I'd just gotten my first look at Robert Camden, a.k.a., Raymond Cicelli. He leaned down close to the girl he was massaging, and she turned her face to give him a peck on the lips. She looked familiar, but it took me a moment to place her. It was Gina Harris, Sara's cousin. Hmmm. That was mildly interesting. Camden continued his circuit of the room, stopping next at the Eastwood table. As I watched him chatting up his famous guest, I had a flash of inspiration. Flagging down the erstwhile Evan, I asked him to bring a bottle of Dom Perignon and three glasses.

Chris's eyebrows quirked up in surprise. "Are we celebrating something — like maybe you just inherited a small fortune so you can afford to pay for this dinner?"

"Just bear with me. I have an idea."

Evan returned with the necessary accouterments, and when the champagne had been plunged into the ice bucket, I said to him, "Now will you please ask your manager to join us? My dinner partner is the food critic for a prominent national publication, and we'd like to congratulate him on the excellence of every element of this dining experience."

Evan flushed and practically saluted. "Right away, Ma'am!"

"What are you doing?" Chris hissed urgently.

But I was busy watching our waiter dart across the room to intercept Camden, who'd just taken his leave of the Eastwood party. As Evan spoke to him, the roué-cum-restauranteur ran a jeweled hand over his carefully greased coiffure, then glanced speculatively at our table. I caught his eye, and he nodded at me, smiling slightly. He patted Evan on the shoulder as if he were a puppy who had performed a clever trick and, altering his course, slid in our direction.

"Beautiful ladies, good evening! It's a great pleasure to have you with us. My name is Robert Camden, and I am here to be of service to you in any way I can."

"Mr. Camden, the pleasure is entirely ours," I simpered shamelessly. "We've just enjoyed the most exquisite meal in this gorgeous setting, and we both felt compelled to congratulate you personally. My name is Ariel Swartout and this," I gestured to Chris, "is Naomi Wainwright. Naomi has just been chosen as the new food critic for *The Christian Science Monitor*, and her first review, her maiden voyage, you could say, into the world of national culinary criticism, might be titled 'An Ode To Fat Farm.' Isn't that right, Naomi?" I gave Chris a sharp kick under the table, hoping to encourage her to quit staring at me as if I'd just sprouted an extra head.

"I'm flattered that you chose us as your first subject." Camden was trying for humble, but it didn't quite track. "And I'm pleased that your experience was satisfactory."

"Oh, so far beyond satisfactory! So far beyond any of our expectations!" I was about to gag on my own obsequious gushing. "In fact, I'd like to propose a toast. Evan, will you please do the honors?"

Evan uncorked the champagne while I batted my eyes at Camden, who'd plastered on his version of a gallant smile. I raised my glass, and the others followed suit. "May your successes continue in an unbroken golden chain!" We drank, though I noticed Camden hesitate; he was probably squeamish about toasting any kind of chain.

"Charming!" he declared as he set his glass down. "And now, fair ladies, I must unfortunately get back to business." He leaned toward us, and his musky cologne nearly brought up my dinner. "I hope you won't mind — I've taken the liberty of ordering your dessert." He grinned, a swarthy shark in a custom suit. "Ciao, Bellissimi!" And with that, he glided off into the artificial pink twilight. Chris threw a stern look at me, and I shrugged, rolling my eyes heavenward. Then we both dissolved in a fit of giggles.

"Naomi?" she gasped. "Where did you come up with that?"

"I like the name Naomi! It's sounds substantial, and very Christian."

"You could at least have warned me what you were going to do! You're outrageous!"

"I would have if I'd planned it. But you did just fine," I assured her.

"I didn't do anything except sit there with my mouth hanging open."

"Relax. It worked out okay."

I did a quick visual once-around-the-room, but nobody was paying any attention to us. I picked up Camden's discarded champagne flute, laid it in my lap, and wrapped my napkin loosely around it. Then I stashed the bundle in my bag.

"I can't believe you just did that! What is going on with you tonight?" Chris scolded in a fierce whisper.

I reached over and put a hand on her arm. "Fingerprints," I said quietly.

His timing perfection, Evan scuttled toward us carrying a tray loaded with a multi-hued fruit tart and a huge slab of chocolate layer cake leaking a creamy filling dotted with fresh raspberries. Instead of icing, the entire concoction had been dipped in white chocolate forming a crisp sweet shell. An insulin chaser should have come with each piece.

"This is better than sex," Chris moaned as she bit into the cake.

"Maybe we should order some to go." I reached across the table for a forkful. "So, in your professional opinion, did Fat Farm live up to its reputation?"

"Oh, yes!" she mumbled enthusiastically, dribbling crumbs in the process.

I studied her over the rim of my coffee cup. "Have you ever thought about opening a place of your own? I've tasted your handiwork, and you're every bit as talented as the people cooking here."

"It's a dream of mine," she sighed, gazing down at her plate. "But it'd mean such a huge initial outlay of capital . . ." She gave her head a little shake and scooped up another hunk of chocolate. "What are you going to do with the glass?"

"Take it to the police to see if their lab can lift any prints to run through NCIC."

"NCIC?"

"The National Crime Information Center. It's a criminal data file maintained by the FBI, and I'm willing to bet Mr. Camden is a member of the club."

By the time we finished our dessert, it was nearly eleven-thirty. I signaled our buddy, Evan, and asked for the check. He smiled broadly and told us our bill had already been settled; our meal was on the house. That made me feel a tad guilty, but only enough to barely prevent me from leaping into the air and clicking my heels. I left him a generous tip, and we set out to rescue the Toyota from the valet parkers. As luck would have it, we got to the door at the same time as Clint Eastwood and his friends. Though she'd never have dreamed of accosting him, Chris still couldn't keep herself from smiling rapturously in his direction as we all converged on the exit.

Mr. Eastwood returned her smile and offered up a cordial, "Have a good evening, ladies," as he held the door for us.

We murmured our thanks and scurried to the valet stand. With an heroic effort of will, Chris just managed to contain her excitement until we were buckled in and chugging up the street. "Totally awesome!"

I showered when I got home and pulled on a threadbare T-shirt as soft as skin. But I knew I couldn't sleep. I wandered from room to room, unable to quell my restlessness. I picked up my knitting needles and started to cast on stitches, but hadn't the patience to sustain such a ritual. I went to the kitchen and poured myself a glass of white wine to take out to the balcony, then on impulse detoured through the studio to grab a newsprint pad and pencil. A little late night sketching in the dark — just the thing to soothe those frazzled nerves. *What a goof you are, McGrath*, I thought as I juggled all my props through the French doors.

A gauzy layer of clouds had slung itself across the sky like a net hanging so close overhead it seemed near enough to touch. I sat outside and sipped my wine surrounded by velvety silence and hundreds of lights winking at me from the hills nearby. The faint glow filtering through the kitchen curtains was enough for me; that night I preferred the softness of the dark. Propping my feet on the balcony's stucco wall and balancing the drawing pad on my knees, I felt more than saw the image take shape on paper.

A face says so much. History is writ large in its topography, the planes and angles worked on day after day by a lifetime's worth of love and loss, triumphs and defeats, secrets shared and kept. God is in the details. By some artistic alchemy, drawing a person's face brings me in touch with that history. As I sketch those planes and angles, I glimpse the roads traveled and emotions spent. I start to know that person.

The whispery scratching of my pencil stopped as it came to rest of its own accord, and I reached for my glass of wine. A cool finger of wind skittered across the hills, tickling up the goose flesh on my bare arms as I stared down at Robert Camden's portrait, drank my wine, and wondered if I could be looking into the face of a killer.

Nineteen

I sat on my balcony the next morning with coffee and the newspaper, wishing I hadn't plotted such an ambitious schedule for myself. It was one of those increasingly rare clear and cool days when I could actually see all the way to the ocean from my house. It would be wonderful to spend some time in the studio with the Eagles and Tom Petty singing to me for inspiration. Of course, that would mean a trip to the art store first and a major investment in replacement supplies. On the other hand, it would also be heaven to just lie around for the better part of the morning with a good book, and that wouldn't cost me a cent. But I knew this wasn't to be.

Glumly, I regarded the beautiful view and took stock of my situation. I couldn't go to Donleavy with the champagne flute. He had no experience with me, no reason to consider me anything other than a meddling nuisance. And while his previous warning had been oblique, he would now most probably order me in no uncertain terms to cease and desist.

I didn't have the network of professional alliances in L.A. that I'd had in New York from my years of police work. Maybe I never would: I'd always be an outsider as far as the cops out here were concerned, my private status rendering my integrity automatically suspect. I shrugged. Couldn't be helped. Gathering resolve, I picked up the portable phone I'd brought outside with me and punched in a familiar number. One I hadn't called in quite a long time.

"Ferris," he answered crisply.

"I didn't know if I'd find you there today."

A stunned silence.

"Is it Maggie?" I was relieved to hear him sound pleased.

"Guilty."

"How are you, girl? It's been too long."

In some ways. Not long enough in others.

"I'm doing great. Truly. I actually even like it out here. Most of the time. How are you, Glen?"

"Oh, you know. Fine. Nothing ever changes."

"How are your kids?"

"Great. Growing. Cathy's in her first year of high school."

"Hard to believe."

"Yeah."

A slightly awkward pause.

"So, you're well?'

"As well as I'll ever be," I replied.

He was silent.

"That was a joke, Glen."

"Oh." He chuckled nervously.

"Life's pretty good. I can't complain. Well, I could, but who'd listen? You certainly never put up with my whining. Dammit."

"And I'm not gonna start now!"

"Whatta pal."

Our banter abruptly lurched to a halt, but the distance between us seemed less.

"It's good to hear your voice, Maggie. You sound like your old self." I could hear the gentle smile in his voice.

"Well, you know. It just takes time," I said softly.

"Yeah. I know."

"And just to prove what a bad friend I am, I've called to ask a favor," I said briskly.

"I'm yours to command."

"I was hired to look into what appeared to be some nasty garden-variety harassment. But the woman's ended up dead — murdered — and I think I've got a guy who looks like he could be good for it. A major contender, anyway. He's got a very dingy background, and I'd like to know more about him. I think his real name's Raymond Cicelli —"

"Hold on, something tells me I need to start writing this down."

I waited while I heard the scrabble of papers being rearranged.

"Okay. Shoot."

"Okay. Raymond Cicelli is supposedly the guy's real name, according to a former girlfriend who's a little hazy about the details. He calls himself Robert Camden now. Runs a restaurant the victim owned. The girlfriend says she thinks he was connected in Las Vegas. Anyway, I've got a glass he handled that I hope might have some useable prints. If I send it to you, can you process it and run them? And also run those two names?"

"You don't want much, do you? This is going to take some finessing."

"You always did have the magic touch."

"You . . ." he growled.

"Can you do it?"

"I could never say no to you."

"That's what I like best about you."

"You're welcome," he said pointedly.

"And I thank you. I'll get it into FedEx today. You'll have it Monday morning. And I'll call you — when?"

"It could take a couple of weeks, Doll. You remember how the finely tuned bureaucratic machinery grinds along. With no deliberate speed."

"I know, I know. So you'll call me?"

"You know I will."

"Thanks again, Glen."

"It's great to hear from you, Mags. Take care of yourself."

We hung up. Two weeks was not acceptable. On the other hand, I had no choice. I leaned back and gave myself a minute to recover. Glen and I had been partners, and we'd always have the kind of bond that comes from being in the trenches together.

He was one of the few people who stuck by me when my life fell apart, and he was the one who finally kicked my butt and got me to start picking up the pieces again. I killed somebody during the course of an investigation, and it nearly did me in. It's not that I wouldn't make the same decision again given the same circumstances, but I don't believe anyone kills with impunity: you just don't end another life and walk away scot free, I don't care who you are.

Up until then I'd led a charmed life: masters degree from John Jay College of Criminal Justice, top ten percent of my class at the Academy, one of the youngest women ever to make detective in the NYPD's history. All that plus I was married to a distant cousin of the Rockefellers, and not so distant that a chunk of their wealth hadn't sprouted on his branch of the family tree. Not to mention he just happened to be the deputy commissioner of police in charge of legal matters, an appointed position intended as a springboard to a career in politics; and believe me, he had his sights set well beyond the five boroughs.

We had a comfortable relationship; I guess I'd characterize it as "comradely." But not deep enough to weather the storm of publicity that battered us from the outside in the wake of the shooting coupled with the stress eating away at me, and therefore the marriage, from the inside. The newspapers had a field day raking me over the coals, even though it was established early on the guy shot at me first, along with the fact that he'd already carved out quite a criminal history for himself. Among other things, he was a crack dealer. He was also thirteen years old. A grand jury exonerated me, but that didn't stop the talk or silence my personal demons. I drank too much, an anesthetic measure that, predictably, failed utterly. I flew into violent rages over nothing. My husband said he didn't know me anymore. I replied that the door was always open, and he always had a choice. He chose to leave. And I couldn't blame him. Hell, I envied him. I wanted to get away from me, too. Knowing my career had suffered irreparable damage, I resigned from the police department, a job I'd loved and that had filled me with a sense of purpose. I cloistered myself in my Upper Westside apartment, shutting out friends and family, drinking all day and staring out the windows at the gray surface of the Hudson River. But Glen refused to respect my privacy and denied my prerogative to flush my life down the drain. He pounded on my door, poured the liquor down the sink, cooked for me, cried with me, and finally dragged me kicking and screaming into the therapy that saved my life.

I learned you can walk through something like that and come out the other side, but like I said before, you can never walk away. You're forever changed. Truth be told, after a time I found I wasn't entirely sorry my life had been re-routed, even if I can't say yet exactly where I'm headed. One thing I do know: wherever I go from now on, that boy will always be with me. That's why I kept my gun in a box on a shelf in the closet. And I knew that was where I'd kept most of my feelings since then, too. Why I tended to keep everyone at arm's length. Why I seemed to have lost my capacity for strong emotion. I closed my eyes and for the hundred-thousandth time thought of the message that came through Jen the first night I met her at Joyce's party. And for the hundred-thousandth time, I tried to believe. "He says he is at peace, and he wants you to find peace, too."

The morning sun felt good, and a gentle breeze stroked my face. "Please let it be true," I whispered.

There's just no getting around it: you know you're creeping toward middle age when you look at yourself and see your mother. But if you're like me, that's not all bad news. A well-ordered thought process is only one of the bonuses I got by jumping in at her end of the gene pool. A penchant for domestic organization is a hallmark trait of ours. My house, like my mother's, is always well-stocked (some might say with seige-mentality quantities) of food, cleaning supplies, batteries, candles, paper products, plenty of fresh underwear, and shipping supplies. I have boxes, I have bubble wrap, three kinds of tape, labels, and beaucoup de sizes and colors of permanent markers.

I transferred the champagne flute to a nest of newspapers I'd wadded up in a box selected from my collection of availables, then taped it shut with an obsessive thoroughness I knew would send Glen into fits of laughter at my expense. That task complete, I showered and dressed in a tailored pantsuit. Best to try looking as much like a grown-up as possible when talking with an accountant. I dropped the flute at the FedEx office on Lexington, then set out for Beverly Hills.

Adolphe Associates was located on the chic 9000 block of Wilshire Boulevard in a multi-story glossy gray office building with an atrium-style lobby that was a jungle of thriving plants and small trees. I double-checked the directory, half-hidden by a ficus, to make certain I'd copied down the correct suite number. At 9:30 Sara still hadn't showed, so I went in search of a pay phone, but the machines picked up at both the Malibu place and the house on Nichols Canyon. At 9:40 I decided it was time to go upstairs, thinking maybe we'd gotten our wires crossed and she'd be there already waiting for me.

The accounting firm's suite of offices was a sleek, austere collage of iron-gray walls and carpets, chrome-and-black leather furnishings. The only person in the spacious reception area was the secretary, a small gray woman who blended perfectly with her environment, and she told me that no one answering Sara's description had been in the office all morning. I couldn't think what else to do, so I asked her to tell Mr. Adolphe that half of his 9:30 appointment had arrived. She buzzed him on the intercom, and I was ushered directly into his office. Back-lit by the morning sun streaming through his windows, Lawrence Adolphe rose and came around his desk to greet me as I walked in the door.

"Good day, Ms. McGrath," he said pleasantly as we shook hands.

His manner was positively chummy compared to our phone conversation the day before, and I wondered what had caused the thaw. He was a tall spare man with striking silver hair that was a startling contrast to his youthful face. I was sure the combination turned heads wherever he went, and judging by the way he preened throughout our conversation, he didn't mind the extra attention.

"I have to apologize, Mr. Adolphe. Ms. Landesmann is late. I just tried calling her, so I can only imagine she's already on her way."

"Not to worry," he assured me. "She phoned late yesterday to say that something had come up — an urgent matter that would force her to miss this appointment. But she said you have her complete confidence and authorized me verbally and by fax to release the information I have to you."

But that struck me as odd: if Sara knew she wasn't going to be there, why hadn't she called me the day before? What could have been more important than this meeting? Whatever it was, she obviously hadn't wanted to tell me about it. Or was I just being paranoid? More likely, she was still in her hiding-out mode, simply not wanting to deal with any of this.

"But a phone call would have been nice," I muttered under my breath.

"I beg your pardon?" Adolphe asked, indicating a chair across from his desk.

"Oh, nothing," I said vaguely, shaking my head. I sat and took out my notebook. He rested his elbows on the arms of his chair and gazed at me expectantly. With his angular limbs and brilliant crest of hair glowing in the sun, he looked like a big silvery bird posed for a wildlife photograph.

"When did you first speak with Faye Symington?" I asked.

"She called me three weeks ago. She was referred by another client of mine, who also happened to be a friend of hers. My specialty is corporate accounting, and I have a reputation as something of a trouble-shooter for businesses experiencing financial difficulties. I enjoy a challenge, and I've often been able to affect a favorable transition when conventional wisdom has pronounced the case hopeless."

He tented his fingers and gave me a beatifically self-satisfied smile. I felt like I'd just been cued to applaud. Or maybe genuflect. But what he'd said made my ears prick up: Faye had first come to him about the time the threats started. Coincidence or cause and effect?

"She said she owned a restaurant," he continued, "that was losing vast amounts of money despite the fact that it was tremendously busy and, to all outward appearance, quite successful. I asked her to bring me the financial records in as much detail as possible for the past three years, the length of time she had owned the business. I gather she had some trouble getting hold of the information, for reasons that soon became all too apparent, but she finally brought the whole muddle in to me last week."

He paused for dramatic effect. Tap, tap, tap went the fingertips. 'Here's the church, here's the steeple.' The childhood rhyme played itself in my head. This guy was getting off on the telling of such a tale way too much for my taste, so I waited him out, refusing him the satisfaction of a prompt.

"So then," he finally went on with an awkward little cough, "I found evidence of fraud on a massive scale, some of it so bold there was practically no attempt to conceal it." He began ticking off infractions on the long thin fingers of one hand. "There were many instances of double-billing for large orders of supplies, and I'm sure if we did a complete inventory, we'd find a number of those orders were entirely fraudulent. The manager, a Mr. Camden, paid himself non-specific consulting fees on a regular basis in addition to a generous salary that included benefits, paid vacation, and so forth."

"He didn't miss many opportunities, did he?" I smiled grimly.

"Oh, but that isn't all! I noticed that several employees cashed their paychecks at the restaurant every week, without exception. That sent up a red flag for me, particularly because of the other irregularities I'd already spotted, so I looked more closely at those records and discovered they were bogus salary lines — those people simply do not exist. Camden must have been cashing the checks and pocketing the money. I'm also certain — though there's no way to prove it — that a fair amount of the restaurant's cash transactions never made it onto the books at all. The percentages of currency versus plastic are way off any normal ratios."

"Did you tell all this to Faye?" I could only imagine what a festive interview that would have been.

"I didn't have the chance. Our appointment was for the morning of the thirteenth. By then she —" He shook his head delicately. "I was going to suggest that we delve into her personal records next. Her business manager had to be in collusion with Camden for the scheme to go undetected so long. I wouldn't be surprised if a review of Ms. Symington's other business transactions — up to and including her tax returns — would reveal more evidence of the same kind of outright thievery."

I have to admit it was all I could do to keep myself from jumping up and hugging that supercilious twit, because he'd just handed me what felt like my first major break in the case. The threats might have been an attempt to distract Faye in the hope she'd abandon her examination of Fat Farm's troubled finances, buying time for any paper trail to be cleaned up or simply destroyed. But once she'd taken the records, the jig, as they say, was up. Now there was evidently another side to this coin, because Faye had been threatening Camden that day I'd overheard her on the phone. He'd stepped out of line, and she was about to lower the boom; and it didn't sound like she was talking about calling the cops. As a motive for murder, self-preservation would have to show up on anybody's top-ten list. But to make any real sense of it, I needed to know exactly what Faye was holding over his head — sooner rather than later.

"Damn it!"

"Ms. McGrath . . ." Adolphe bristled.

"I wasn't talking to you," I said irritably. "Just thinking . . . do you still have all the Fat Farm records here?"

"Yes," he nodded.

"Why didn't you contact the police with this information when you heard about the murder?" I didn't even try to keep the criticism out of my tone.

His silvery feathers remained unruffled. "Well, now you touch on my dilemma. I had no idea if the information was relevant to the investigation. And I have a reputation to protect. I've never run into this kind of situation before, and I wasn't certain what the legal ramifications might be if I turned over confidential financial documents given to me in trust by a client to the police department without authorization or an instrument of legal compulsion such as a court order." He spread his hands, palms up, in a gesture that begged the question. "I might have exposed myself to a punitive lawsuit by Ms. Symington's estate. When you called, I was quite at sea about the matter. You fortuitously provided me with the most discreet and correct avenue to handle it." He steepled his fingers again, obviously pleased with himself and his little speech. *What a self-serving chicken-shit ass*, I thought. But he'd been a helpful ass, no question.

"I need to ask you to hold the records in trust for Ms. Landesmann for a few more days. I assume you're prepared to be officially deposed about all this?"

"Of course. I was engaged to serve Ms. Symington's interests, and I shall continue to do so." But he didn't look all that pleased with the situation.

I handed him my business card. "I may call you if other questions come up in the next day or so."

"All right," he frowned. "Do you have any idea about your time frame on this?"

"My guess is soon." I fear my smile lacked warmth.

"Very well, then," he said stiffly. "I'll wait to hear more from you or Ms. Landesmann."

I thanked him and left.

I retrieved the Toyota from the parking garage. The only thing I can say in favor of Beverly Hills, the nation's capital of conspicuous consumption, is that they've managed to provide plenty of facilities that offer two hours of free parking. As I headed back toward the office, my irritation at Sara for ditching the meeting resurfaced. But I reminded myself to cut her a break: she'd absorbed a lot of trauma — the death of her mother and the end of her marriage — all in the space of a week. More than enough to entitle her to a time-out.

When I got to Auntie Em's, the spaces behind the building were full, and I soon discovered there was not a parking place to be had within a four-block radius. I'd forgotten this was the beginning of Joyce's weekend-long "Ides of March Madness" sale. After circling the area several times with no luck, I gave up, disgusted by my own laziness. When I'd lived in Manhattan, it was nothing to walk ten or fifteen blocks to do an errand. Since I'd moved to California, I grumbled inwardly, I'd gotten soft, depending on a machine to carry me within a few steps of my destination. On that note, I drove over to the Vons supermarket on Virgil Avenue and left the Toyota at the north end of the parking lot. Then I hiked back to the office, feeling virtuous.

I peered in Auntie Em's big front window as I went around the corner to my private entrance. The store was packed with shoppers, and I could see Joyce and Gail, both wrapped in togas, laurel wreaths slightly askew, frantically bagging purchases and making change. I caught Joyce's eye and waved; she smiled happily and gave me a thumbs-up salute.

I let myself into my office, thinking as I often do upon entering that the place was long overdue for a good dusting. The usual mound of junk mail was heaped just inside the door; I groaned as I scooped it up and deposited it all in the middle of my desk. While I punched in the code for my voice mail, I gave the stack a cursory once-through and tossed the bulk of it in the wastebasket. Oh, hello! A check I'd been expecting for a month now. I'd had to hound the guy for payment, but he'd finally come through.

There was one message, from Claire Harris, asking that I return her call. I'd just tapped out her phone number when another envelope caught my eye. It was small, like a note card, and made of good quality pink paper. The return address was a label: "Landesmann" with the Malibu address printed underneath. A Friday A.M.

postmark. I hung up the phone and tore open the envelope. It contained a single sheet of matching pink paper, folded once:

> Dearest Maggie,
> I can't believe we met only a few days ago.
> Your support and compassion have helped me
> during this past awful week more than I can
> adequately express. But I have traveled as far as
> I can on this journey. There has been too much
> sadness, too much lost.
> As I write this, I am looking out over the
> sea, and I can think of nothing I long for more
> than to be enfolded by such a blessed, endless
> tranquillity. To finally sleep in oblivious peace,
> insensitive to pain. I thank you from the bottom of
> my heart for all you've done. Please don't judge
> me too harshly.
>
> Affectionately,
> S.

My throat closed in panic; I couldn't get my breath. I punched in Claire's number again, shivering with dread. I heard the receiver being lifted on the other end and didn't wait for a greeting. "Claire, it's Maggie McGrath."

"Maggie, I'm so glad —"

I cut her off. "Have you talked to Sara today?"

"Why, no," catching the tension in my voice. "What's wrong?"

"I got a letter. We have to get over there, Claire. Now. She's going to kill herself."

"Oh, my Lord."

"Go!" I shouted. "You're closer! I'll call 911 and be there as soon as I can!"

I tried to be calm as I related the situation to the emergency dispatcher, then I ran out to the car, fighting down the roiling knot of anxiety that threatened to explode in my chest. Malibu might as well have been on the other side of the universe. I shot onto the freeway dodging from one lane to the next, looking for any opening that would allow me to go faster. A morbid chill gripped me; my hands felt like blocks of ice on the steering wheel. Blood pounded in my ears and became a pulsing silent chant as I sped across town: "Please not that. Anything but that." When I finally pulled up in front of the house on Malibu Colony Drive, a sheriff's car and ambulance were already parked outside. I sprinted to the front door and hammered on it frantically. Claire opened it, her face ashen and drawn. When she saw me, she clamped both hands over her mouth and burst into tears. Suddenly unable to support my own weight, I sagged against the doorframe feeling light-headed and woozy. I reached out to her, and she collapsed in my arms.

Twenty

The next couple of hours were spent answering questions for the two sheriff's deputies. They'd arrived at the house first, and after receiving no response when they knocked on the front door, they'd gone around to the back and found the French doors to the patio standing open. Entering the house, they'd found it deserted. No sign of a struggle, no note. Nothing.

"Did she seem despondent when you left her the other morning?" This from the taller of the two, a lanky young man with curly brown hair and aviator-style glasses.

"She seemed thoughtful and a little sad. She talked about how much she missed her stepfather. But no, I didn't think she was dangerously depressed." *Or maybe you were just too preoccupied to notice*, I thought with a pang. Then I glanced over at Claire, who was staring at me in undisguised horror. I looked a question at her, but she turned away, her face an unreadable mask.

"Had she ever talked about suicide to either of you?"

We both shook our heads. Claire covered her face with her hands and began to weep again, softly.

"Is there any reason to think she might've just taken off?" the deputy persisted. "From what you've said, it sounds like she's been through a lot lately. Maybe she just needed to get away for awhile."

"I wish I could believe that," I said slowly. "And I haven't known her long enough to know her well . . ." I looked to Claire again, but she'd completely withdrawn. "Sara wasn't given to histrionics. She kept a lot inside. If she'd just disappeared, that would be one thing. But the note . . ." I closed my eyes and let out a sigh. "Is her Jeep in the garage?"

He nodded and motioned to me; I got up to walk a few steps with him.

"We'll want to keep the note she sent you," he said, squinting at the curving stretch of rocky beach to the south of us. "And you might want to fill out a missing person report. Couldn't hurt anything." He looked back at me. "We'll make a sweep along the coast for a few miles, but the currents being what they are here, depending how far out she got . . ." He shifted his eyes away from mine. "It's a goddam shame."

We might never find her, I thought with a shudder. I hated to think of her out there in that unfathomable darkness, all alone.

After the deputies had gone, I offered to drive Claire home.

"No, I think I'll stay here for a little while."

"Claire, this isn't such a good idea. Let's get you home —"

"I'm not ready to leave yet," she replied firmly, the edge of tears in her voice. She was staring out the windows toward the sea. The western sky was beginning to be tinged with a golden pink that bled into the water along the horizon.

"All right, then. We can stay for awhile," I said gently.

"Maggie, you needn't —"

"I'm not leaving you here alone." It was my turn to be firm.

She sighed. "Suddenly I'm completely exhausted." She pushed herself up from her seat and smoothed her skirt with an automatic, unnecessary gesture. "I'll make us a cup of tea, Dear."

A cup of tea. Another unnecessary gesture, a ritual pretense of comfort and order restored. But I followed her into the kitchen, grateful to escape from that wall of windows overlooking the ocean. She prepared the tea in silence. I could think of nothing meaningful to say; her attention was turned inward. I sat at a worn oak table tucked into the breakfast nook and watched her go through the motions. My brain had hit the "pause" button: I observed her activity without assigning it significance or measuring its progress, in a mental state of suspended animation. Claire set a mug of fragrant tea in front of me, and I cupped it in my hands, soothed in a small way by its warmth. We sat for some time in silence before she spoke.

"This is my fault, of course," she said in a flat voice. "I should have known she was in crisis —"

"Claire, it's pointless and destructive to blame yourself," I interrupted wearily. "You can't take responsibility for anyone else's actions."

"But I knew, you see." Her voice had dropped to a whisper. "I knew the history, and I should have seen the signs."

"Had she tried before?"

She stirred her tea, gazing at the swirling liquid in her cup. "She threatened to right after Hugh died. The poor girl was completely undone by his death. Faye even had her committed for a time."

I heard a note of disapproval.

"You thought that was a bad decision?"

Claire set her spoon down carefully and looked at me. "I thought the child needed to be cared for by people who loved her, surrounded by familiar things. Not thrust into a clinic to be scrutinized by strangers. She was grief-stricken, not insane."

"But if she was talking about suicide, Faye must have been understandably concerned. For her own welfare —"

"Faye never gave a damn about her daughter's welfare!" Claire snapped. "She turned her back on Sara years ago. All that girl ever wanted was someone to love her. And when she needed her mother's protection and guidance most, Faye turned a blind eye to the situation because that suited her own selfish purposes best."

The flesh on the back of my neck tingled unpleasantly.

"What are we talking about now, Claire?" I asked quietly.

Her eyes slid away from mine and she spoke so softly that I had to lean forward to hear her. "The relationship between Hugh Forsythe and his stepdaughter was unnatural. From the time she was just a child . . ." Her voice caught and she shook her head sadly.

"And Faye knew?" I whispered.

"From the beginning. Hugh took few pains to hide it. One day, when I was over visiting them, I wandered out to the back patio and found Sara sitting on his lap. They were having a game of tickle, and she was laughing madly — she would have been about nine at the time — and Hugh had his hands all over her. Rubbing over her chest and up between her legs. I was absolutely appalled, and I took him aside to tell him that his behavior was not only inappropriate, but confusing to a young girl. He only laughed and said Sara wasn't confused at all, and that I should mind my own business. So I went to Faye. She was furious! Not with Hugh, mind you, but me! She said she wouldn't put up with my meddling in her family, and she ordered me out of the house."

Claire's voice was thick with fresh tears. I realized I was barely breathing and looked down to find I'd torn the paper napkin in my lap to shreds.

"That was almost fifteen years ago. Faye and I never spoke again after that day. I kept in touch with the girls as best I could, but the situation was so distorted, so painful." She reached for her cup and took a small sip of tea, eyes glistening. With a sickening insight, I thought back to the picture of Forsythe and the prepubescent Sara, finally understanding why it had looked so familiar. It was very like the photograph of Forsythe and his first wife at the movie premiere.

"What about Jeri? Do you think—"

"I don't know. Probably. Jeri was younger . . ." She gestured helplessly.

"But why would Faye —"

"She had everything she'd ever wanted, and she had no intention of rocking the boat," Claire said bitterly. "A wealthy husband, plenty of good projects because of his connections, beautiful homes, clothes, the opportunity to travel, and complete freedom. Hugh made no demands and placed no restrictions on her so long as she didn't interfere."

I closed my eyes, remembering the fragile girl with the feathery voice and anxious hands who'd come to my office overwhelmed by concern. For the mother who had so wholly betrayed her trust. My instinct that day had been to reach out to protect her. Yet another unnecessary gesture, many years too late. I looked at the faded woman who sat across the table from me now. It wasn't my place to judge her, but as usual, that didn't stop me. What would I have done in her place? I couldn't honestly say. But I hoped with all my heart that I wouldn't have simply walked away.

"It's time to go, Claire," I said quietly.

This time she didn't argue.

I bypassed the office and went straight to Sav-On Drugs because liquor is a couple of bucks cheaper there than at the grocery. No sense spending more than you have to when all you want is to get thoroughly sloshed in the peace of your own home. I picked up a fifth of Stoli and a jar of chunky peanut butter (I've found peanut butter is always good for a hangover) and proceeded to the check-out. Of course, there was only one register open, and ahead of me stretched a looong line of short, squat people tending to heavily loaded carts, looking for all the world like a band of refugees fleeing with as much junk food as they could carry.

I looked around, hoping against hope to see a light blink on at another register. No dice. So I picked up a copy of *Soap Opera Digest* and amused myself by trying to pinpoint the qualities that set soap stars apart from normal people, even normal actors, for that matter. I mean, a soap hunk is pretty specific to his genre, am I right? These guys look like they should be swinging a jock strap at Chippendale's, not declaiming Shakespeare or even Neil Simon. I decided it's mostly in the teeth and hair. Soap actors seem to have a lot more of both than the rest of us.

"Hey, Maggie," called a voice down the line.

I tossed the evidence aside and peered over to see who'd busted me reading *Soap Opera Digest*.

"Oh, hey, Rick," I smiled wanly.

The boy cleaned up well. He was wearing black jeans and a light blue sweater that brought out his eyes. I, on the other hand, looked like a slob.

"You live around here?" I asked. "Hasn't anyone told you this is an unsavory neighborhood?"

The grin he gave me was a heart-stopper. "I've been here for about six months. I'm house-sitting for a buddy of mine who's doing a TV series up in Canada. Until Lynn and I can figure out what we're doing about the house." He shrugged, and the grin faded.

I'd miraculously reached the head of the line, so my attention was diverted while I paid for my stuff. I turned to wave, and he said, "Wait up for a minute, okay?"

Trapped. Trapped like a bedraggled rat under unflattering fluorescent lights. This is what I get, I thought bitterly, for not paying closer attention to personal grooming every single solitary second of my life.

Rick was buying a carton of Camels.

"Those things are like gold now," I said. "What is it, something like thirty-five dollars a carton?"

"Yeah, guess it's about time to quit."

I held up my bag of treats. "Well, between the two of us, we've got several of the most important vices covered."

"So, were you just headed home?" he asked.

"Pretty much."

"Anybody waiting for you?"

"Nope."

He nudged me with an elbow. "You plannin' on drinking all that vodka by yourself?"

"I plan on making a sizeable dent in it," I said too brightly.

He put a hand on my arm. "Rough day?"

The simple gesture nearly undid me. "Yeah, you could say that."

"Well, I was thinking about having a drink myself, but I don't much like drinking alone. You want to go someplace and talk a little while? I'm buying," he added quickly.

"Since you put it that way . . ."

I followed him over on Hyperion to a little place called The Flying Leap Cafe. Inside there was a small oak bar and about a dozen tables. Also a four-foot model of a red bi-plane hanging from the ceiling.

"The food's pretty good," Rick said, steering me to a table in the back, "and the people who run it are very cool."

"I'm not really hungry," I said. Ever the gracious lady.

"Well, I am," he said, "and you might just change your mind once you've seen the menu."

We sat in a back corner and ordered drinks, a Red Wolf Ale for him, a double vodka for me. I was determined to stick to my plan of getting shit-faced.

He touched his glass to mine. "To new friends."

"New friends," I murmured. I felt detached, as if I were hovering just above my body, observing the situation. "So, how are you feeling about things?"

"Not bad." He shrugged and set his glass down with a tap. "It's been going on for so long now, I've had a chance to get used to it gradually."

"You have children?"

"No. She never wanted any. Now I think that's maybe just as well. I don't know if I could handle it if there were kids involved. How about you?"

"Kids? No." I shook my head. "I wouldn't want to inflict myself on innocent children. They'd end up as ax murderers."

He laughed. I guess he thought I was trying to be funny. "And, so, how are you doing?" he asked.

"Fine."

"Really?"

I ran a hand through my hair. "Really, I don't know. It's been a hard day." I took a gulp of my drink and shivered at the 80-proof bite of it. "I think I lost a friend."

"You feel like talking about it?" he asked.

A wave of heat, part sorrow, part shame, rushed through me, and I stood suddenly, toppling my glass over. "Damn, now look what I've done." I grabbed my napkin and started mopping up the mess, then sat back down and burst into tears.

Rick was beside me. "It's okay," he said and put his arms around me. I buried my face on his shoulder, and he stroked my hair, humming something soothing, like a lullaby. It made his chest rumble and took me back to a time I only half-remembered, sitting on my father's lap while he sang to me. "You okay?" he asked, and I realized I'd stopped crying.

"Oh. Yeah." I pulled away from him and wiped my eyes. "Sorry about that."

"Don't be." He handed me his napkin so I could blow my nose.

"Well, I'll bet this has gone a long way toward cheering you up."

"Come here."

He kissed me gently. His lips were soft, and he tasted like cold dark ale.

"Let's get you home," he said.

He followed me over to my house. I held the metal gate for him, then unlocked the front door and turned on a lamp by the couch. He walked over to the windows.

"Beautiful view."

A pale moon and Venus dangled over Hollywood.

He turned back to me. "You going to be okay if I go?"

I reached out and took his hand. "You don't have to go."

He looked at me and smiled. "You're a sweet woman."

"Well, that just proves how —"

He put a finger against my lips. "Don't joke about this," he said. "You use sarcasm to keep your distance." He raised his eyebrows.

"I plead the Fifth."

"But if I stayed here tonight . . ." He shook his head. "It's not the right time for either one of us."

I stood back and stared at him with my hands on my hips. "Are you for real?"

He smiled crookedly. "I'll probably be kicking myself all the way home."

"Well, I should hope so."

He kissed me again at the door. "I think we're signing the papers next week. The divorce papers." He cleared his throat. "Would it be okay if I called you sometime soon? Maybe we could actually sit down and eat a meal together next time."

I wanted to shriek, *When? When?*

"I'd like that," I said.

He turned to go, then shook his head and turned back to give me a hug. "Go easy on the Stoli, okay?" he whispered in my ear.

"Okay," I said softly as I watched him walk down the hill to his car, blonde hair shining silver in the moonlight.

Twenty-One

On Sunday the haze was back, veiling the hills of Silverlake and nearly obscuring the buildings of the downtown skyline. The bleak and colorless morning was the mirror of my spirits. I'd hardly slept, but the coldness of the light when it finally came did little to encourage me to leap out of bed to greet the new day. Depression weighted my limbs and sapped my energy. I still hoped Sara would turn up alive, but I knew the truth was, she'd been destroyed long ago: she'd never had a chance. What was the point of getting up to participate in a world where people so routinely brutalized and damaged one another?

A quick inventory of my options did not, however, supply me with a desirable alternative. Heaving myself out of bed, I padded directly to the shower and stood underneath a pelting stream of hot water. Half an hour later, washed, fluffed, combed, and dressed, I set out for the office. Moping would accomplish nothing. It was time once more to pull myself up by my fraying mental bootstraps and get on with the business at hand.

It was still early, and all was quiet at Auntie Em's. I parked behind the building, feeling a syrupy surge of gratitude for the comfort of routine, for my cubbyhole of a workplace, even for the layer of dust that coated every surface and object in the office. I got busy making a pot of coffee. Then, fortified by the prospect of caffeine on my horizon, I thought about how to proceed.

The more I learned about Faye, the less I was saddened by her passing, but I had promised her daughter I'd try to find the person responsible, and I was determined not to be another in the long line of people who'd abandoned Sara. If anything, her death would render that promise more binding.

I picked up the phone and called information for Truckee, California. Then I poured a cup of coffee before trying the number for the Moose Head Lodge. A man's voice answered, roughened some by age but still vigorous and deep.

"May I please speak with Ben Hudson?"

"You got him," he rumbled.

"Mr. Hudson, this is Maggie McGrath. I'm a detective working in association with the Los Angeles Police Department on a murder investigation. (Okay, not completely kosher, I admit, but I was willing to go out on that ethically questionable limb if it got me some answers.) "Do you have a minute to talk with me now, sir?"

"Mebbe."

"I'd like to ask you some questions about your nephew and former employee, Raymond Cicelli."

I thought I heard his breath catch, then there was a long pause.

"Mr. Hudson?" I prompted.

"Is Ray okay?" he finally asked.

"Yes, he's fine."

He hung up.

Damn the old scofflaw! Was that any way to respond to an official police inquiry? I banged out the number on the phone pad again.

"Moose Head Lodge."

"Mr. Hudson, I don't think you appreciate the seriousness —"

He slammed the phone down with a deafening report that made my ear flinch. Muttering obscenities, I flipped to "Airlines" in my rolodex and called the toll-free number for Reno Air. I was expecting one of those annoying recordings that gives you a list of eighteen confusing options, so I was thrown when a human voice coming from a live female person answered.

"Reno Air."

"Oh! Hi! Uh, do you fly to Truckee, California, or Lake Tahoe?"

"No, ma'am," she replied, her tone tinged with regret on my behalf.

"Do you know if any commercial carrier flies into either of those cities?"

"I don't think so," she said doubtfully, "but let me check for you."

I dug out my Master Card while I waited.

"Ma'am, Reno is the closest commercial airport to both those destinations."

"How far is it from Reno to Truckee?"

"About forty-five miles."

I booked a flight leaving at noon, then put in a call to Sylvia Forsythe. She was an interesting conundrum, living over there in that parallel universe of hers. Still, I could've sworn she'd been working me some. But whether or not she was completely nuts or just angling me, her stance had proved an effective dodge: I hadn't gotten much out of her at all. And yet, I caught myself feeling vaguely guilty about getting her all stirred up; that episode had been real enough. I must have let the phone ring at least twenty times to give her the chance to notice it over the clamor of her television, but there was no answer, and I promised myself I'd check in on her when I got back from Truckee. I have to admit my motives weren't all that altruistic — I still wanted to talk to her son.

At LAX's Lot B for long-term parking I left the Toyota by a light pole with the two-fold hope of discouraging vandals and giving myself a leg-up when it came time to find it again; then I caught the shuttle to the terminal. By some miracle the plane took off on time, and I went immediately to sleep. Air travel always acts like a sedative on me: no matter what the time of day or my general state of wakefulness when I board, as soon as the plane is airborne, I'm snoozing.

We landed at Reno International Airport at around 1:45. Still groggy from my nap, I deplaned to a rude awakening — the terminal was a bilious green hive of frenetic activity and noise. Everywhere I looked there were slot machines whirring, dinging, and clanging. At the end of the gangway a hugely fat woman was staked out in front of one on a metal stool that looked challenged by her bulk. Her hair had been tortured into a platinum beehive that stood a good six inches high, gleaming under a coat of spray lacquer. She wore yellow shorts hiked up on her thighs to reveal a considerable acreage of dimpled white flesh and a bright red T-shirt that blared I GOT MINE IN RENO — THE BIGGEST LITTLE CITY IN THE WEST. I shuddered to think what that meant. A blue plastic bucket of quarters was balanced on one pale plump knee, and she was flinging coins in the slot and yanking on the mechanical arm with a fierce concentration that gave me the creeps. I could smell her sour tension sweat as I hurried past and plunged into the thick pall of cigarette smoke that hung in the air. I was in Marlboro country now — with a vengeance.

A low-rent cousin to Las Vegas, Reno is as ugly a city as you could ever hope to avoid visiting; it strikes me as the kind of place people go when they can't afford a real vacation. Everything about it screams "second-rate," from the $1.99 all-you-can-eat salad bars awash in iceburg lettuce and freeze-dried bacon bits to the cut-rate rooms where all the furniture is bolted to the floor. They even skimped on the neon, so at night Reno's strip glows with all the magical appeal of a down-at-the-heels red-light district.

I went straight to Enterprise Rent-a-Car and by 2:15 was on the road in a purple vehicle optimistically called an Aspire, which I promptly rechristened "Expire." It was about the size of a dog cart with no power steering and a wheezing air conditioner that spit more water than cool air. I steered the car (not without considerable effort) onto I395 North and sped away from Reno as fast as four gasping cylinders could carry me. Once I got out on the open road, the surrounding countryside was beautiful — a vista of unspoiled mountains and clear skies — something we don't see much of anymore in Southern California.

I transitioned to I80 heading west, pondering the question of how to best approach Ben Hudson when I arrived unannounced on his doorstep, the fly in the ointment being I had no idea what kind of man he was. Was his nephew a renegade from the family fold or a chip off the old block? I might have done better to put in a little time checking up on the uncle first, but there was no help for it now. I'd just have to play it as I saw it when the time came.

After a drive of about forty minutes through densely wooded landscape with a backdrop of picture-perfect mountains, I pulled into Truckee proper and stopped at a Unocal station. The car hadn't used much gas, but I refilled it anyway, then nipped into the station's little convenience market for a couple bottles of spring water and one of those pre-packaged tuna salad sandwiches, the kind that come in the white plastic triangle with the window of cellophane across the end. Completely nutrition-free. One of the secrets I won't share with even my closest friends is that I love those sandwiches. The heavy-set woman behind the cash register had a broad, pleasant face and permed hair that clung to her skull like a cap of tightly coiled springs. She wore an oversized denim shirt with a bolo tie sporting a piece of turquoise carved in the shape of the state of California as its slide mechanism. While she was making change for my purchases, I asked her for directions to the Moose Head Lodge.

She gave me a quizzical smile. "Are you plannin' to stay there, Honey?"

"Possibly."

"Well, I don't mean to be tellin' you what to do," she said with a doubtful shake of her head, "but there's lots nicer places nearby and no more expensive."

"I appreciate your concern," I smiled, trying not to sound impatient, "but I particularly want to get a look at the Moose Head Lodge. I work in the film industry, and we're considering it as a potential location for a movie."

Sometimes the lies just seem to make themselves up.

Her eyes flew wide open. "What movie are you all doin'?"

"I'm not supposed to say," I demurred. But she looked so disappointed that I leaned over the counter and whispered, "But it's for Tom Cruise's production company, if that gives you a clue."

"Oh, I love him!" she squealed, jiggling with excitement.

I touched a forefinger to my lips in warning; she mimed pulling a zipper across her mouth in response.

"Now, Ma'am, how do I get to the Moose Head Lodge?"

Darla Jenkins (that was the cashier's name) was very sweet and most helpful. She drew what proved to be quite an accurate map of the route out to the Moose Head Lodge, which was located on the northwest edge of Truckee. As I drove toward my destination, I felt a prickle of regret about fibbing to her. But for now it seemed advisable to cleave to the better part of valor as a matter of course.

On the outskirts of town, I turned onto a winding two-lane road that led into an undeveloped, heavily forested area. After about half a mile, just as Darla had told me, I saw on my right a simple painted wooden sign: MOOSE HEAD LODGE. One side of the sign had been shaped like a pointer and was positioned to indicate a narrow asphalt road ascending the side of a mountain. The Expire coughed up the precipitous incline and just as I thought it might give up, hurtling me back down the slope, I pulled into a level clearing in front of a large two-story building made of hand-hewn logs. The roof, steeply pitched with dormers that looked out from the second story, was bracketed by two rough stone chimneys. A glassed-in sun porch spanned the front of the structure. A breeze whispered in the branch-tops of the beautiful old pine trees that crowded up next to the lodge, cloaking the surrounding property in sun-dappled shadow. Undisturbed by my intrusion, a couple of squirrels were enjoying a raucous game of tag, but a blue jay of monstrous proportions and brilliant plumage cursed me heartily with indignant, rasping squawks.

I found it all completely delightful.

The only other vehicle in sight was an old Ford 4x4 truck covered with a patina of fine dirt and so bleached and rusted that its original color had been transformed to a soft, uncertain shade of brown. I noticed a scattering of outbuildings, probably cabins available to guests who craved more privacy, although, judging by the deserted grounds, privacy was not a gripping concern here.

I climbed the front steps and entered the lodge through the sun porch, which was furnished with substantial angular wooden chairs liberally strewn with cushions covered in heavy, bright fabrics that made me think of Hudson Bay blankets and lumberjacks' shirts. Beyond the porch was a large open room with a high raw-beamed ceiling. A worn sofa and two easy chairs were arranged in a conversational grouping beside a massive stone fireplace that dominated the wall on my left. Straight ahead was a wide wooden staircase with a carved balustrade leading to the second floor. The dark wooden reception desk for check-in was on my right. I was relieved to see no evidence of an actual moose head on the premises.

On a counter behind the check-in desk stood a wooden rack divided into pigeon-holes to hold the keys and messages for each room. It was apparently a slow day for messages, but there were lots of keys. The lodge was obviously not a busy establishment, but despite the want of bustle, its atmosphere bespoke more tranquillity than disuse.

I still hadn't encountered a single soul. No one was at the front desk, so I helloed up the stairs and down the hall that ran alongside the staircase toward the back of the building. Then I tried ringing the bell sitting on top of the desk beside a hand-lettered sign requesting "Please Ring Bell for Service." Nothing.

Presently I heard a door close somewhere at the back of the lodge. Heavy footsteps approached, and a man in his late sixties came in from the hall. He wore no-nonsense work boots, jeans, a denim jacket, and a black cowboy hat. His face was as creased and leathery as a piece of beef jerky but his blue eyes glowed like two beacons shining from a lighthouse.

"Well, hello there!" he greeted me. "You been waitin' long?"

"Not so terribly."

"Why didn't you ring the bell?"

"I did."

"Oh." He grinned sheepishly. "I was out back — guess I just didn't hear. You lookin' for a place to stay?" he asked, looking at me skeptically.

He removed his hat, revealing a luxuriant thicket of gray hair trimmed close at the back of his neck. There was something about him — a physical ease, an air he projected of self-confidence and good-will — he was an extremely attractive man.

I didn't know what to say. I opened my mouth but nothing came out, so I clamped it shut again in the manner of a fish-out-of-water gasping for air. So much for the "play it as you see it when the time comes" school of thought. My confusion was compounded by the tell-tale tingling in my cheeks that told me I was blushing.

He chuckled sympathetically but misinterpreted the symptoms. "The place is mighty quiet. I don't wonder you'd have second thoughts. I can't compete with the fancy ski resorts. Don't want to. I run a place for folks who want to get away from all that touristy crap, 'scuse my language. Wouldja like a glass of lemonade?"

I nodded dumbly, and he motioned toward the sun porch. "Why don't you go sit out there, and I'll get a coupla glasses for us."

I did as I was told, selecting a chair cushioned with multi-colored pillows, and sat gazing out at the clearing with the late afternoon sun's slanting rays streaming through the branches of the trees. I would have been happy to sit there all afternoon — or all week, for that matter. The serenity of the spot liquefied my thoughts, bringing the same profound sense of peace I felt when I painted. And for the first time since the break-in, I found myself longing at the soul-level for canvas and brushes. He returned shortly and handed me a glass full of ice and tart lemonade. I fished out a slice of fresh lemon and chewed it, thinking how to begin.

"So what brings you all the way out here, young lady? Something tells me this isn't an entirely recreational visit," he said, smiling.

"Why, you old fox!" I blurted.

He laughed, a deep, rich baritone.

I shook my head, laughing in spite of myself. "Excuse me. I didn't mean to be so fresh."

"No offense taken," he assured me, his eyes twinkling. "I like it when pretty young women get fresh with me. Doesn't happen nearly often enough to suit me."

"Maggie McGrath," I said, extending my hand.

"Ben Hudson." And as he took my hand, I could tell he was trying to remember where he'd heard my name before.

I was sorry to have to spoil our rapport. "I'm the investigator who called you this morning from Los Angeles. About your nephew."

"Ahhhh . . ." He withdrew from me instinctively. "I had you pegged for a realtor. They keep wantin' to buy this parcel up for a condo development. Come to think of it, though, they aren't gen'rally so polite."

"I'm sorry to ambush you this way, Sir, truly —"

"Call me Ben, Maggie." He looked at me calmly, his merry eyes now very serious. Not as friendly as before, but not hostile, either.

"Ben," I amended, "a few days ago a young woman came to see me, terribly upset because of some anonymous threats her mother had been getting, and she asked me to help find out who was responsible. The very next night, her mother was murdered, and the circumstances point to the killer being someone she knew." I hesitated under his steady gaze. Even though I'd met him only a few minutes before, I liked this man. "Your nephew worked for the murdered woman. He manages a restaurant she owned. And he's been stealing from her, embezzling money from the business. There is positive documentation. She'd discovered that and was about to take action against him."

Ben sighed and ran a hand over his face. None of this seemed to take him by surprise, but I could tell it hit him hard, anyway. He suddenly looked old. "You think he killed her."

"I think it's possible," I said carefully. "The day she died, I overheard her arguing on the telephone with someone called Robert — he goes by the name Robert Camden now. It sounded to me like she was accusing and threatening him."

The pain in his eyes told me I'd opened an old wound, and I felt a pang of regret that made me look away. He reached over and took my hand. "None of this is your fault," he said gently. "He never has been any good, and I've known for a long time it'd fin'lly come to this."

He sat gazing into space for a moment or two, absently rubbing my hand. Then he blinked and came back from wherever his thoughts had wandered. He patted my hand and let it go. "What is it you want to know?"

"What is your nephew's real name?"

"You had it right when you called up here. His name's Raymond Cicelli. He's my sister's boy."

"Was he working for you here before he went to L.A.?"

"For a time," he nodded.

"What name was he using at that point?"

"He was already callin' himself Robert Camden by then."

"Why is he using an alias, Ben? He lied about his employment record when he went to work for my client. What's he hiding?"

Ben started to say something, then shook his head. He sat so still for so long I thought maybe he wasn't going to answer at all, but then he threw me an agitated glance and got up to pace over to the windows at the far end of the sun porch. "Ray's tryin' to hide from himself — that's about what it amounts to. It'll all catch up to him, though. Only a matter of time. The boy never learned that," he said softly, "and now it's too late." He ran a hand through his hair. "I'm just grateful Marie's not alive to see it. Lord knows he gave her enough heartache while she was here."

I sat quietly, content to let him tell it in his own way, his own time.

"We grew up in Northern California, and there was just the two of us, my sister and me. Both our folks died when we was youngsters, and our ma's brother took us in. He didn't know much about kids, but he did his best, I guess. Anyways, Marie and me was always close." He sighed and came over to sit down beside me again. "But then she got married and went out East to live. Never did think much of her husband. Ray's their only kid and, like I said, he was a bad 'un from the get-go. Always in some kinda trouble — shoplifitin' and petty vandalism when he was a youngster. They couldn't control 'im. Marie hoped he'd outgrow it . . ."

He shrugged and shook his head again. "But it just got worse, the older he got. Stealin' cars and dealin' drugs — anything to keep from doin' an honest day's work. It broke Marie's heart. She sent 'im out to me one summer when he was in high school. I had a workin' ranch back then. The kid damned near burnt my barn down, just out of boredom and spite. I washed my hands of 'im then. Sent him packin'."

Ben stopped, caught by the past. The sun was low in the sky now; it was twilight in the clearing. "My sister passed away shortly after that, and I never heard another word from Ray till he showed up here a little more'n four years ago, askin' me to take 'im in." Off my troubled expression, "I know what you're thinkin', but he was scared. I could see that right off, even though he handed me some bullshit story 'bout how he quit his job back East. Said he come out here to make amends since we're all the fam'ly each other's got and to start over." He smiled grimly. "I told 'im he better start bein' straight with me or he'd find himself out the door on his behind just 'bout right away. And he started to cry." Ben's voice was surprised and tender at the recollection. "He cried like a baby and he fin'lly told the truth. His drug dealin' 'd got him noticed early on back in New Jersey. Some local hoods come callin' and off'red 'im the choice of a job with them or a pair of cement shoes." He shrugged philosophically. "Now, I'm sure Ray was happy enough to go to work for those folks. And he must've done a damn fine job for 'em 'cause it got 'im noticed again. Only this time they moved 'im out to Las Vegas and give 'im a casino to run. But then Ray got greedy."

I winced.

"Yeah, well, the boy's no rocket scientist. He started a little free-lance drug business on the side financed by skimmin' from the casino. And it sounds like his bosses were just gettin' ready to fit him with those cement shoes they'd talked about before when the Federals picked 'im up. Seems he'd been dealin' to one of their agents, and they had 'im big as life on all kinds of videotape."

"Oh, my God!"

"You're not kiddin'. They laid out his options, real clear and simple. And he turned like the worm he's always been."

"Can't say I blame him."

Ben tipped his head to one side, acknowledging my point. "They stuck 'im in that federal witness protection program. He testified against his bosses, made the cases that put away some big-time criminals, to hear him tell it. And when it was over, the Federals give 'im a new name, a house, a car — hell, they even got 'im a job. But then somethin' went wrong." Ben's open expression clouded over. "Someone got paid their price is what happened, and one day when Ray got home, those boys from Vegas was waitin' for 'im."

"Oh, shit."

"Yeah, you could def'nitely say that. So, that's when he come to me. He had no place else to go, no one else he could trust."

"No corner of the world that was safe for him," I murmured.

He stirred restlessly again and got up to cross back to the windows. "I don't know how he got away from 'em. Prob'ly left a body or two behind. That part I didn't care to know." His gaze was distant, haunted by memory and loss. "He's my sister's boy. I couldn't turn 'im away."

"Of course you couldn't," I said softly.

Ben looked back over his shoulder at me. "I knew he wouldn't stay. He hated the isolation. Hated the quiet. Started up with his old ways, started chasin' women. Not that I've really got anything 'gainst that," he winked at me. "But he got 'imself mixed up with a coupla real gem-stones. That one from Los Ang'les, 'specially. Whooeee! What a bitch!"

"I couldn't agree with you more heartily. Did Lillian come up here often?"

"That's right. Lillian." He smiled to himself. "Funny I couldn't recall 'er name. Nature takin' care of me, I expect. But yeah, she come up here ev'ry coupla weeks for 'bout six months. Then Ray took off. Said she was gonna set 'im up in bus'ness. Asked me for a stake to get 'im down there." He snorted scornfully. "I told 'im all he'd get from me was a swift kick in the butt if he didn't have inny better sense'n to mess with trash like that."

"Have you been in touch with him since he went to Los Angeles?"

"Not a peep."

I nodded, wondering how much Lillian actually knew about Camden's extra-legal activities — and how far she might go to help cover for him.

Ben leaned against the doorframe and folded his arms, staring out into the clearing and the gathering dusk. "Well, that's all water under the bridge now. Can't do nothin' about it. Never could." He looked at me kindly. "You've gotta be whipped; you've prob'ly been on the road all day. I'm pretty handy with the grill, and I got a coupla nice steaks that need cookin'."

I considered it. There was nothing I would have liked better than to stay in that lovely, tranquil place, to have a good meal in good company, and forget about the mess in L.A. — at least for one night. But the pull to go back was almost physical, like someone tugging at my sleeve. "Could I have a rain check? I feel like I need to get back, and I can make the eight-fifteen flight if I leave now."

He walked me out to the purple horror. Taking my hand, he kissed me gently on the forehead. "You be careful, now."

"I'll call you when I have any news about all this. And thanks, Ben."

"You're welcome here anytime, young lady. Remember that," he said gruffly.

For once, I couldn't sleep on the plane, so I kept turning it all over in my mind on the way home .If she'd managed to ferret out the details of his past, as she seemed to have done, then Camden certainly had plenty of reasons to want Faye dead. Too bad I didn't have anything even resembling a shred of evidence. Aside from that, I had to wonder who else stood to profit from her death, especially if Sara was out of the way now. That thought sent a chill rippling through me. Add to that the Galen Landesmann wild card. I still didn't see a motive there, but he had disappeared right after the murder. But then, he and Sara clearly had a very shaky marriage, and Galen had a weak character. Not a propitious combination. Coward that he was, he'd probably simply chosen that moment of confusion as a smokescreen to grab what money he could and slip away. There were a couple more things I wanted to check out. Then I'd take the information I'd gathered to Donleavy and let him decide what to do with it. At the very least, Camden could be charged with embezzlement. That was something. *But it's not justice,* that stubborn little voice rattling round my brain argued. *Not if he killed her.*

Twenty-Two

I was still wired when we landed at LAX, and since I was already on the west side of town, I decided to make a small detour on the way home. Which is why I was parked on Alta Avenue in Santa Monica at eleven o'clock that night, just down the block from the fake Georgian monstrosity of a house where Lillian lived. You've seen the kind of thing: all the proper stylistic components are there but modernized and in skewed proportions yielding a hideous result. The house was too large for the tiny patch of grass that passed for a yard; the white columns studding its facade were spindly and graceless. But the tinted windows were easily the worst features: the dark gaping panes made the house look more like a bank.

But that night I wasn't interested in the aesthetic shortcomings of the place as I contemplated the scene. No gold Mercedes in the driveway; no lights on in the house. There was probably an alarm system, but I figured I'd have a good ten minutes after I set it off before the security guys showed up. And then all I had to do was be cool. It had happened to me once before at a friend's house: I'd tripped the alarm when I went in to water his plants because I had the wrong security code. When the patrol came to investigate, I showed them my driver's license and explained the situation. No big deal. I could always say I was staying with Lillian while my house was being fumigated. I didn't think she'd be eager to press charges once she and I had a chat about her relationship with Camden.

The moon was obscured by overcast, the street in this upscale neighborhood well-lit but deserted. I flipped the glove compartment open to dig out my Swiss Army knife and a flashlight. I stuck the knife in my pocket, then got out of the car clutching the flashlight at my side and walked purposefully toward Lillian's front door, like a friend paying a visit. As a precautionary measure I rang the doorbell. If Lillian was at home, I preferred to find out before I broke in, though I hadn't a clue as to what I'd say if she actually opened the door. Maybe something like "Here, Lillian, I've brought you a flashlight." That had a friendly ring to it.

The files in her office, which she'd said was in her house, were my objective. It was time to find out more about Lillian and her business. And I wasn't above using any guilty knowledge I might soon acquire as leverage with her. She could be the key I needed. I was willing to lay odds that she knew all about Camden's thieving; if her lover was a murderer, I had to believe she knew that, too. But the prospect of a grimly unfashionable future garbed in those unflattering prison schmattas might be just the incentive she needed to convince her to come clean and make a deal.

When there was no answer to the bell I trotted around to the back of the house, where a granite tiled patio led to a set of sliding glass doors. That's right — sliding glass doors in a house modeled on eighteenth-century architecture. But I was happy to see them because they're a cinch to get into. I opened the knife and slid one of the blades into the lock mechanism, jiggling it up and down until I felt the catch release. Then I slowly eased the door open, steeling myself for the whooping assault of the alarm. But nothing happened.

"Could be a silent alarm, so don't get cocky, McGrath," I muttered.

Once inside, I switched on the flashlight. I'd entered a sitting room of sorts. An entertainment center with a stereo system, TV, VCR, and about a million videotapes filled one wall. I followed the connecting hallway past the kitchen to a circular entryway at the front of the house. Like one of those traffic rotaries dreamed up by some highway engineer from hell, the rest of the rooms on the first floor spun off from this central point. I checked the alarm key pad by the front door. I needn't have worried — it wasn't armed.

Viewing the layout like the points on a clock with the front door at 6:00, the living room was at 3:00, the hall I'd come from at 1:00, a stairway leading to the second floor at 12:00, and at 11:00 and 9:00, two doors that were closed. I opened the one nearest the stairs. The room was dominated by a large oak desk that sat in front of one of those God-awful tinted windows. I closed the door behind me and padded across the thick plush carpet for a closer look. On either side of the desk were two file drawers, locked tight. I started with the top one on the left and jimmied it open with my knife. I didn't know exactly what I was looking for, but three files labeled "Symington Taxes" for '97, '98, and '99 caught my eye because of Adolphe's speculation on the subject. I pulled the bulging folders out and was just beginning to sort through the first one when I heard the front door open, then slam.

Shit!

I slid the drawer shut and looked around frantically for an escape route. Heels clicked in the entryway. There was a door to my right. I yanked it open — a supply closet. No time to quibble. There was just enough room for me to squeeze into the shallow space and pull the door closed. I was standing in front of shelves filled with binders, legal pads, manila envelopes, and the like. I only hoped Lillian wouldn't come looking for a box of stationery.

I heard the door to the office open, then the lights flicked on. Footfalls muffled by carpet crossed to the desk. I held my breath, hoping she wouldn't notice the file drawer. She picked up the phone and punched in a number.

"Bob, I don't know if you're screening your calls, but if you're there, you'd better damned well pick up," she said, her voice dripping icicles. *Tsk, tsk, tsk, Lillian.* I wanted to tell her she'd catch a lot more flies with a little bit of honey.

A short pause, then, more plaintively, "Bob, this isn't fair. You promised we'd see each other tonight. Call me the minute you get in no matter what time it is. We have to talk about these partnership papers. I did a helluva job on

Faye's signature, if I do say so myself, but — Oh!" She cried out in surprise. I heard her drop the receiver back in its cradle.

"My God, you startled me!" Now she was speaking to someone in the office. "Why haven't you returned any of my phone calls?" And she was annoyed. From her tone, I guessed it was the wayward paramour. This eavesdropping thing was really working out for me. I pressed my ear to the door, hoping for a long, enlightening discussion.

Then, fearfully, "What are you — ? What?!"

Two gunshots rang out in rapid succession. Like an idiot, I burst out of the closet.

"N-O-O-O-O!!"

Running footsteps charged out the front door. I didn't get so much as a glimpse of the retreating figure. I grabbed the phone and hit 911, then bent over Lillian. She was lying behind her desk, a crumpled heap already awash in blood. The two bullets had hit her squarely in the chest. She reached toward me spasmodically, a drowning creature clutching at the last shreds of life as they slipped through her fingers. She was breathing in shallow, wet gasps, choking on her own blood.

I grasped her hand. "Who did this to you?"

"Nine-one-one operator."

"A woman's been shot. Sixteen thirty-two Alta Avenue in Santa Monica. Get them here now. She's dying."

"They're on their way. What's your name?"

"Just get them here. First floor, front of the house. The room to the left of the stairs." I repeated the address.

But Lillian was already dead. Her grip went slack; unfocused eyes stared up at me looking flat and opaque now that the soul was gone. I laid her hand at her side and leaned over to press my fingers against her neck, checking for a pulse, knowing I wouldn't find one. I stood up and started to go out front to wait for the paramedics and police. Then I saw the gun. I couldn't believe it. How could he have been so careless? I must've really scared him, popping out of the closet like some demented jack-in-the-box. It was a Smith and Wesson .38 caliber revolver, with a customized black rubber hand grip.

Then I did something that went against every iota of investigative training I'd ever received. Something unthinkable at the undocumented scene of a homicide. I went over and picked up the gun.

Because I knew it was mine.

Damn it! How could *I* have been so careless? The gun had been taken days ago when my house was vandalized, but I hadn't even noticed. Or reported the theft. Now it was a murder weapon, and there I was conveniently helping to set myself up by not getting the hell out of there. No way was I going to hang around to try and talk my way out of this one.

Using the hem of my shirttail, I swiped over the phone, file drawer, and doorknobs, then I hauled ass down the brick walk in front to my car. This was no time for delicate subterfuge. I jumped in the Toyota and gunned it out of the parking space, not caring which direction I was going so long as it was away from Alta Avenue. I drove blindly toward the beach, stopping only when I got to the sandy edge of the parking lot at the end of Rose Avenue by the board-walk in Venice.

All the shops and restaurants were closed for the night; the whole area was deserted except for the homeless people who live on the beach. Two shadowy shapes crouched at the base of a palm tree, probably sharing a bottle or a cig-arette. I sat in my car staring out at the Pacific, breathing in the sharp sea air. There were a couple of big ships out in the bay, but the night was so dark I could barely make out their silhouettes against the horizon. Off to the south the sweeping curve of the coastline was outlined by the glittering tracery of the lights of Santa Monica.

What to do, what to do? We had some trouble now, Girlfriend. Lillian's killer had hoped to get two birds with one stone, and he might have managed to do just that with a little help from this particular pigeon. I knew I should get rid of the gun, but I was suddenly feeling the need to hang onto it for my own protection. My aversion to the little sucker was receding swiftly before the incoming tide of convenient morality. I didn't like being on the defensive. Not one bit. It scared me. It also pissed me off. I looked at my watch. Nearly 1:00 A.M. My nerves were sending shock waves through my system. I was closing in on complete physical and mental exhaustion. I didn't think it was smart to go home, but I needed a place to rest. I was panicked to still be so far from the truth with a rapidly mounting body count and a killer who was outsmarting me at every turn. I got on the freeway going east, back to Silverlake and checked into the Elysian Motel, a shabby little dive just off Sunset. After a long hot shower, I climbed into bed between sheets as cool and rough as two pieces of paper. But sleep was a long time coming. I lay staring at the plastic curtains of the room's only window until dawn seeped in around the edges. Then I didn't drift off so much as pass out.

Twenty-Three

I went out early the next morning to the twenty-four hour Thrifty drugstore on Vermont Avenue and bought several pairs of underwear printed with teddy bears, some socks, and a couple of T-shirts. I picked up a bagel and coffee, then returned to the Elysian.

"Claire, this is Maggie McGrath," I said when she answered the phone.

"Oh, Maggie, I'm so glad you called! Have you heard about Lillian?" Claire sounded hoarse and a little hysterical.

"No. What's happened?"

"She was murdered last night! Shot to death in her own house!"

"Do they know who did it?"

"I don't think so. The police came over to talk to me this morning. Those same two detectives who came to the house after Faye was killed."

"Donleavy and Ames." I winced, thinking about the 911 tape. Would Donleavy be able to recognize my voice? I rubbed my suddenly clammy palms on my jeans.

"It's so awful! I didn't like the woman, but nobody deserves to die like that! And Faye and Sara . . . I just feel like the whole world is falling to pieces!" she wept.

"It's been a horrible time, Claire. I wish I could think of something to say that would make it better," I said, feeling as lame as I sounded.

By now she was crying so hard she could barely get the words out. "They found Sara yesterday."

"Oh God." I felt the blood drain out of my brain, and I dropped my head between my knees.

"I tried to reach you —"

"Yes, I'm sorry. Some things have come up," I said vaguely, willing myself to focus. "Where did they find her?"

"Someone walking along the beach near Trancas," she said through her tears. "Gina went with me to see her. They warned us it would be difficult, but I had to. Oh, Maggie, that beautiful girl! They took us into a little room with a television hanging from the ceiling, then they put her up on the screen. I couldn't believe it was really happening. My poor, sweet girl. It was the most awful thing I've ever seen."

I could well imagine. I closed my eyes, swallowing bile. Bodies that have been floating are worked on by the water in a way that's ghastly and distinctive. The fatty tissues puff up in a poisonous bloat, and with time, little by little and cell by cell, are transformed into a yellowish waxy substance called adipocere. It's hard to accept such a sight was once a human being — even before the marine scavengers go to work.

"They're positive it's Sara?"

"Gina fetched the records from her dentist. But I knew . . ." Her breath caught. "I knew because she was wearing the sweater I made for her two Christmases ago."

"The one with the heart on the sleeve," I said faintly.

"How did you know?"

"She was wearing it the last time I saw her. I'm so sorry, Claire."

"I know. Thank you. I am, too . . . so very sorry for so many things."

I was gripping the receiver so hard my fingers were cramping. "Claire, there are some things I'd like to go over with you again." I worked to keep my voice even. "I'm feeling stuck, and I'd like to use you as a sounding board. Are you up to it?"

There was a moment's hesitation. "Oh, my. Well, I don't know how much more help I'll be. But I suppose if you'd like to come out to the beach house, I'm going to be there today packing up Sara's personal things."

"Claire, why would you put yourself through that now? There must be someone who can do that for you."

"Absolutely not." Her voice wavered again. "It's the last thing I can do on this earth for that child. Lord knows I did little enough while she was alive."

I could think of no reply to that. "All right, then. What time were you planning to be there?"

"I was just about to leave when you called."

"I'll meet you there shortly, then."

We said goodbye. The next call was a little tougher to make, but it's times like this when my stubborn independence kicks up its heels. Maybe I should have dumped it all in Donleavy's lap right then, but I was afraid of putting my fate in someone else's hands. I couldn't just sit by, watching and waiting. I wanted to take a crack at Robert Camden before he could get himself barricaded behind a bunch of lawyers. I thought I might be able to use what I'd learned about him to force his hand.

A man picked up on the other end. "Hello."

"I'm trying to reach Robert Camden."

"Who is this?"

"I have information about some missing records that I think will interest you."

"Records?"

"Am I speaking with Robert Camden?"

He had to think about that. "Yes."

"I'm talking about the cooked books from Fat Farm that Faye Symington took."

"How much do you want?" he said flatly.

"I don't want money. I'd like to set up a meeting with you later today."

"Who are you?"

"I'm not a cop, and I'm not affiliated with your former employers. That's all you really need to know."

I could almost feel his tension crackling through the phone line.

"What are you after?"

"I just want to talk. Now, do you want those books back or not?"

"Yeah. Okay," he said. "Why don't you come on over to the house?"

"No. Not a chance. We'll meet at Fat Farm later today, once the lunch crowd has had a chance to assemble. Let's say, two o'clock."

"How will I know you?"

"Just be in the dining room. I'll find you."

"You'll bring the stuff with you, right?"

I hung up without saying anything more.

I thought about calling Joyce and Chris to tell them not to worry, but they would anyway, and I didn't want to put them in the position of having to lie to the police if they came around asking after me. I checked out of the Elysian. Feeling like a vagabond, I threw my pathetic sackful of dimestore possessions into my trunk and got on the freeway for the now-familiar drive to Malibu.

Although it had been sunny and as clear as L.A. ever gets over in Silverlake, the west side was gloomy and overcast. The ocean was a forbidding metallic gray, and I had to force my mind from thoughts of Sara's last moments trapped beneath its surface. The front door of the house on Malibu Colony Drive was ajar when I arrived. I pushed it open and called out. "Claire, it's Maggie."

"In the study, Dear."

I found her seated on the floor packing a stack of books into a box. She made a motion to stand.

"Don't get up."

"Honestly, I'm very glad to see you. This is more difficult than I'd suspected," she said.

I looked around the room. It was crammed with pictures, books, and objects, mounds of the flotsam and jetsam we all use to accessorize our lives. Several cardboard boxes and a pile of newspapers stood waiting in one corner.

"Quite a task."

"Yes, and I believe your advice was sound," she said, pushing a wayward strand of hair back from her face. "I do need help. I'm just not equal to it — not alone, anyway."

I shed my jacket and tossed it on a chair. "I'll be glad to help while we talk. What would you like me to work on?"

"That would be so kind." She pointed to a shelf beside the windows where a beautiful amethyst geode sat in the middle of a forest of framed photographs. "You can pack all that."

I grabbed an empty box and several newspapers. "Claire, has anyone . . . has Faye's lawyer been in contact with you regarding the terms of her will?" I asked, watching her out of the corner of my eye.

"Yes." I sensed her discomfort.

"Who will benefit most from it?"

"Well, Dear, strangely enough, and much to my surprise, Gina and I will," she replied, her hazel eyes clouded by — what? Grief? Confusion? Guilt? All of the above?

"That's really not very surprising, now that Sara's gone. You have no other close family, then?"

She shook her head. "None living."

I wrapped and packed photographs while we talked. As I thought about how to phrase my next question, I glanced down at the picture in my hand and gasped, nearly dropping it.

"What's the matter?" she asked in alarm.

"Do you know who the people are in this photograph?" I noticed my hand was shaking as I held it out to her.

She leaned forward to peer at the photo. "Yes, that's a picture of Galen as a young boy with his mother."

"Did you ever meet his mother?"

"No, she passed away when Galen was still quite young. Shortly after that was taken, I believe."

"Who told you that?" I asked sharply.

She stared at me. "Why, Galen did."

"When did Galen and Sara meet?"

"About a year and a half ago. And they married very quickly," she said with a frown. "I always thought their haste unwise. I never felt the boy was substantial enough for Sara —"

I cut her off. "Hugh Forsythe was already dead by then?"

"Yes, he was." Claire was thoroughly bewildered by my questions.

"Of course, he had to be," I muttered. The photograph I held was identical to the one I'd seen on top of the television in Sylvia Forsythe's house. Galen Landesmann's mother was the wife Hugh Forsythe discarded in order to marry Faye.

"I have to see someone," I said, shrugging back into my jacket. "May I borrow this?" I held up the photograph.

"Where on earth are you going?"

"To visit a ghost. I'll explain later!" I called over my shoulder as I dashed out the front door.

I drove toward Marathon Street, thinking back to my first visit to the beach house. How did I miss that picture? It had to have been there. Keeping it so prominently displayed was pretty ballsy of Galen, considering the likelihood that Faye had seen photographs of Sylvia as a young woman. But then I remembered Sara saying that Faye rarely went to the beach house, that she hated being so near the water.

I screeched to a stop in front of Sylvia's sad-looking little bungalow. As I hurried up the cracked front walk a fiftyish man came out her front door dragging a bulging plastic garbage bag. He wore a flannel shirt and gray twill work pants slung low on his hips to accommodate the belly that hung over his belt like a bundle of laundry. He was also sporting a particle mask and rubber gloves.

"Hey! Who are you?" I challenged him.

He pushed the particle mask up on his forehead and squinted at me in annoyance. "And just who the hell are you? You're on my property, so I guess I'm the one who gets to ask the questions, Girlie."

I could tell he and I were going to be fast friends. "My name's Maggie McGrath. I'm looking for the woman who lives here."

"Lived."

"What do you mean?"

"She's gone. Cleared out." He grimaced. "I shoulda been so lucky. I mean, I wish she'da cleared out. She left everything behind." He jerked his head back over his shoulder. "Buncha junk. Place's a mess."

"How can you be sure she's really gone for good if all her stuff's still there?"

"Gotta call."

"She called you?" This was like pulling teeth, and it was making me cranky.

"No. Some other lady. Younger gal."

"When was this?"

"I dunno . . . coupla days ago, maybe?" He shrugged and hitched up his pants, which were threatening to slip past the point of no return.

"What did she say?"

"Well, ain't you just little Miss Twenty Questions?"

I gave him my most winsome smile. "Please. It might be important."

"Not to me."

I dug in my bag, pulled out a twenty-dollar bill, and held it up between my fingers. He grabbed at it, but I was quicker. "Unh-uh. You first."

He sighed. "She said she was the old broad's daughter and she was gonna take her home to Utah. Or maybe it was Omaha — someplace like that, anyways."

"Did she give you a forwarding address or phone number?"

"Nope, 'n I didn't ask."

"How can you be sure Sylvia's not in some kind of trouble?"

"Girlie, that ain't even a question I'm askin' myself," he said with a laugh that showed off a mouthful of truly repulsive teeth. He brushed by me, plucking the twenty from my fingers.

But Galen didn't have a sister — at least as far as Sara had known.

I slipped into the house for a quick look around. Everything looked much as it had on my first visit. He hadn't yet made a dent in the layers of filth, and the pervasive disorder seemed no better or worse than it had before. I don't know what I was hoping for. A scribbled note? A travel itinerary? A map sketched out in the grease on the stovetop? There wasn't even a hint about where Sylvia might have gone.

I went back to my car to do some semi-private mulling. The early afternoon heat had made a sauna of the Toyota, so I switched on the ignition and cranked up the air. I find it hard to think straight when my thighs are sticking to the upholstery. Here was an interesting wrinkle. What if Galen Landesmann married Sara strictly to get even with her mother, the woman he blamed for the destruction of his family? If that was the plan, maybe it had always been in his mind to kill Faye, or maybe he'd plotted a more subtle revenge — tit for tat, as it were, torturing her daughter with his constant infidelities while living off his mother-in-law's largesse. And maybe in the end that just wasn't enough to satisfy him. Then, panicked by the police interrogation, he fled with whatever he could scoop up in a rush. If I was barking up the right tree here, then I wouldn't bet the farm at this point that Jeri and Sylvia were with him, but I'd almost guarantee they'd gone because of him. Willingly or not? I couldn't hazard a guess.

I went hunting for a pay phone, punched in the number for the station on Wilcox, asked for Lieutenant Donleavy, and promptly hung up. Was I nuts? (Don't answer that.) What did I really have to tell him? Nothing factual. No carved-in-granite truths that would hold up in court. Just a lot of supposition that would probably net me a backlash of pointed questions I couldn't and/or didn't want to answer. I picked up the phone again. There was another base I needed to touch.

"Maggie, where are you?" Claire's voice was filled with concern.

I ignored her question. "What's Gina's address?"

"Maggie, dear, you have me completely mystified. What is going on? Is Gina in some kind of trouble?"

"No, not at all. I just want to talk to her, Claire," I sighed, unable to keep the exasperation out of my voice.

"I see." She sounded hurt, but she gave me an address in Venice, and I told her I'd check in with her later.

I hesitated a moment, then picked up the receiver once more. There was someone else I needed to talk to first.

Twenty-Four

"Come on, come on," I muttered. Six rings and the machine still hadn't picked up.

"Tolan here," she chirped.

"Jen." I clutched at the sound of her voice and held on.

"Maggie, what's the matter, Luv? You sound frightful."

"Oh, God, Jen." Relief flooded me, and I realized how isolated I'd become. "It's so damned good to hear your voice. I don't know where to start. I'm in trouble, Jen."

"Take a deep breath, Luv," she instructed. "Then tell me everything."

And I did. I talked for twenty minutes. Jennifer listened without interrupting, but I could feel her steady concentration at the other end of the line.

"Maggie, you must listen to me carefully now," she said slowly. "This energy you've engaged is very dark and twisted. It's almost as if it's been mangled. That's the closest image I can come up with."

"That much I pretty well figured out already," I snapped. "Sorry," I added quickly, not sounding it. "This shit's really working my last nerve." I allowed a tiny bubble of hope to rise in my breast. "Anything you can see that might help?"

"I can only tell you what they're showing me. This presence, this evil I'm sensing is dangerous, and it's stalking you now. It wears a face of expedience for the world, but that's false. Its real face is too hideous to show. Oh, Maggie, please don't pit yourself against this energy!"

"Jen, I have no choice!"

She was quiet for a moment. "Then get to a safe place and stay there. I'll come to you. We'll work on it together. You mustn't try to do this alone."

Despite the heat, I found myself shivering. "I can't wait, and I can't get you involved. I'm obliged to you for the warning. I'll call soon." And I hung up quickly before my resolve faltered.

As I threaded my way through the cross-town traffic, I reflected that it was too bad I wasn't being paid by the mile. In point of fact, I wasn't being paid, period. The thousand-dollar advance was all I'd ever see out of this one, since both my clients were dead. It had been exactly seven days since Sara first walked into my office. Not a brilliant week's work, I mused grimly. The impatient blare of a horn brought me back from my woolgathering. My road mates had grown restless. I ducked my head in embarrassment and shifted the car into second gear. *Here's a clue for you, McGrath: the light's green.*

The address I'd gotten from Claire belonged to a wooden A-frame house plunked at the edge of one of the small canals that provided inspiration for the city's name. The parallel is merely conceptual: the system of canals in Venice, California is a miniaturized and purely decorative homage to its European counterpart. Gina's house was painted a grayed-out avocado green and was bordered on three sides by a fence overgrown by pink and peach bougainvillea intertwined with vibrant purple morning glories. The unfenced front of the house overlooked the canal.

It seemed I was in luck: a white Honda Civic was parked in back beside the fence with its nose poking right up into the flowering vines. I tried the back gate and found it was bolted shut, so I went around to the front of the house. A neat gravel path led to an oak front door with a porthole-shaped security window made of amber glass. I rang the bell, heard it chiming inside. There was a scuffling noise on the other side of the door, then Gina's voice, high-pitched and agitated, demanded, "Who is it?"

"It's Maggie McGrath, Gina. May I talk to you for a minute?"

The porthole window opened slightly, and Gina peered out at me, her annoyance unmistakeable. "Can this wait? I'm just on my way out, and I'm late for an appointment."

"Actually, Gina, it can't wait. May I please come in for just a minute?" I couldn't have cared less about inconveniencing her, and that was plain in my tone.

"Well, no. I'm too embarrassed." She glanced back over her shoulder at the room behind her. "The house is a complete disaster, and I really am terribly late."

I stood my ground but said nothing more. Gina sighed in irritation. "I've got to get going. I'm just going to put on some shoes, and I'll be right out."

She shut the window with a little thunk. *What's up with that?* I wondered. It seemed unlikely she'd be in such a nervous snit over an untidy house. As I was mulling that over, Gina came out, opening the door just enough to slither through the narrow aperture with the speed of a snake darting out of its hole. Whatever her urgent appointment was, she hadn't bothered to dress up for it. She was wearing turquoise-and-black bicycle shorts, an oversized T-shirt with the neck cut out, and flip-flops. Without so much as a look at me, she strode purposefully down the path and around to the back of the house, her wealth of dark curls dancing angrily. I had to trot to keep up with her.

"I just wish you'd called before you came by. I'm sorry to be rude," (yeah, sure) "but I really am strapped for time today."

"Don't worry, Gina, I understand," I said soothingly. "But I do have a couple of questions I need to ask you."

"Like what?" she sighed impatiently.

"Like have you maybe heard anything from Jeri and Galen since they supposedly disappeared?"

"Supposedly?" she echoed in a strained voice. She stopped in her tracks and turned to face me with her hands on her hips. "They're long gone with the money they ripped off from Sara. They're probably out of the country by now."

"Maybe. Maybe not," I baited her, intrigued by the reaction I was getting.

She shifted her weight uneasily from foot to foot. "And what is that supposed to mean?"

"It's just a loose end, you know? Loose ends bother me. I can't leave them alone."

"Whatever." She turned away.

"What's your relationship with Robert Camden?"

She froze for an instant, then turned back again. "We're friends. More like acquaintances, really. He manages my aunt's restaurant."

"Yeah, I saw you there with him the other night. You two looked very friendly to me."

"What's your point?'

"My point is, there's more going on here than meets the old naked eyeball. And it probably has something to do with money. Doesn't it always?" I said conversationally. "A big payday coming up for somebody. As a matter of fact, I was just over visiting with Claire. You two ladies stand to inherit a big chunk of change now, don't you?"

"Are you accusing me of something?" she demanded hotly.

"Not at all, Gina," I said easily. "Just thinking out loud. And I'm thinking I should call the sheriff's department to be certain someone's doing a careful autopsy on Sara's body and that her suicide note is being inspected thoroughly. Just to be sure she didn't have some assistance making that sad choice."

"I don't have to stand here and listen to this crap," she spat.

"Suit yourself, Gina," I shrugged. "But a word to the wise — the people close to this case have a high mortality rate lately. The way things stack up now, you're just about at the top of what's become a very short list. If this is all part of some master plan that's spinning itself out, you'd better watch yourself to make sure you don't get ground up in the mechanism."

"Thanks for the warning, Bitch," she snarled as she flung herself into the Honda. She rolled down the driver's side window as she started the car and backed away from the fence. "Now fuck off," she suggested as she hit the gas. The car shot down the tiny alleyway behind the house, hardly pausing at the intersection before it sped onto Ocean Avenue.

I sighed. Ah, well, another Christmas card I shouldn't be expecting this year. I'd certainly hit a nerve. I was still standing beside the fence, trying to decide what to do next, when a dark little ripple of dread skittered up my spine, making my hair stand on end. Every muscle tensed involuntarily. I'd received a telepathic warning — the instinct of the prey announcing the presence of the predator. As if I were being watched. The feeling was kin to one I'd had as a child when I'd have to walk home from my best friend's house after dark. We'd moved to Indiana after my father's death, back to the small country town my mother had come from. We lived on the outskirts in a quiet family neighborhood where the houses were only a couple of hundred yards apart. But to a child with an overactive imagination, the dark was peopled with malicious beings and evil spirits. To undertake that journey alone was to run a gauntlet of terror.

I began to stroll nonchalantly toward my car. Could my imagination have geared into hyperdrive as it had on those dark homeward walks of my childhood? What was making Gina so damned skittish? She was acting like a cornered animal lashing out to protect itself. I stopped abruptly and looked around. *Well, why not?* One B-and-E or two — it hardly made a difference at this point. Oh, and the little matter of my gun showing up as a murder weapon. It wasn't like I was saving space on my wall for my Good Citizen's plaque.

I hurried to the car and took the gun from my bag. Darted a look up and down the alleyway and stuck it in the back waistband of my jeans. It felt solid and reassuring, and I adjusted my T-shirt to hide the tell-tale bulge as much as possible. I shoved my hand in my pocket to make sure my Swiss Army knife was still there.

"Okay, let's do it," I muttered to cheer myself on.

I retraced my steps around the house and up the front path, then slipped into the tiny side yard behind the fence. I circled the house, peering into the windows, which were long narrow casements covered by screens. The house looked cozy in a cloying Laura Ashley sort of way, and if the perfect order I saw within was Gina's idea of housekeeping gone awry, I cringed in sympathy for any man who might find himself expected to toe such a stringent line of domestic idealism. Gleaming wood floors were strewn with multi-colored throw rugs. Lots of floral chintz upholstery and ruffled curtains. A big canopy bed overwhelmed the small bedroom, also smitten by the relentless tide of floral ruffles.

Nothing looked amiss. I pulled out my pocket knife and slipped a blade under the bottom edge of one of the screens. It took a minute of maneuvering to catch the metal loop stuck over a single nail that held the screen in place, but once I got it, it slid off easily, allowing me to slip the screen out of its frame. The window itself was secured on one side by a short, single-levered handle. It proved sticky and resistant to my prying knife, but persistence paid off, and it finally yielded, flipping up and out of its cradle.

I folded the knife, put it back in my pocket, and looked around once again. I didn't see how anyone could be observing me. There'd been no traffic through the alley while I'd been at it, and the wall of flowering vines made the yard very private. Moving carefully, I pushed the window open and stepped into the bedroom. All was quiet except for the subliminal hum of electrical appliances one only notices in an empty house. A dark cherry wood quartz clock ticked on the table beside the bed. I'd do a quick scan of every room before I got into any serious snooping. I checked my watch. I'd allow myself thirty minutes, max. I didn't believe Gina had an appointment, but I thought she'd stay away at least that long to be sure I was gone when she returned.

The bedroom was neat — nay, immaculate — spotless ruffled comforter in place, rugs clean and set at perfect angles on the dust-free hardwood floor. I started down the hallway and peeked into the kitchen, where the floral motif had been supplanted by fruit. Flounced curtains printed with cherries hung cheerfully in the windows; a ceramic fruit-basket clock sat on top of a refrigerator adorned with dozens of fruit-shaped magnets holding a gallery of snapshots in place. I'd have to come back for a closer look at that.

I continued to tiptoe down the hall toward the living room, the largest one in the little house. When I'd looked in a side window, there appeared to be a small loft above the main room that took advantage of the "A" shape of the structure and extended in depth back over the kitchen and part of the hallway. Shafts of sunlight alive with dust motes streamed through the windows, although here, as in the rest of the house, the dust was obviously not allowed to settle comfortably on any surface for long. A floorboard creaked beneath my foot and I stopped, listening once more to the quiet. Satisfied, I proceeded. As I stepped through the doorway into the living room, I sensed more than saw a flash of movement to my left. But I never felt the blow.

Twenty-Five

Consciousness was a gradual resurfacing through layers of murky dream images and pain — like waking up from a nightmare with a terrible hangover. Everything hurt. That was my first bit of awareness tinged with any real clarity. I was lying on my back with my neck crimped at an uncomfortable angle. My entire body ached as though it had been used as a target for some kickboxing festival, and the back of my head throbbed with a painful pulse all its own. Better to go back to sleep for a week or so.

But I was cold, too. And I needed to pee. Damn. I wanted to turn over on my side and scrunch up to conserve body heat, but my brain was resistant to sending out those signals to the pertinent muscle groups.

"No, you idiot!" it screamed. "You think you feel bad now, just try rolling over. Then you'll understand what real agony is all about!"

But did I listen? Sadly, no. I shifted my position slightly, a little warm-up for the full body roll, and let out an involuntary groan worthy of a mortally wounded buffalo. Now I was awake. I opened my eyes and found myself staring into a blank darkness that seemed to hover just above my head, as impenetrable as a wall of cement. I searched my memory for a clue about where I might be expecting to find myself and how it was I got there, but came up with zippity-do-da.

And this was when I began to be concerned. Feeling smothered by the heavy blackness that swaddled me, I sat up too quickly and was hit by a wave of dizziness that forced me to slump back. It was then I noticed the acrid smell of gasoline hanging in the air, biting my nostrils and making the gorge rise in my throat. I closed my eyes against the black whirlies and waited for the sickening spinning to subside. When I finally opened them again, I lay still, gazing into the void around me until they began to adjust, picking out a charcoal landscape of indistinct shapes and patterns of shadow. I was lying on a bed.

Then all at once it came crashing back: Gina's little house in Venice — and the flash of movement I'd glimpsed just before the lights went out. I automatically reached back to feel for the gun in my waistband, but of course it was gone. I put a careful hand up and gingerly prodded the back of my head. Oh yeah. There was a big old knot where they'd socked me. But where was I now? The area around me felt too open and spacious, the walls too far away from the bed, to be part of that tiny house.

I sat up, this time with greater care, and swung my legs over the side of the bed. The dizziness wasn't as bad as before. I depressed the stem of my watch to activate the luminous dial. 2:00 A.M. Quite a nap I'd had. The light from my watch was enough to show me I was in a large bedroom. There was a lamp on the nightstand beside the bed, but when I turned the switch nothing happened.

I heaved myself up on rubbery legs to make a tour of my quarters. A set of heavy floor-to-ceiling drapes swathed what appeared to be the only window. I crept up to one side of it and pulled the fabric back to peer out at the night. The window was high and completely covered by security bars. This was not an exit. A thin, watery glow filtered in from a moon partially wreathed in clouds, lessening the utter darkness of the room. I squinted through the glass. I couldn't see much — no lights from another house or road nearby — but I had the impression of trees and vegetation sloping down and away from my window. Then I gasped as a quick blade of fear sliced through me. It wasn't as though I'd made a logical deduction, but I suddenly knew where I was. The Symington house in the canyon.

"Okay, okay, okay," I muttered. Not okay at all.

A small wooden desk and chair stood against the wall opposite the bed. I pulled the chair over to the window and spread the drape across it to allow a bit of light into my cell. If my inner compass was accurate, the window was on a west-facing wall, which meant the door to the room was on the east wall. I tiptoed across the carpeted floor. The pungent gasoline smell was stronger by the door. I put my ear against its wooden surface, barely breathing. I didn't hear any sound at all coming from the hallway, but there wasn't much comfort in that. And yet I had to make a move; waiting for a match to be struck didn't seem like such a good idea. Someone, and I thought I knew who, was out there putting the finishing touches on plans for a barbecue with me cast in the role of charcoal briquette.

I gripped the glass door knob and twisted it to the right with a barely perceptible creak. It caught after only half a turn. I pulled but the door wouldn't budge. A trickle of sweat slipped down my back. Slowly, slowly I rotated the knob to the left — same result. The damned door was locked. What a surprise.

I turned and stole over to the desk to look for something to use for a tool, but the desk was bare and its drawers were empty. The nightstand also yielded nothing, not even a bobby pin. At my wits' end, I sank to the floor in a dispirited heap when something jabbed me in the thigh. I leaned back and stretched my leg out so I could stick my hand in my pocket. Snugged deep in a fold of fabric was my Swiss Army knife. Hallelujah and good morning!

It's funny how your mind will grasp at little straws of hope that way — it's not like my prospects were so swell, but finding my knife felt like a huge victory at that moment. I went to work on the lock with renewed vigor. It was an unsophisticated mechanism meant to do nothing more than insure a superficial measure of privacy; still it was slow going. Every scrape and click of metal on metal sounded amplified to my ears, an ungodly racket alerting one and all that I was up — and up to no good. By the time the lock finally yielded, I was drenched by the rivulets of tension sweat pouring down my sides. There was one last click, and the door started to gently tip open as the mechanism let go with a soft metallic sigh. I heaved a sigh of my own and checked my watch. 2:25. I opened all the appliances on my knife to maximize its ripping and tearing potential, then eased the door open a crack.

The hallway had been sluiced with gasoline — with the door open, the fumes were overpowering. I stuck my head out. No lights in the hall itself, but an ambient glow at the far end told me there were lights on in the living room. No one was in sight. I knew from walking the property the day we'd installed the motion sensor lights that there was no exit from this wing of bedrooms. I'd need to get out to the kitchen, where there was a stairway to the lower level and back entrance, or I had to get to the front door through the living room. Either way, this hallway was my only way out.

All the doors lining the corridor were locked. I know because I tried each in turn as I made my way along that noxious passage, leading with my left shoulder to make myself as flat and narrow as possible and wishing I'd thought to pack my cloak of invisibility. I gulped air through my mouth in an attempt to steady my rapid, shallow breathing as I choked back nausea brought on by the gasoline-saturated atmosphere.

I came to the end of the hallway and stopped. I could hear music being played low in the living room. A heavy bass line. Something I recognized but couldn't immediately identify. I froze in place, straining to listen over the roar of blood in my ears for sounds of activity in the next room. But I couldn't hear anything aside from the low, insistent pulse of the music and, as I waited with the seconds ticking by, a little voice began to whisper in my inner ear. What if I was standing petrified in this hallway and there was no one at all in the living room? Maybe (for example) they'd planted a bomb set to detonate at a certain time, trusting to the explosion and accelerant to do the job. What if I was standing there like a moron just waiting to be blown to kingdom come?

I wiped my palms on my jeans, got a firm grip on my knife, and dropped to a crouch, inching toward the doorway to the living room. I plastered myself right up against the doorframe and peered around its edge, trying to extend my eyeball like a periscope. Stravinsky's "Rite of Spring" — that's what was playing. A slightly hysterical giggle bubbled up in my throat as this useless nugget of information popped into my head, but it died before it reached my lips. The Symington living room was ablaze with candles. It was lit up like a religious shrine, an eerie tableau vivant dancing with light and shadow. Candles of all shapes, colors, and sizes flickered on the dining room table, the windowsills, the mantel, and the coffee table. At center stage of this bizarre theatrical a young woman sat motionless on the hearth with her back to me. She had a graceful willowy figure and light brown hair shimmering in the fitful glow from the candles like an unsteady halo. She was dressed head to toe in white, her pose as reverent as a postulant at prayer. Jeri was staring at the grate, where a lively fire snapped and chewed at a fragrant log.

There wasn't a sign of anyone else, but I could only see partway into the kitchen from my look-out. That room was dark, but on the counter silhouetted against the windows were two one-gallon metal cans, one of them topped by a funnel. A hulking five-gallon can with a spout attached rested on the floor below. I continued to study the puzzling scene playing "what's wrong with this picture," my bludgeoned, gasoline-soaked brain fumbling to make sense of the images. And then I spotted it nestled on the cushions of one of the sofas. My gun.

I didn't have a lot of choices here to work with. I could try for one of the doors, hoping it wouldn't be locked, hoping Jeri couldn't get hold of the gun before I made it out, hoping no one waited on the other side — a lot of unsubstantiated hoping, to my way of thinking. Or I could arm myself first and take my chances from there. I scanned the area once again. It was all strangely peaceful in a macabre sort of way. Candlelight. Music. A fire in the grate. The scent of gasoline in the air.

I folded the knife and slipped it back in my pocket. Centering my weight over the balls of my feet, I made a hunching run, snatched up the gun, and squatted behind the sofa, resting the barrel of the .38 atop its tufted back to steady my aim as I sighted on Jeri. With a small cry, she twisted herself around to face me.

The shock nearly finished me off. The pieces of my reality suddenly shifted like a kaleidoscope to rearrange themselves in an entirely new design, and I found myself staring dumbly across the room at Sara Landesmann.

She smiled, taking it all in stride with perfect composure. "Well, well, so you're up." She nodded approvingly. "I suppose I should be used to you creeping up on me by now; you always seem to do that." Her tone was good-natured. "How do you feel, Maggie?"

I felt like I might faint dead away, but decided not to mention it. "How —?" I croaked. But then I knew. "The body that washed up was Jeri."

"Of course it was." Sara rolled her eyes. "Who else?"

"But the dental records?"

She looked at me curiously. "Are you planning to shoot me, Maggie?"

"I don't want to." I swallowed. My throat felt tight and dry as sandpaper.

She nodded again thoughtfully. "Well, the dental records were the easy part. I arranged all that months ago," she said breezily. "First I switched to Jeri's dentist. Then I fed him some tale about putting together a scrapbook for Mother. I told him I wanted to include my own and Jeri's dental charts, our baby footprints, locks of hair, photos — you know the sort of thing." A languid smile played on her lips. "Faye would have loathed it."

"And then you changed the names."

"Maggie, I'm here to say hooray for technology!" She clapped her hands in delight. "The whole world is computerized — even dentists — and it makes everything so much simpler. I took Jeri's chart, scanned it into my PC, typed in my name, and printed it out again. Easy-peasy!"

"And Gina knew all about it?"

She lifted her chin and peered down her nose at me. "Well, what do you think?"

"I think she was in it for the money, the inheritance."

"Brava! Nothing much gets by you, does it?" she said with a laugh.

"So where's Gina now? And Galen?" I darted a look around to make sure no one had joined us unannounced.

She smiled coyly, one finger pointed at her own chest. "That's for me to know and you to find out." She pointed at me playfully.

"Okay," I sighed. "I'm tired of this game now. Let's go, Sara." I stood up.

"Where shall we go?" she asked brightly, not moving.

"You're sick, Sara. You need help. We'll go someplace where you'll be taken care of."

She threw back her head and laughed. "Oh, Maggie, you are priceless! What a good little Girl Scout you are!" She gave me a mock salute.

"Fine, have it your way. I'll just call the police now and they can sort it out."

I crossed to the kitchen and picked up the phone. The line was dead. Great. Just great. I went back into the living room. Sara was standing in front of the hearth now, clutching the poker from the fireplace set at her side. She looked at me expectantly. "What, no answer?"

I put my hand out as if she were a strange beast I might gentle with a reassuring gesture. "Sara, let's be calm here. The last thing I want to do is hurt you."

"I know," she nodded, and I could have sworn her eyes were moist. "Dear Maggie. You only ever wanted to help."

"That's right," I said softly. "I wanted to help you." Even now my heart went out to her. "Why, Sara? Why did you even come to me?"

"It was all part of the script," she shrugged impatiently. "Distraught daughter hires detective to protect beloved mother. I thought that played rather well, if I do say so myself. I didn't think you could be very good, or you wouldn't be working out of that hole on the east side. And I certainly never thought you'd be so persistent," she said peevishly.

"So it was you all along. You engineered the campaign of threats."

She cocked her head and fixed me with a penetrating gaze that bored straight through me, riveted by visions I couldn't even guess at. "When Faye was nominated for the Oscar, I knew it was a sign to me. Time to act. It was the thing she wanted most in the world. I couldn't have borne it if she'd won."

I thought I might weep. "Oh, Sara," I whispered.

"How dare you judge me?" she cried furiously, her mood doing a gut-wrenching 180. She took a menacing step toward me "That bitch hated me as much as I hated her! She took great pains to prove that every day of my life!"

"So, how did Galen fit into all this?" I asked soothingly. My mind was racing. How was I going to get her out of there without hurting her?

"Oh, Galen. Galen was a mistake," she said simply. Something in her tone sent a chill through me. Galen and Jeri were together, after all. But neither had gone willingly.

"He didn't run off with the money, did he?"

Her answer was a brilliant smile. Eyes glittering, she started toward me, still gripping the poker.

I took a step back. "Sara, don't do this," I pleaded. "I swear I'll shoot you if I have to!"

"No, I don't think you will," she crooned.

I aimed the gun at her feet and squeezed the trigger. The hammer clicked as the .38's empty cylinder rotated impotently.

"Shit!"

I hurled the gun at her, dodging as she lunged for me. But I wasn't quick enough: she landed a sharp, glancing blow on my shoulder, and I felt a warm trickle of blood run down my arm. Yelping in pain, I lashed out with my foot and caught her squarely in the stomach. Her breath rushed out with a satisfying whoosh, and she doubled over, dropping the poker as she fell to the floor. I kicked her again as she toppled and connected with her chin. Her head snapped up and she fell back against the coffee table, sending candles flying in every direction. The two sofas went up like kindling.

Sara was out cold, lying on her back just inches from the fire. I grabbed her feet and dragged her away from the flames, bumping her across the floor like a sack of potatoes. I cast around for something to use to fight the fire, but there was nothing close at hand. I raced back down the hall to the room I'd been locked in and pulled the comforter off the bed just as the smoke alarm in the living room started its high-pitched pulsing wail. The air was thick and foul with the chemical stench of burning man-made fibers. I started beating at the flames with the blanket, grateful that the fire was still concentrated around the sofas. I had to stop it before it reached the gasoline-doused carpet in the hallway.

The next thing I knew I was sprawled face down on the floor, thrown off my feet by a walloping tackle from behind. A sharp splinter of pain shot up my arm as I landed on my elbow with a bone-jarring thud. Sara was on top of me, straddling my back and ripping at my face like a rabid harpy. I managed to get my hands planted flat, and I pushed up to a kneeling position, bucking and twisting to shake her off, but she'd gotten an arm locked around my neck. I jabbed with my elbows, but I couldn't quite get at her. She wrapped her legs around my waist, riding me piggyback and choking me from behind.

The fire exploded into the hallway with a blistering roar, sending a blast of heat billowing back into the living room as it raced down the corridor to consume the rest of the house. Smoke alarms screamed in all the rooms now. I was blinded by tears as smoke stung my eyes, poisoning the little bit of air I was able to drag into my lungs. My strength began to flag. I staggered upright on trembling legs only to be pulled down again by Sara's weight. Grunting and snuffling like a wounded animal, I clawed at her arms, but her grip was too solid. She allowed herself to slip down on my frame like a dead weight, pulling my head back to effectively cut off the last of my air supply. I could feel myself fading, my focus racheting down like a fish-eye lens as my oxygen-starved brain cells began to check out en masse. The fire didn't worry me anymore; I couldn't think about anything but my need to get the next breath. Soon now, that would be a moot point. With darkness crowding in, I stumbled toward the flames and spun around, making myself go limp into a dead-fall backward. We landed on a sheet of fire, and in some dim corner of my mind I heard Sara shriek in pain as she gave up her hold on me. The darkness washed back as I gulped air along with a chestful of smoke, and I rolled, spurred by a searing pain high on my back and the smell of my own charred flesh — and I kept on rolling until I was clear of the flames.

I got to my knees. By now the fire was everywhere, roaring throughout the house. The air was hot and dense with smoke. I could hardly see to the other side of the room and every breath brought a spasm of coughing. There was a solid wall of fire between the kitchen and me — I'd never make it out that way. And it wouldn't be long before the flames got to those cans of gasoline.

The French doors to the deck seemed like my best bet, even though that meant a fairly long drop to the hillside below. They were out in the open and closer than the front door. If I got into that front foyer and found the door locked, I might not be able to get back again. I made a running leap at the double glass panes and yanked on the handles. They were bolted shut. I whirled in panic and grabbed one of the dining room chairs to use as a battering ram just as Sara came charging through the smoke, wielding the poker and screaming like a banshee. I ducked as she swung at me, using the chair as a shield to fend off the blow. The force of the impact snapped off one of the legs and sent shock waves up my arms as she wound up for another go at me.

"You crazy bitch! We've got to get out of here!" I screamed.

But she was beyond reason. She jousted wildly again, and I hauled off and hit her with the chair. For a fraction of an instant that seemed to last forever, it was as if time stopped, and she appeared to hover there. Her eyes bounced into focus and held me with a look of piercing amusement, and then all at once she was gone, arms flailing, to be swallowed by the fire. I squeezed my eyes shut against the sight and turned blindly to fling the chair at the doors, diving after it through the jagged shards of glass. The cool desert night folded around me like a blessing as I lay on the rough wooden surface of the deck, gasping and bleeding. I wanted nothing more than to lie there drinking in clean air with the pale moon and stars winking overhead, but I knew there was no time. I crawled to the edge of the deck and used the wooden railing to haul myself upright with every muscle and joint screeching its protest. I stood for a moment gazing down into the dark silence of the canyon. Then with a moan, I climbed over the railing to drop and roll down the cool damp of the grassy slope below.

A minute later the flames overtook the gasoline in the kitchen. I leaned against the trunk of an oak and watched in awe as a fireball blew out all the windows on that side of the house. And I heard the first of the keening sirens echoing up the canyon.

Twenty-Six

The badly burned bodies of Sara Landesmann and Gina Harris were recovered from what was left of the Symington house late the following day. The coroner found it impossible to determine if Gina was dead before the fire started, but I'd say it hardly matters at this point. I was hospitalized with second-degree burns over 15% of my body, but after a week in bed being pumped with megadoses of antibiotics, they sprung me on out-patient status. I'll be nearly good as new before long — physically, anyway — though I have an angry purple scar on my left shoulder where the fire bit deeper. It'll fade some with time I'm told, but I'll carry it the rest of my life. In many ways, that's the least of it: I know how lucky I was.

Hikers discovered two partially decomposed corpses in a Range Rover in the Santa Susana Mountains last week. The vehicle was registered to Galen Landesmann and the bodies — a man and a woman — were identified as Galen and his mother, Sylvia Forsythe. Both had suffered gunshot wounds to the head from a .38 caliber weapon.

Of course the ordeal goes beyond all the physical anguish meted out. Donleavy was livid at first and even raised the question of a partnership gone sour between Sara and me. But I don't think he ever really believed that. I've endured innumerable lectures from all quarters and finally lapsed into a state of non-resistant depression. The only bright spot for me has been Skunky's homecoming. He accepted my tearful hugs and kisses with cool reserve until I softened him up with broiled chicken.

Robert Camden was arraigned on embezzlement charges and retained a high-priced lawyer, but out of that whole situation has come an unexpected benefit. Emotionally devastated by all that's happened and overwhelmed by the responsibility of the enterprise, Claire simply wanted to be rid of Fat Farm. But I introduced her to Chris Jameson. For a dollar, Chris bought a half-interest in the troubled restaurant and has quickly taken the first steps toward getting the place back on financial terra firma.

And just in case you're wondering, I have to give the guy credit: Rick did call. But I'm just not ready for that yet. I do manage to drag myself into work every day, and that helps to some extent. Joyce spends most of her time hovering anxiously just outside my door. She's trying so hard to rein in her desire to smother me with care-giving. Yesterday, she brought me two beautifully stretched canvases along with a set of oils and an array of good sable brushes. I took them home, put them in the studio, and closed the door. I know I'll probably feel a lot better once I motivate myself to get back in there, up to my elbows in paint. But I'm not ready for that yet, either. Make no mistake, I'm grateful to have friends like that, and I'm glad to be alive, but my depression persists, along with the nightmares. Or rather, one recurring nightmare. It always starts with a child crying, a little girl. I can't see her, but I can hear her clearly. We're in a building, some sort of institution made up of gray hallways with no rooms laid out in a peculiar angular pattern. I'll start searching for the child, then be confused, lose my sense of direction, come to a dead end. Or realize that the route I've chosen is actually taking me farther away from her cries. I become frustrated, then frantic, unnerved by the heartbroken sobs echoing through the maze. Suddenly, I turn a corner and there she is, her hair pulled back in a ponytail, tears streaming down her tiny perfect face. Gasping with relief, I hold out my arms to her. That's when I always wake up. I'm never able to hold the child in my arms. Never able to comfort her.

There is an old saying: "No man is your enemy, no man is your friend. Every man is your teacher."

Some lessons are harder than others.

Carolyn Morese

Marjorie McCown lives in Los Angeles and has worked in the film industry for the past ten years.